James Craig has worked as a journalist and consultant for more than thirty years. He lives in London with his family. His previous Inspector Carlyle novels, *London Calling*; *Never Apologise, Never Explain*; *Buckingham Palace Blues*; *Th* *A Man of Sorrows*; *Shoot to Kill*; *Sins* *Hero*; *Acts of Violence*; *All Kinds of D* *Goodbye*; *Dying Days* and *Into the Vall* Constable.

Also by James Craig

Novels
London Calling
Never Apologise, Never Explain
Buckingham Palace Blues
The Circus
Then We Die
A Man of Sorrows
Shoot to Kill
Sins of the Fathers
Nobody's Hero
Acts of Violence
All Kinds of Dead
This is Where I Say Goodbye
Dying Days
Into the Valley

Short Stories
The Enemy Within
What Dies Inside
The Hand of God

JAMES CRAIG

CIRCUS GAMES

CONSTABLE

CONSTABLE

First published in Great Britain in 2021 by Constable

Copyright © James Craig, 2021

1 3 5 7 9 10 8 6 4 2

The moral right of the author has been asserted.

A CIP catalogue record for this book is available from the British Library.

ISBN: 978-1-47213-276-5

Typeset in Times New Roman by Initial Typesetting Services, Edinburgh
Printed and bound in Great Britain by Clays Ltd, Elcograf S.p.A.

Papers used by Constable are from well-managed forests and other responsible sources.

MIX
Paper from
responsible sources
FSC® C104740

Constable
An imprint of
Little, Brown Book Group
Carmelite House
50 Victoria Embankment
London EC4Y 0DZ

An Hachette UK Company
www.hachette.co.uk

www.littlebrown.co.uk

For Catherine and Cate

This is the fifteenth Carlyle novel.
Thanks for getting it done go to
Michael Doggart, Krystyna Green,
Rebecca Sheppard and Hazel Orme.

'Human beings suffer,
they torture one another,
they get hurt and get hard.'

Seamus Heaney

'Open wide.'

'Akkkkkkkkkurgh.'

A golf-ball-sized object was forced into the man's mouth.

'In case you were wondering, this is a V40 fragmentation grenade.'

A dirty index finger appeared in front of his face.

'Made in Holland – you wouldn't have thought the Dutch indulged in that sort of thing, but there you go.'

The finger wrapped itself around the pin sticking out between his teeth.

'The fuse delay time is four seconds . . .'

ONE

'That's not something you see every day.' Commander John Carlyle considered the crumpled body chained to the toilet seat. 'Where's his head?' He felt irritated and titillated at the same time. 'It's like I've been transported into an Elmore Leonard novel.'

'Hm.' Inspector Karen O'Sullivan, a single mother of two, didn't have much spare time for reading crime novels.

'There was one that started with a guy being blown up on the loo.' Carlyle struggled to remember the title.

'Vaporised.'

'No, I think he was blown into the street, or something.' Carlyle was still talking about the book – maybe it was *Freaky Deaky*.

'I'm talking about our guy.' O'Sullivan pointed at the mess on the walls. 'Not much left of his head.'

'It's not going to make identification any easier,' Carlyle acknowledged. 'Anything in his pockets?'

Careful not to get any mess on her jacket, O'Sullivan quickly checked the victim's clothes. 'They're empty,' she confirmed. 'No ID.' A young constable stuck his head through the door. As he clocked the headless corpse, the colour drained from the lad's face and he retreated.

'We should give him a name,' Carlyle suggested. '"The Man

With No Head" is a bit of a mouthful, don't you think?' He racked his brains for ideas. 'There's a Murray Head, actor and singer,' he offered up an excruciating chorus of 'One Night In Bangkok', 'or Travis Head, a cricketer.'

'Travis,' said O'Sullivan, 'if only to shut you up.'

Carlyle was struggling to come up with a witty reply when they were interrupted by the sound of retching from outside the cell. 'Who's the snowflake?'

The inspector glared at him. 'You can*not* say things like that, these days.'

'You've gotta be able to look at a dead body in our line of work,' Carlyle protested.

'And you've got to be aware of changing standards of workplace behaviour. Remember what happened to Kelvin.'

'Yeah.' Superintendent Jake Kelvin had been sacked after an ill-judged joke about a glazed ring went viral. A twenty-three-year career up in smoke because someone had taken offence at a somewhat risqué doughnut gag. Carlyle had laughed out loud when he'd heard it.

'The union are fighting to try to keep his pension.'

'Poor sod.' The smell of vomit wafted through the cell. Carlyle wrinkled his nose in disgust. 'Talk about contaminating a crime scene.'

'Keep your voice down. You don't want Gervase to make a complaint.'

Gervase? Carlyle stifled a chortle.

'He's a good boy, just a bit sensitive.' O'Sullivan went to check on their colleague.

Carlyle listened as she sent the youngster out to get some fresh air, along with some coffee, before turning his attention back to the corpse. 'What the fuck happened here, eh?' This was clearly not a random killing. The victim had been brought to an abandoned building and executed in a unique way. It was personal *and* professional. The guy's head had been efficiently destroyed, leaving the rest of the body largely intact. The corpse was well dressed, suited and booted in an expensive fashion – Paul Smith, if he'd identified the lining of the victim's jacket correctly. 'Nice schmutter.' The ensemble was finished off by a polished pair of double monks. 'Nice shoes, too.'

O'Sullivan reappeared, a paper cup in each hand. She offered one to Carlyle. 'Double macchiato.'

'That was quick.' Carlyle vowed to give young Gervase the benefit of the doubt, for now at least.

O'Sullivan took a sip of her latte. 'I bet you didn't expect to be back here, huh?'

'I only moved out about a month ago.' Carlyle drank his coffee in two quick gulps. 'I was one of the last to leave.' Paddington Green police station had been sold off and he had been sent back to his spiritual home, Charing Cross. 'Some of the stuff that took place in these cells . . .' He let the thought trail off. 'This used to be our only purpose-built facility for terrorists. Al Qaeda, the IRA, they've had all sorts in here.'

'And now it's going to be turned into luxury housing.'

Carlyle grunted. People always moaned about property developers but at least they built stuff. He turned his attention back to the stiff. 'He couldn't have been here long – doesn't smell too bad. Then again, it's like a refrigerator in here.'

'The woman who found him, is she one of the squatters?' A group calling itself the Anti-Capitalist Rainbow Front had broken into Paddington Green earlier in the week and announced plans to convert it into a community centre.

O'Sullivan consulted her notebook. 'Laura Taylor. She was having a look around and found a key to the cell block.'

'It was locked?'

'Apparently. Anyway, she went upstairs and told her mates. They held a vote and decided to call the police.'

'I suppose we should be grateful.'

'I got diverted here on my way to work. When I saw it was an unusual one, I thought you'd be interested.'

'Thanks.' Carlyle had first come across O'Sullivan on his return to Charing Cross, but he had already marked the inspector's card. In his book, she was a good cop and a reliable colleague. 'What does the pathologist say?' It suddenly dawned on him that they were alone. 'Where is everyone?'

O'Sullivan pointed at a fragment of twisted metal lying on the concrete floor. 'Your man Travis had his head blown off by a grenade. Someone suggested the rest of the body might be booby-trapped, so everyone's downed tools. They're waiting for the bomb squad.'

'Booby-trapped.' The commander's eyes widened. 'But you just stuck your hands in his pockets.'

O'Sullivan was unconcerned. 'If there was another bomb,' she reasoned, 'the squatters would've set it off.'

'Maybe . . . but maybe not.' Not wishing to test her theory, Carlyle promptly ushered her out of the door. 'Let's go upstairs.'

'This used to be my office.' The furniture hadn't been removed and a couple of paint pots stood in the corner, testimony to a protracted redecoration project, which had only been completed the week before he left and the station closed.

'Handy for going down to the cells and torturing people, I suppose.' Sitting in front of his desk, Laura Taylor didn't look up from her phone. The green-haired eco-warrior didn't smell too good, but she was fresh-faced and clear-eyed. Beneath a patina of grime and attitude, the commander imagined she was quite pretty. Her given age was twenty-four, she looked barely out of her teens, and he estimated she was a rough contemporary of his own daughter.

'What were you doing down there?' Carlyle belatedly noticed

6

the bruise on her cheek. There were deep scratches on the back of her right hand as well.

'I was having a look about.'

'Put the phone away,' he said brusquely.

The woman looked askance but did as she was told.

'You were exploring,' Carlyle recapped.

Taylor clasped her hands together and placed them on her lap. 'I needed a bit of time to think.'

'About what?'

'Stuff.'

'About the guy who hit you?'

She touched her face. 'How did you know?'

Lucky guess. 'What happened?'

'I thought you wanted to talk about the dead guy.'

Travis wasn't going anywhere: he could wait. Carlyle softened his tone. 'Just tell me what happened to you.'

Silence.

'He hit you?'

'I won't press charges.'

'One step at a time. Maybe I'll just take him down to the cells and rough him up a bit.'

'You?' She looked at the physical specimen in front of her, clearly unimpressed. 'I don't think so.' The beginnings of a smirk appeared at the corners of her mouth. 'You're old enough to be my dad.'

'Older,' Carlyle admitted. 'But I'm still sprightly enough to handcuff him to a toilet and break out the electric cattle prod.'

Her face hardened. 'Fascist.'

'That's right, I'm a fascist pig, whose job is to smash the . . .' he paused to check the flier on his old desk '. . . Anti-Capitalist Rainbow Front and shut down your basket-weaving workshops.'

Taylor looked genuinely confused. 'Basket-weaving workshops?'

Carlyle changed tack. 'Just tell me the name of the bloke who hit you or I'll have you and all your mates taken to a police station that's still open and placed in the cells there for a few days.'

'This is police brutality.'

Carlyle casually confirmed it was so.

'I don't talk to cops.' Taylor pouted.

Carlyle smiled. 'Neither do I.'

Staring into space, she mumbled, 'Reuben's not a bad guy. He's not violent.'

'He hit you, though.'

'We had a fight. He caught me with his hand.'

He punched you in the face. Carlyle took a deep breath. 'I'll have a quiet word.' She started to protest but he cut her off. 'Don't worry, he won't be arrested.'

'It was an accident.'

'Well, if there's another accident, give me a call.' He held out a business card until she took it. 'I'm sure the Anti-Capitalist Rainbow Front doesn't endorse that sort of thing.'

First impressions count. Carlyle's initial take on Reuben Barnwell was less than favourable. The guy oozed slacker arrogance. 'Shouldn't you be focusing on the guy whose head was blown off?'

'Do you know anything about that?'

'No, why should I?' Barnwell looked round the room. 'This is harassment. I should complain to the IPCC.'

Carlyle was surprised the squatter had heard of the Independent Police Complaints Commission. 'This just is me doing my job,' he said equably.

'No one could ever doubt it,' came the sarcastic reply.

'Why did you hit your girlfriend?'

'It was an accident.' Barnwell tried to change tack. 'Laura told me you used to work here.'

'I did.'

'You must've been sorry to see it close.'

'It's just a building. I do wonder why so many police stations are closing, though.'

'You're losing the battle.'

'What battle?'

'The battle to save capitalism.'

'Uh-huh.'

'Capitalism will destroy our planet and ultimately our civilisation. Only by ending capitalism, and finding a new system, immediately, can we hope to survive in any meaningful way to the end of this century.'

The guy sounded like an actor reciting his lines. Something was a bit off. 'How old are you?' Carlyle asked.

Barnwell stiffened in his seat. 'What's it to you?'

'You're way too old for a teenage girlfriend.'

'Mind your own business, copper. Anyway, for your information Laura's twenty-four.'

'However old she is, if you hit her again, I'll have you arrested.'

Barnwell stroked his chin. 'Are you threatening me?'

'Yes, I am.'

'Good. Well, I'm glad we sorted that out.' Jumping from his seat, Barnwell bounced towards the door. 'Nice meeting you, copper. I'll give Laura your best.'

TWO

Assistant Commissioner Gina Sweetman looked aghast. 'How much did they cost?'

'Bloody hell, Gina, what kind of a question is that?' Superintendent Susan Moran looked around the dimly lit dining room. It was well after midnight and they were almost the last diners in the hotel restaurant. Not that the place had been packed to begin with. For the cost of a single starter, they could have enjoyed a full meal at Pizza Express down the road. Moran hoped her boss would be picking up the tab on her expenses.

'Go on, I'm curious.' Sweetman took a slug of Chardonnay, wincing as the wine settled uncomfortably in her stomach. It was their third bottle of the evening and she was doing most of the drinking. 'How much?'

Moran swilled the wine in her glass. 'Five and a half grand,' she whispered. 'Plus VAT.'

'Jesus.'

'I should've got a doctor's note saying it was for medical purposes, rather than a cosmetic thing – would've saved me the tax.' Moran peeked at her boss's chest. 'Remember that, if you ever think about—'

'Not a chance,' Sweetman scoffed. 'I wouldn't waste my money. I'm sorry to say it, Susan, but you've been a right mug.'

'It's my money.' Moran overlooked the fact she had availed

herself of the Monkseaton Clinic's zero per cent financing offer to get the job done. 'And it's my business.' She searched in vain for a waiter who could bring them the bill. The final day of their Senior Women in Policing conference was due to commence in less than five hours. Moran had signed up for a networking breakfast on the theme of Sexual Harassment in the Workplace and How to Stop It. As far as her career went, stopping harassment in the Metropolitan Police was at least two decades too late, but hey-ho. Maybe the next generation of female officers would benefit, or the one after that. Ultimately, it was the superintendent's considered view that the only way you could ever deal with the problem was to staff the force entirely with women. It was a good idea, but not one that would ever come to pass.

Finally, she caught the eye of a nearby waiter and signalled they wanted to settle up.

'We haven't finished the wine yet.' The assistant commissioner grabbed the bottle, filling her glass almost to the brim.

'I've had enough. Time to call it a night.'

'Never could stand the pace, could you?'

'What?'

The assistant commissioner's eyes blazed with alcohol-fuelled righteousness. 'We've worked together for, what, fifteen years?' Her words were becoming more slurred by the minute.

'No, sixteen.'

'Eighteen.' Moran could still clearly remember her first posting, Stockwell police station. She had met Gina Sweetman, already an inspector and marked for greatness, at the end of her second week out of training college. Over the years, Moran had clawed her way further up the greasy pole than seemed possible for a girl from a poor part of north London. Sweetman, meanwhile, had risen to dizzying heights, promotion after promotion, until she'd found herself only two steps away from the Metropolitan Police's top job. Virginia Thompson had won the

11

race to become London's first female police commissioner but there was no reason why, with a bit of luck, Sweetman couldn't follow in her footsteps.

'So how come you do this without talking to me about it first? It doesn't matter how hard you work now, you'll always be known as the woman who had the boob job.' The assistant commissioner gulped more wine, as if she feared the drink might be taken from her at any minute. 'Your career is finished.'

She was woken by a text from Gina Sweetman: *Too much booze. V. sorry. Think you are great professional. Bygones?*

Bygones, my arse. Resisting the temptation to send a sharp reply, Moran struggled out of bed and slipped into the shower. Turning the water up as hot as she could stand it, the superintendent tried to wash away the profound irritation caused by her boss's inappropriate tirade.

The sorry episode had left her as upset as anything that had happened to her during her time on the force, with the possible exception of the initiation ceremony she had been put through in her very first week on the job. Decades later, she still bridled at the memory of being branded in a back room of the Griffin public house. Bent over the snooker table, skirt up around her ears, gritting her teeth while a couple of senior officers had inked her backside with the station stamp.

Embarrassed at the memory, she angrily soaped the violated buttock. It couldn't happen today. At least, she hoped it couldn't.

Downstairs, Moran found herself sitting in the middle of the hotel's misnamed Grand Ballroom, the only woman at a table of six at the Sexual Harassment networking breakfast, gulping down some much-needed caffeine. Sweetman was nowhere to be seen.

'The rules of the game have changed.' On a platform at the far side of the room, the event's sponsor, an entrepreneur called

Victoria Dalby-Cummins, was droning on about the need for men to start bucking up their ideas, big-time.

I bet no one's ever inked your arse cheek with a rubber stamp. Moran caught the eye of Terry Brunel, a loud Yorkshireman on the Met's Approved Contractor list, who had recently won a contract to refurbish half a dozen police stations in north London. The procurement panel of the Building and Infrastructure sub-committee of the Capital Projects Group had awarded the deal; Moran was a member of all three entities. Brunel was hosting the breakfast as a thank-you. As the speech ended, he nudged Moran's arm with his shoulder. 'Gina told me about your . . . thing.'

'Wha-at?'

Brunel's eyes flicked down to her chest. 'I thought you looked different. I couldn't put my finger on it.'

You're not putting your fat fingers anywhere, Moran vowed.

'I've always wondered, you know, if they feel like the real thing.' Brunel wiggled his fingers in anticipation.

'Terry, for Christ's sake.' Flushing with embarrassment, she pushed back her chair, trying to get out of reach of the Yorkshire Groper.

'Are you pleased with them?'

'Are you kidding?' Moran got to her feet before the pervert could lunge at her. 'Fuck off.' Resisting the urge to punch the man in the face, she stormed from the room.

Hermione Lacemaker wandered through the hotel lobby, glancing at a sign advertising a Sexual Harassment breakfast in the Grand Ballroom as she made for the lifts. A young concierge started to smile then checked himself, not wanting to appear uncool. Hermione was pleased at being recognised, despite hiding behind a pair of ostentatiously large sunglasses. Then again, *Goodbye Crazy* had opened last week and her face was on posters everywhere. According to her agent, the film had taken less than twenty thousand on its opening weekend, making it one of the ten worst performers of the year so far. That wasn't Hermione's problem, though. With more than seven hundred thousand Twitter followers and her own YouTube channel, she was a performer in demand.

Waiting for the lift, she ran through a list of some of the scripts currently before her. There were a couple of family cartoons, a toy tie-in, a superhero flick in which they wanted her to play a badger, and a couple of rom coms. For a woman who had already played Ophelia at the National, not to mention lead roles in a couple of well-received BBC dramas, it was all rather thin artistic gruel, if well remunerated. Hermione craved cash *and* kudos. Hopefully, Kenny Schenk would come through with both. Over the last four decades, the producer's movies had grossed seven Oscars and twenty-two nominations, not to mention incredible amounts of cash.

Hermione's agent, Graham Hughes, had called, burbling about an 'incredible' script. 'Take this part and a nomination's guaranteed, absolute bare minimum.'

In Nice, celebrating her BFF's birthday, Hermione scanned the synopsis. 'It's a medical movie, right?'

'Jeez, Hermione, it's a *love* story. Didn't you read the synopsis I sent you?' Hughes began reading: '"After contracting a fatal illness at the age of twenty-five, Seymour Davis is sent to a sanatorium and given only months to live. There, he strikes up a bromance with crazy-genius inventor Philip Bunce and devotes the rest of his life to helping his fellow patients and the disabled." It's wonderful, truly amazing. No robots. No aliens. No cartoons.'

'Sounds interesting,' was as far as Hermione was prepared to go at this stage.

'There's not even any sex in it, as far as I can see.'

14

'At the moment.' Hermione knew how easily that could change.

'The script's got Oscar written all over it. You're up for the part of Davis's wife.' Hughes named a handful of Hermione's peers. 'There are other names in the frame but, from what I hear, you're currently their number-one pick. It's not a lot of screen time but a shoo-in for a Supporting Actress nod.' He paused for breath. 'They want you to take a meeting, here in London, tomorrow morning.'

'For God's sake, Graham, I'm having a few days off.' Hermione chugged a beer as she watched Ella, the BFF, allowing herself to be chatted up by some Latin-looking bloke at the bar. 'What's the rush?'

'Because Kenny's in town.' Hughes named a hotel on Park Lane. 'He wants you to have breakfast in his suite.'

Hermione's stomach lurched downward. 'You've got to be fucking kidding. Everyone knows the guy's a total pervert.'

'A pervert with more Oscar nominations than almost any other person on the planet.'

'Remember how Becky said he tried to rape her once?'

There was silence on the line. Then Hughes responded, in a low voice, 'Remember how Becky used to have a career? Last I heard, she was auditioning for a job on a Turkish cruise ship.'

Finishing her drink, Hermione looked over to the bar. Ella and the Latin guy had vanished. The clock behind the bar told her there was still time for her to make the last flight of the day back to London.

'Do you know how hard I've had to work to get you this meeting?' the agent whined. 'I need you to be there. This is a great opportunity – it'll help take your career to the next level.'

'If he gets out of line,' Hermione insisted, 'I'm outta there.' She wondered why the line sounded familiar before recalling it came from her first big Hollywood movie, *Space Convicts*. She'd had four lines and that was the only one that hadn't ended up on the cutting-room floor. Still, *Space Convicts* had proved a valuable career stepping-stone. Her love scene with a werewolf-like alien had been voted the forty-sixth Best Sci-Fi Movie Moment by readers of the They Live fan website. Hermione was very glad her parents, who were more into Truffaut and Godard, had never seen the film.

'It'll be fine,' Hughes insisted. 'Kenny's dynamite. He needs to explode sometimes.'

'Well, he's not exploding over me.'

'Ha-ha. Look, there's nothing to worry about. He never travels alone – there'll be lots of his people around. And you're a big girl. You know how to look after yourself.'

THREE

You know how to look after yourself. Coming out of the hotel lift, Hermione wondered if she should have brought her pepper spray. It was illegal, but pretty effective. One of her exes, Giles, had volunteered to let her test it on him; the poor boy had never been the same since. She giggled at the memory of Giles rolling around on the floor, squealing like a stuck pig.

If things did get lairy, there was a rape alarm in her bag. The alarm wasn't as good a pervert-deterrent as the pepper spray, but it made a hell of a racket. Hermione doubted whether the noise would be enough to get the hotel's management to open up an eight-grand-a-night suite in good time, but it had to be better than nothing.

Striding down the corridor, she arrived at the Clinton Suite and rapped firmly on the door. After a few seconds, a pale assistant, dressed head to foot in black, opened the door. Hermione was vaguely aware of meeting him at a party in New York with Giles. To the best of her recollection, he was called Wayne, or Dwayne, something in that general ballpark of crap names.

'Right on time.' The gofer smirked. 'Thank you for coming.' Stepping aside, he watched her enter a reception room that was bigger than her entire flat in Shepherd's Bush. The far end was given over to a large picture window that looked out over Hyde

Park. In front of it a table had been set for breakfast: two places, with enough food for about a dozen people.

'Please help yourself to coffee and some fruit, or maybe one of the pastries.' Wayne-Dwayne-Whatever giggled, as if eating a pastry was the most *outré* activity imaginable. 'Mr Schenk will be with you in a minute.' Without waiting for a reply, he skipped into the corridor.

Hermione listened to the door click shut, then stepped over to the table. Placing her bag on a chair, she reached for the heavy silver coffee pot sitting in the centre of the table. Filling a cup, she lifted it to her lips, barely taking a sip. The room was silent, save for the gentle hum of six lanes of rush-hour traffic rising from Park Lane on the other side of the double-glazed windows.

Hermione contemplated the ghost-like reflection in the glass. Her look – minimal make-up, black jacket buttoned to the neck – was sombre and professional. It was true that her black jeans were so tight they might have been sprayed on but they, too, were a deliberate choice. It had taken her the best part of five minutes to squeeze into them; if things really went south, Schenk would have a hell of a job trying to get them off.

The thought sent a jolt of electricity through her chest. She giggled nervously. Conscious of her elevated heart rate, she ran through what she wanted to say to the producer: 'Thank you for considering me. The part sounds interesting, but I was wondering—'

'Hermione, how nice to see you.' The man himself appeared from an adjoining room. Wearing a hotel dressing gown, Kenny Schenk looked like he'd just rolled out of bed, which he probably had. Yawning, he ran a hand across his shaven head. 'Your people told me you came back specially from France to take this meeting. I appreciate it. Demonstrates the kind of commitment you need to make a Kenny Schenk movie.'

Trying not to think about what was – or wasn't – under the

man's dressing gown, Hermione gave her host a professional smile. 'Thank you for inviting me, Mr Schenk.'

'Kenny.' He beamed.

'Kenny.' She offered a couple of rushed air kisses before dancing out of his reach. 'Lovely to see you.'

'Mmm. The coffee smells good.' Pottering over to the breakfast table, Schenk waved at one of the chairs. 'Sit, sit.'

'Thanks.' Hermione stayed on her feet.

Schenk reached for the coffee pot. 'I need a couple of cups of Java in the morning before I get going.' He held up the pot. 'This is Java, right?'

'Uh. Hmm.' Hermione had no idea. 'Sure.'

Schenk poured himself a cup, downing it in a single gulp, then turned his attention to the food crammed on the table. 'Hungry?'

'I'm good.' Hermione stared at her boots, hoping the patent leather Dr Martens underscored the *Don't mess with me* vibe.

From behind his coffee cup, the producer gave her a sickly smile. 'I remember you in that hot scene in *Badass Bears . . .*' He picked up a slice of pineapple and dropped it into his gaping maw.

Hermione felt her cheeks start to burn. 'That was a body double.'

Schenk's eyes grew wide. 'No way.' He wiped some pineapple juice from his chin before reaching for another slice.

'My agent said there's a script.'

'Getting right down to business, huh?' Schenk's eyes narrowed. 'How badly do you want this part?'

Hermione looked down into her coffee. 'I want the part – in principle. It sounds interesting.'

Schenk reached inside his robe. 'How about we go and discuss it some more next door?'

Without thinking, Hermione took a step forward and threw the remains of her coffee into his face.

'Bitch.' Lunging at her, Schenk tripped on the belt of the dressing gown and went sprawling across the carpet. 'Ow.'

'Serves you right.' Buzzing, Hermione grabbed the coffee pot. As Schenk got to his knees, she brought it down across the back of his skull.

'Fuck.' Schenk sagged, but did not go down. It took a second blow and then a third before the producer hit the floor, face first. Once she was sure he wasn't getting back up, Hermione used the toe of her shoe to roll him onto his back. Dismayed to see an erection poking through the dressing gown, she quickly took a succession of photos with her phone.

'I would be great for the part in this movie,' she proclaimed, enjoying the adrenalin rush that came from battering one of the most important men in Hollywood and taking down a sex pest all in one go, 'and I fully expect to get it.' With his eyes rolled back in his head, all Schenk could manage by reply was a groan. 'And if I *don't* get it, these pictures'll go viral.'

'Fuck you,' a fluttering voice hissed.

'I don't think so, Kenny. How long do you think it would take for these photos to destroy you? Hours, I'd say – certainly no more than a few days.' Grabbing her bag, Hermione headed for the door. 'Thanks for breakfast, by the way. All in all, I think it was a very productive meeting.'

Carlyle fiddled aimlessly with his coffee cup as he watched people walking up and down Park Lane at speed. Everyone seemed to be in a blind hurry, even the beggars.

The arrival of a hard-faced but very attractive thirty-something woman put an end to his people-watching. 'Thank you for agreeing to meet me, Inspector.' Victoria Dalby-Cummins took the seat opposite. A slender young man emerged from the throng behind her and joined them without saying a word.

'Commander.' For someone who had never cared much for

titles, Carlyle found himself profoundly irritated when people failed to give him his due.

'My apologies.' Dalby-Cummins did not introduce her companion. 'Congratulations on your promotion.' She looked the policeman up and down. 'Presumably they give you a uniform.'

'I don't wear it very much.' Carlyle buttoned his jacket, in an attempt to conceal the crumpled Clash T-shirt underneath. At least it was clean.

'Imposter syndrome can be a bitch,' she smirked, 'so I understand.' Sensing his irritation, she moved on. 'It was a shame you didn't manage to come to visit my farm.' Dalby-Cummins ran stables and a large organic farm near the Welsh borders.

'That was a while ago now.' Carlyle recalled accepting the invitation. Then something had come up and he'd forgotten all about it.

'The offer remains open.'

'You're very kind.' Allergic to the countryside, Carlyle had no intention of schlepping out to God-knew-where. He couldn't remember why he'd said yes in the first place. 'I'd love to visit but, you know, getting time in the diary can be difficult.'

'I suppose, in your new job, you must be very busy – all those meetings.'

'Yes.'

'You even missed our breakfast.'

Carlyle had noticed a sign for the event on the way in: Sexual Harassment in the Workplace and How to Stop It. 'Wasn't it women-only?'

'Not at all.' Dalby-Cummins looked vaguely affronted. 'Everyone needs to engage with this issue. How are we going to educate men if we don't talk to them, explain what they're doing wrong?'

'Hm.' As a middle-aged man, Carlyle felt this was a topic best avoided. Engagement, he was sure, would lead only to disaster.

He had decided a while ago that keeping his mouth shut and his hands to himself was the sensible option.

'Of course, you know a bit about sexual harassment, with the Umar Sligo situation.' Sergeant Sligo, a close colleague of Carlyle's, had been forced to quit the Police Service after emailing photographs of his genitals to female officers. 'It's exactly the kind of unprofessional behaviour we were talking about this morning. It's simply not acceptable, these days.'

'That's why he had to resign,' Carlyle replied evenly, 'and work for your old man.'

'Why Harry hired Umar, I have no idea.' Harry Cummins, Vicky's late husband, had found a certain celebrity as Britain's self-styled Poshest Pimp. 'At least he stopped photographing his thing . . . and moved on to shagging one of Harry's girlfriends.'

Carlyle feigned ignorance. 'I was sorry to hear about what happened – to both of them.' Harry and Umar had both perished violently during a turf battle with a no-nonsense gangster called Vernon Holder.

'I wasn't,' Dalby-Cummins declared. 'Harry was an idiot and Umar, well, clearly, he was a sex pest.'

No need for condolences, then, Carlyle thought. It was well known the widow had dried her tears in double-quick time, then gone into partnership with the same Vernon Holder.

'What makes a man want to display himself, d'you think? Is it to do with some kind of trauma in childhood? A lack of proper toilet training perhaps?'

Carlyle felt himself redden slightly. 'No idea.'

Dalby-Cummins turned to her companion. 'What about you, Sandro? Do you feel the need to go about exposing yourself to all and sundry?'

The man has a name, Carlyle thought.

Dalby-Cummins clarified the question, in response to Sandro's blank look: 'Do you ever get the urge to wave your penis about in public?'

'A man who does that,' Sandro said quietly, 'is sick in the head.'

'A fair summation.' Dalby-Cummins belatedly made the introduction. 'Sandro's been a great help since Harry's death.'

Carlyle tried to move the conversation on. 'How is Vernon, these days?'

Dalby-Cummins didn't miss a beat. 'He spends most of his time in the Caribbean.'

'He's retired?'

'He's a sleeping partner.' She smirked.

'Give him my best next time you speak to him. And remind him that next time he's in town I'd like a word.'

Dalby-Cummins raised an eyebrow. 'About anything in particular?'

'Just a few loose ends.' The woman was beginning to annoy him, and Carlyle wished he had somewhere else to be. 'Tell me,' he asked, 'the people at your breakfast on sexual harassment, do they know you're a madam?'

Dalby-Cummins ignored the barb. 'I have a broad portfolio, Commander. Harry's legacy businesses are only a small part of my operations.'

Enough chat, Carlyle decided. 'What did you want to talk about?' Before he could get an answer, he was conscious of someone hovering at the edge of his vision.

'Excuse me, Inspector?'

'Commander.' Getting to his feet, Carlyle offered a hand.

'Ros McDonald. Head of hotel security.' She gave Dalby-Cummins an apologetic smile, still addressing Carlyle: 'Could I have a moment?'

Walking towards the lifts, Carlyle had the sense of a marker being called in. 'You helped me one time at the Garden Hotel.'

McDonald was pleased he remembered. 'I worked there with Debbie Burke.' She pressed the call button for the service lift. 'I moved here about a year ago. To be honest, it's been a lot quieter than I was expecting. Until now.' The lift arrived promptly. The doors opened and they stepped inside. McDonald pressed the button for the top floor, waiting for the doors to close before saying more. 'We've got a problem upstairs. I was going to see if I could get someone from the conference in the basement when I saw you in the café with Ms Dalby-Cummins.'

'You know Vicky?'

'She stays here sometimes, gets a special rate. She owns a few rooms.'

'She *owns* them?'

'You can buy individual hotel rooms. It's a popular form of investment, these days.'

'Uh-huh.' Carlyle's salary had almost doubled when he was made commander, but his pay packet still didn't allow him to think about investing in hotel rooms.

They rode the rest of the way in silence. When the lift doors opened, Carlyle found himself in a seemingly endless corridor. It took him a moment to realise something was wrong with the picture in front of him – there were no doors. 'Where are we going?'

McDonald signalled right with a plastic door key. 'It's all the way to the end and then left, the Clinton Suite.' She set off and Carlyle followed.

FOUR

It felt good, standing in a hotel room with a corpse at his feet. 'Did you call 999?' Carlyle circled the body without getting too close.

'Not yet.' Standing near the door, Ros McDonald folded her arms. 'One of the maids found him, about half an hour ago, when she came in to clean the room. I sent her downstairs for a cup of tea – she was a bit shaken.'

'I'm not surprised.'

McDonald flicked her chin in the direction of the man's death erection. 'How long's it gonna last?'

'No idea.' Carlyle peered at the gash above the stiff's left eye. 'He's taken a nasty smack, but it probably wasn't fatal. Maybe he had a heart attack.' He moved onto autopilot. 'I'll get Forensics. And call up a pathologist.'

'What about an ambulance?'

'There's no rush. The team'll find out what happened here and then we'll take the body away. In the meantime, keep the room clear. Make sure the maid is okay but don't let her go home. Someone'll need to take a statement from her.'

McDonald lifted a linen napkin from the breakfast table. 'And what about the, erm, guest?' Shaking it out, she waved it at Carlyle. 'Should I cover him up?'

'We don't want to contaminate the scene. Better leave him as he was found.'

'But it looks so gross.'

'He's not gonna look a lot better with *that* covering his modesty.' Carlyle chuckled. 'And, anyway, he's past caring.' He called Joaquin.

'*Hola, El Jefe.*'

The commander quickly ran through what he needed.

'What about your diary this morning?' The PA recited a list of meetings, which had Carlyle itching to jump out of the window.

'Clear my diary for the day.' Maybe the stiff wasn't such bad news after all. 'I need to focus on this for the moment.'

'Are you sure?' Joaquin had inherited from his predecessor a seemingly genuine concern for Carlyle's appalling performance statistics. 'The Quarterly Meeting Attendance Tables are due to be compiled next week and you're gonna be in trouble again.'

Carlyle didn't need to be told he would be at, or very close to, the bottom of the list. 'It's fine,' he insisted. When Joaquin demurred, he added, 'Get hold of Karen O'Sullivan. I need her here urgently.'

'You need her *where*?'

'The Clinton Suite.' Carlyle gave him the name of the hotel. 'I have a suspicious death here – a big name . . .'

'Ooooh.' Now Joaquin was interested.

'Keep it to yourself.' He winked at McDonald. 'I'll give you the juicy details later.'

'Yes, boss.'

'I need O'Sullivan, Forensics, all the usual bells and whistles.'

McDonald watched as he put his phone away. 'The owners hate this kind of publicity. The media will be all over it. There was a case, not long before I arrived – the servant of a Saudi prince was found hanged in one of the other suites. That was bad enough, but when it's a celebrity, it's even worse.'

Carlyle studied the corpse. 'This guy's a celebrity?'

'Don't you recognise him?'

The commander didn't have a clue. 'Who is he?'

'Kenny Schenk. He's a big film producer.'

'Was.' Carlyle texted Vicky Dalby-Cummins to let her know their meeting would need to be rescheduled. Her reply was immediate: *No probs. Maybe later in the week?* He resisted the temptation to propose a new time. Better to see how the current problem played out, rather than risk blowing out the Godmother for a second time. 'Surely a film producer isn't much of a celebrity.'

'He is in Hollywood.' McDonald reeled off a list of the dead man's movies. Carlyle had heard of most of them – he'd even seen a couple. 'I'm surprised we haven't had any press calls already.'

'Only three of us know,' Carlyle pointed out, 'you, me and the maid.'

'And the person who bashed his head in.'

'Four, then. Maybe more. Was he here on his own?'

McDonald confirmed there was an entourage. 'His production company's called Perendi Films. They've got an office in Soho.'

Carlyle noted the table, set for two. He resisted the temptation to swipe a pastry. 'Do we know who he was having breakfast with?'

'I'll check with the staff downstairs, see if they were told to expect anyone.'

'Hold off for now. Let's not feed the rumour mill.' There was a sharp knock on the door. 'For now, draw up a list of people we'll need to talk to.'

'Sure.' McDonald cautiously opened the door.

'Police.'

McDonald stood aside, allowing Karen O'Sullivan to enter.

Carlyle was pleased to see the inspector. 'You got here quick.'

'I was at a networking breakfast downstairs.' O'Sullivan was going for the *Matrix* look in a full-length black leather coat and black jeans.

'Handy.' Carlyle made the introductions. 'The inspector's the best person to handle a delicate situation like this,' he told McDonald.

'You're too kind.'

O'Sullivan contemplated the victim's priapism without comment. 'Everything's in hand. Forensics are on their way and the pathologist should be about twenty minutes.'

'Good.'

'Who's the dead gentleman?'

Carlyle was delighted not to be the only person in the room who didn't recognise the film producer. 'This is – was – a film producer by the name of Kenny Schenk. American national.'

O'Sullivan let out a disapproving cluck. Foreign deaths meant more paperwork.

'A famous guy.'

Another cluck.

'I would say he's in his sixties.' Carlyle looked in vain to McDonald for confirmation. 'Late middle-age, anyway.'

'What happened?'

'Someone gave him a smack on the head, which may or may not have killed him. That's about all we know at the moment.'

'And this is the primary crime scene?'

'Looks like it,' Carlyle confirmed. 'He was found by a maid.'

'About an hour ago now,' McDonald chipped in.

'Ms McDonald alerted me.' Before O'Sullivan could ask, Carlyle added, 'We go way back.'

'You were at the breakfast, too?'

'I was taking a meeting downstairs.'

'I bumped into the commander in the lobby,' McDonald confirmed, 'and he very graciously agreed to come up here and provide what assistance he could. The room's not been touched. I was going to compile a list of people you might want to talk to in the hotel.'

Carlyle waited for the head of security to leave, then said, 'You're in charge here, Karen. I thought I might go and talk to the staff in the dead man's Soho office.'

O'Sullivan's eyes narrowed. 'Isn't that way below your pay grade?'

'Some of us like to roll our sleeves up. And, anyway, I promised Ros we'd deal with this discreetly.'

'It'll be dealt with *properly*,' the inspector insisted.

Carlyle couldn't disagree. 'Properly *and* discreetly.'

The quote had been painted onto the meeting room wall: *Leadership is the art of getting someone else to do something you want done because he wants to do it.* Carlyle couldn't work out if it was cynical or just honest.

'Eisenhower.'

'Sorry?' The commander turned to face a thin man in an expensive suit, with a pale blue, button-down shirt open at the neck. He had a shock of white hair and the healthy glow of someone who spent a lot of quality time with a personal trainer.

'Dwight D. Eisenhower, thirty-fourth President of the United States.' The man had one of those irritating mid-Atlantic accents that made him impossible to place – he could as easily have hailed from Bolton as Boston. Taking a seat opposite Carlyle, he slid a business card across the table: Rick Ford, Co-founder, Perendi Films. 'Would you like some coffee?'

'I'm fine, thank you.'

'Are you sure?' Ford seemed genuinely disappointed at the rebuff. 'We've got a very nice Cuban blend.'

'It's fine,' Carlyle repeated. 'I promised myself a trip to Bar Italia once I'm finished here.' The famous café, barely a two-minute walk away, had fantastic coffee, not to mention the best cheesecake in London.

'Good choice,' Ford agreed. 'I go in there every morning.' He clasped his hands together, as if in prayer. 'Meantime, what can we do for you?'

Having been kept waiting for more than twenty minutes already, Carlyle was not going to break the news gently. 'Your associate, Mr Schenk, was found dead in his hotel room this morning.'

'Oh, my God.' Ford looked shocked but Carlyle suspected it was an act. Perhaps he had known this day would come.

'I was wondering if you might be able to tell me why Mr Schenk was in London,' Carlyle said briskly, 'in particular, what his schedule was this morning. What meetings did he have in his diary? In particular, who was he having breakfast with?'

'What are you saying?' Parking his grief, Ford immediately got down to the practicalities. 'Did someone kill Kenny?'

Carlyle defaulted to official-speak. 'At the present time, no determination has been made as to the cause of Mr Schenk's death.'

'But the police wouldn't be here if . . .' Ford's brain started buzzing with the possibilities. 'You wouldn't be here if there wasn't a suspicion of foul play.' He seemed slightly elated at the prospect.

'Mr Ford, our investigation is only beginning. At this stage, speculation of any kind is both pointless and counter-productive, a waste of time.' Carlyle lifted his gaze past the film producer to the window and the Soho rooftops beyond. 'The information I am sharing with you at this time should be treated in confidence until we can inform Mr Schenk's family.'

'I can help.'

'Good. Ideally the family will find out properly from us, not via the media.'

'There's two ex-wives, a sister and Kenny's mother. All of them are in the States. No kids, thank God.' He reached for his phone. 'I'll get you their details.'

'Thank you.'

30

'Kenny's diary might be a bit harder to decipher. I'll need to talk to his PA in LA.' Ford consulted the chunky watch on his wrist. 'She won't be up for a while.'

'Doesn't anyone in London have access to his diary?'

A look of discomfort crossed Ford's face. 'Kenny's London PA resigned a couple of weeks ago. We haven't got round to hiring a replacement yet.'

Pining for his slice of cheesecake, Carlyle allowed it to slide. 'Give me the family contact details now and I can get the rest later.'

Delighted to snag one of Bar Italia's pavement tables, Carlyle gave a cheerful waitress his order. As he waited for his cheesecake, a woman took the seat opposite. 'Inspector Carlyle,' she gazed at him as a hungry fox would look at a chicken, 'long time no see.'

Sitting up in his seat, Carlyle did nothing to hide his dismay at being denied his me-time. 'It's Commander Carlyle.'

'Are you kidding?' Abigail Slater raised an eyebrow but managed to stop short of bursting into laughter. 'I never had you pegged for senior management.'

'Neither did I.' Carlyle appreciated the lawyer's direct manner, if nothing else. He tried to remember the last time they had met. Ten years, give or take, was his best guess. Slater didn't look much older. The possibility of plastic surgery crossed his mind. 'How about you? Still working for the kiddie-fiddlers?'

Slater grimaced. 'I'm working for myself, these days. I left the Catholic Legal Network a long time ago.'

'Couldn't stomach working for predators like Father Francis McGowan any longer?' McGowan was a sex offender who had fallen to his death from a church rooftop while Carlyle had been in close attendance. Did he jump, or was he pushed? In all honesty, the commander couldn't remember.

'Come on, Insp— Commander, you were never much of

a moraliser. We're in the same game, more or less. You come across all sorts. We've both had to deal with much worse than the odd troubled priest.'

'McGowan was a—' Carlyle stopped himself. The waitress arrived with his cheesecake and promised the coffee would soon follow.

'Interesting choice.' Smirking, Slater ordered a small bottle of San Pellegrino.

Carlyle made no move to reach for his fork. 'To what do I owe this pleasure? Or was it a pure coincidence you were walking past?'

'Rick Ford said I'd find you here.' Slater fished an envelope out of her bag and handed it over. 'He asked me to give you this. He would have emailed it, but you didn't leave him your details.'

Carlyle opened the envelope and pulled out a single sheet of A4 paper.

'Kenny Schenk's next of kin,' Slater confirmed.

'You know about Schenk?'

She waved her phone at him. 'The story's been online for almost fifteen minutes.'

Carlyle issued a reflexive curse. Stuffing the list into his pocket, he checked his own phone. The death of Kenny Schenk had already generated more than a hundred stories and was trending on Twitter.

He also had a text from O'Sullivan: *Presser at 5.* Taking the list back out of his pocket, Carlyle snapped it with the phone, sending the image to the inspector with an instruction to inform the next of kin ASAP. Hopefully, the time difference would work in their favour: if family members were asleep in the US, there was at least a chance that local law enforcement could reach them before the media arrived on their doorstep.

Not a good start.

Putting the list away again, he turned his attention back to

Slater. 'What's your involvement in all of this?' he asked. 'Are you working for the film company?'

'No, no.'

The waitress returned with their drinks. Carlyle downed his coffee in a couple of quick gulps. He'd get another to go with his cheesecake once the lawyer had left.

'I represent Hayley Briggs.' Slater unscrewed the cap and took a slug of water straight from the bottle. 'Hayley worked as an assistant to Kenny Schenk at Perendi Films. She resigned after Mr Schenk performed a sex act in front of her in the back of a taxi on the way to a film premiere.' The lawyer looked around, keeping her voice low. 'We're suing Schenk, Perendi Films and the Kenny Schenk Foundation for harassment, sexual assault, sexual discrimination and constructive dismissal. This morning, I was due to have a meeting with Rick Ford, Kenny Schenk and Perendi's lawyers. They were supposed to be tabling an offer for an out-of-court settlement.'

'I suppose your client's chances of a big payday have gone up in smoke,' Carlyle said.

'Not at all.' Slater looked at him like he was terminally stupid. 'Dying does not absolve you of your sins. We can still go after Kenny's estate, the assets of the company, and those of the charity. Plus, now he's dead a lot of women are going to be coming out of the woodwork with similar stories. Every new claim will increase the pressure on Rick Ford and the family to reach a sensible settlement.'

Carlyle patted the list in his pocket. 'You seem to be on pretty good terms with Rick Ford, all things considered.'

'We've worked together in the past,' was all Slater would divulge. 'It's *never* personal. Plus, Rick knew the risks when he got into bed with Kenny, so to speak. It was widely known Kenny Schenk was out of control, a serial sexual predator. No one in the industry ever did anything about it.'

33

'Whatever happened to *Everyone loves you when you're dead*?' Carlyle wondered.

'Kenny will be the exception that may or may not prove the rule. It's a shame he didn't face proper justice before he died.'

'Like Jimmy Savile.'

'Like a lot of men,' Slater said coolly. 'But belated justice is better than no justice at all. Mark my words, now Kenny Schenk's gone, many, many women will come forward, all of whom will need legal representation.'

'You ambulance-chasing bugger,' Carlyle blurted. 'You want me to drum up business for you.'

Slater placed a business card on the table. 'I want you to give my details to Hermione Lacemaker.'

'Who?'

If Slater was surprised by his ignorance, she didn't let it show. 'Hermione is one of our finest young actors.'

Carlyle noted the choice of word. It seemed 'actress', among others, had fallen out of favour.

Slater reeled off the names of various films Carlyle had never heard of and a TV series he vaguely recalled his wife watching. 'More important, though, Hermione is a hero of our time.' Slater paused, her eyes twinkling with mischief as she took another drink from her bottle of water. 'The woman who bashed Kenny Schenk's skull in.'

FIVE

'How'd it go with Kenny?'

'How did you expect it to go, Graham?' Hermione Lacemaker paced around the tiny office of GHT – Graham Hughes Talent – like a caged animal, the hum of traffic from the Edgware Road in the background.

'Did you get the part?'

'We never got round to discussing it.'

'No?' Not much of an actor, the agent couldn't bring himself to sound surprised.

'The pig was in his dressing gown and— Urgh.' Coming to a halt, Hermione fiddled with her favourite Dunhill lighter. She had given up smoking months ago but, right now, her desire for a cigarette was almost overwhelming. An actor had once told her you never really quit – 'All you do, darling, is extend the pauses between fags' – and Hermione knew he was right. 'It was horrible.'

Slumped in his faux-leather executive chair, feet on the desk, Graham Hughes seemed supremely unperturbed by his client's distress. '"It's exciting because he isn't quite normal."'

Hermione rolled her eyes. 'Where do you come up with such nonsense?'

'It was a line in a movie,' Graham confessed.

'Well, Kenny's all-too-normal; a fat bloke with too much

power and too little self-control. I can't think of anything less appealing.'

'You handled him, though?'

'I handled him.'

'Good girl.'

Fuck off, you berk. Not for the first time, Hermione fantasised about ditching Graham and signing up with a proper agency, a big American firm with nice offices in Soho, Nespresso coffee machines and decent biscuits. Graham had delivered her first break, a supporting role in a Jane Austen adaptation, while she was still at university. By now, though, Hermione felt she had paid the guy back many times over. With every passing month, Graham's ability to take her career to the next level seemed more in doubt.

'Kenny's always been a bit edgy. He demands more of the talent.'

'Yeah, right, like a hand-job before breakfast.'

Graham's eyes widened. She could see the movie playing in his head and she didn't like it. Lifting his Nikes off the desk, he sat up. 'You didn't?'

'No, of course not.' Hermione clenched the lighter tightly in her fist. If she didn't get her hands on a Marlboro in the next ten minutes, she feared her head might explode.

'Hm.'

'What the hell does that mean?'

'It means "hm". Kenny doesn't take rejection very well.'

'The guy's a classic sexual predator.'

'Never been convicted . . . as far as I know.'

'If his movies hadn't made billions, he'd have been in jail years ago.'

'It was ever thus.' Leaning back in his chair, Hughes stuck his hands behind his head. Hermione considered the torn jeans and outsized trainers with dismay. The guy was ancient – he had to be pushing forty – but insisted on dressing like a teenager. 'Kenny offers as close as you can get to guaranteed success.'

'Great, next time *you* can go over there and let him . . .'

The agent's expression grew grave. 'I hope you didn't piss him off too much.'

'I think you can safely write it off.'

'Herm—'

'Don't start whining, Graham,' she snapped. 'You're an agent, not a pimp.'

Hughes muttered something about semantics.

'We need to move on. What else is in the pipeline?'

'Nothing we haven't discussed already.' The agent ran through a list of deeply unappealing projects.

'What about the women-only version of *Julius Caesar*?'

'It's already been cast. Anyway, it doesn't fit with the arc of your career. The pay's shit and its total global audience is a couple of hundred overeducated lesbians.'

'Graham!' She aimed a half-hearted kick at the desk.

'Well, it is. If I don't spell out the realities of the marketplace to you, who will?'

'We need to think outside the box.' Hermione's father was a City banker – his extended financial support had allowed her to hone her craft in the early years – who always talked about thinking outside the box. 'What's the innovative solution to our current situation?'

'Well . . .' the constipated look on Hughes's face indicated an attempt at thought, '. . . there's always panto.'

'Panto?'

'Yeah, you know, the thing they do at Christmas: *Aladdin, Cinderella, Jack and the Beanstalk.*'

'I know what panto is.'

'I got an email about it the other day.' Mistaking her incredulity for enthusiasm, Hughes pointed at the dark screen of the expensive iMac he never bothered to switch on. 'They're doing *Dick Whittington* at Wimbledon and *Cinderella* at the Palladium. I'd have to see, but you might get offered Prince Charming.' Sifting through the clutter on his desk he named a couple of others up for the part. 'If I can find my bloody phone, I'll show you the email.'

'Are you serious?'

'Yeah.' He started throwing papers into the air. 'I had it and then, I dunno, I didn't. God knows what I've done with the damn thing. My whole bloody life's on that phone. I'm buggered if I've lost it.'

Hermione couldn't have cared less about his phone. 'I mean about me doing panto.'

Muttering to himself, Hughes tossed a bunch of files on the floor. 'Yeah, why?'

'I'm not some reality-TV saddo,' she hissed. 'Why would I do panto?'

'Lots of big names do it, these days. One of the guys from Spandau Ballet did it the other year. *Peter Pan*, I think, in Birmingham.' Hughes giggled. 'Not that I'd make you go to Birmingham – it's a long time to be away from home. I'm only looking at things in and around London.'

'I don't do panto . . . anywhere.'

'You want to think outside the box,' Hughes counselled. 'Panto's thinking outside the box.'

'Well, obviously, Graham, we're talking about different boxes.' While he continued to search for his phone, Hermione made her exit. 'This is not good enough,' she declared. 'You're fired.'

The first Marlboro tasted like heaven. The second, not so much. Flicking the cigarette into the gutter, Hermione checked flights to Nice on her phone. For once, BA seemed to be running to schedule, so there was no reason why she shouldn't be back on the Riviera in time for dinner. Booking a flight out of City Airport, she texted Ella with her arrival time, adding, *Lots to discuss.*

In her official capacity as Hermione's BFF, Ella would doubtless have some good ideas on what to do next, career-wise. To date, Ella's own acting career had proved to be a slow burn, but she was represented by a proper agency – they had Sam Mendes *and* Glenda Jackson on their books, as well as managing image rights for Oliver Reed's estate – and Hermione had no doubt her friend would get there in the end. That Ella was up for a part in the next Spielberg movie was proof positive she was moving in the right direction. And Ella, Hermione was sure, would *never* take a meeting with a guy like Kenny Schenk in his hotel room. The girl had inner steel that Hermione lacked. She was a genuine friend, though, and Hermione was sure Ella could be prevailed upon to get Hermione a meeting with her own agent. The guy was a bit too smooth for Hermione's taste, but he was a definite step up from Graham.

Waiting to cross the road at a set of traffic lights, Hermione checked her Twitter account. Much to her annoyance, her follower numbers still languished below ten thousand. She vowed to have some strong words with her social-media guy. Perhaps Graham wasn't the only one who would be getting dropped from Team Hermione. A fat finger brought up a list of the top trending stories. Towards the bottom of the usual mix of the bizarre and the depraved, the half-witted and the self-obsessed, Hermione's eyes landed on 'Kenny Schenk'.

'What's the fat bastard done now?' The lights changed and she stepped into the street, tapping the story as she did so.

Top Hollywood producer found dead in his hotel room.

'Oh, my God.' Hermione giggled. 'Really?' Stopping in her tracks, she flicked through a procession of tweets reporting the news. 'Shit, shit, shit.'

Slowly, she became aware of a succession of blaring horns. The lights had changed again, and she was standing in front of a long line of traffic. Holding up a hand in apology, she rushed to the far side of the road and into the sanctuary of the Underground.

'Fancy a quick one, love?'

Carlyle felt himself blush as he tried – and failed – to come up with a witty reply. Being identified as a potential punter wasn't exactly a compliment but it was kind of nice to be asked.

'We've got special offers all this week.'

With the hags' laughter ringing in his ears, he continued down Rupert Street, on his way to meet Helen for lunch.

'Commander?'

Carlyle blinked, catapulting himself forward the best part of thirty years. Across the road, the corner where the elderly hookers had teased him was now a building site, part of the neighbourhood's gentrification. Soho's going to be the New Covent Garden, he reflected, sanitised and dull. The café they were sitting in had – until not so long ago – been run by an Italian family who'd owned it since the end of the Second World War. Now it was part of a ubiquitous chain – there were at least a dozen others within a five-minute walk.

The meeting – he couldn't bring himself to call it a brainstorm – had been his idea. He turned to Danny Hunter, a long-time acquaintance, and said, 'Someone put a grenade in Travis's mouth and pulled the pin.'

'Travis is the name we've given him,' O'Sullivan explained, 'until we make an ID.'

Hunter was a former military policeman but even he found the MO unusual. 'Had a kid with a fake grenade stuck up his backside once,' was the closest he could come up with. 'The poor sod ended up having a mental breakdown.'

40

'This one was definitely real, a V40,' Karen O'Sullivan showed him a picture on her phone, 'made in Holland.'

'Easy enough to acquire,' Hunter advised, 'if you have a few contacts.'

'You think we might be looking for a military guy?' Carlyle asked.

'Not necessarily. I mean, how hard is it to pull the pin out of a grenade?'

'The killer wanted to make a point,' O'Sullivan suggested.

'It was personal,' Carlyle added, 'and planned.'

'The location might be significant,' Hunter mused. 'Once you can put a name to the victim, it might start to make sense.'

O'Sullivan stared into her tea. 'It's not easy.'

'Sorry not to be more help.' Hunter finished his coffee and got to his feet. 'I'll have a think, ask around. If I can come up with anything, I'll let you know.'

Carlyle half rose out of his chair and shook his hand. 'Appreciate it.'

O'Sullivan watched him go. 'Whaddya think?'

Carlyle's mind was blank. 'We've got our work cut out on this one,' he said finally, 'and no mistake.'

'On the other thing you asked me to look at . . .'

'Yes?' Carlyle tried to remember what it was.'

'I can't find anything on Reuben Barnwell.'

Ah, yes, the little shit who hit his girlfriend. 'Nothing at all?'

'Not even an NI number,' O'Sullivan confirmed. 'The guy doesn't seem to exist.'

Carlyle didn't know what to make of that. 'Keep looking.'

'Is it that important?' O'Sullivan bridled. 'I mean, Travis and Kenny Schenk are rather more of a priority.'

The commander had to admit she was right. 'Let's divide and conquer. You keep trying to ID Travis and keep digging on Barnwell. I'll handle Schenk.'

O'Sullivan smelt a rat. 'Have you got a lead on Kenny?'

'I need to speak to a guy.' Unsure about the quality of Abigail Slater's information, Carlyle didn't want to bring his colleague into the loop just yet. 'We'll see.'

'Hermione sacked me but the good news is I've found my phone.' Graham Hughes waved the handset in front of Carlyle. 'If I'd lost that, I'd've been up Shit Creek, know what I mean?'

Carlyle wasn't interested in the man's phone. He stared at the cheap movie poster on the wall: *In a Lonely Place*. Humphrey Bogart and Gloria Grahame: '*I was born when you kissed me. I died when you left me. I lived a few weeks while you loved me.*'

A great movie, in the commander's estimation, a great book, too, for that matter. 'Was your sacking connected to Hermione's meeting with Kenny Schenk?'

'Not really.' Hughes tossed the phone onto his desk. 'It was only later, after she'd left, I found out the man had died.'

Carlyle stood on a dirty rug, arms folded in a no-nonsense pose. Marking Hughes down as a bullshitter, he wasn't in the mood to be messed around. 'Why did she sack you,' he asked, 'if you didn't have a falling-out over Kenny Schenk?'

'Talent is mercurial.' Hughes tried to sound philosophical about being dumped. 'It comes with the territory.' After some gentle probing, he continued, 'We were talking about job opportunities. Hermione got pissed off because I said she might want to think about doing panto. Some people are still sniffy about it, but there can be good money in it. Plus, you don't need to take your clothes off and simulate sex with some fat bloke old enough to be your grandpa.'

A significant plus, Carlyle acknowledged.

'Lots of big names do it, these days: Robert Lindsay, Jimmy Osmond . . . the Fonz.'

'The Fonz?' Carlyle was impressed.

'Yeah, he's done it a few times, I think.'

'Wow.' It took a moment for Carlyle to remember he didn't give a monkey's about panto. 'How did the meeting with Kenny Schenk come about?'

'I got a call from one of Kenny's people a couple of days ago. There was a part they were considering Hermione for in their next movie. These things often come up at the last minute. They wanted to arrange a meeting while Kenny was in London. Hermione was in Nice when I called her on holiday. It's fair to say she wasn't best pleased about being dragged back to London, but she agreed to the meeting. Which was the right decision. You don't say no to Kenny Schenk.' Hughes paused. 'At least, you didn't.'

'It was an important part?'

'Definitely. The kind of role you win awards for.'

'Who called you to set it up?'

'Dwayne.'

'Surname?'

'I know him as Dwayne. He organises Kenny's calendar.'

'Procures girls for him.'

'It wasn't like that,' the agent insisted. 'At least, not with *my* people. I don't pimp out my clients.'

'No.'

'This was a professional business breakfast to discuss a particular role. I wouldn't have sent Hermione otherwise.'

'But Ms Lacemaker wasn't keen to go. Presumably she was concerned Schenk would be . . . How best to put it?' Carlyle paused. '*Unprofessional.*'

'Kenny was a pantomime villain. Hermione could look after herself.'

The guy wanted to stick to his script. 'Where's Hermione now?' Carlyle demanded.

'No idea. She told me I was sacked and walked out. Do you think she killed Kenny?'

'Our enquiries are ongoing,' Carlyle replied. 'We cannot assume anything about the causes or circumstances of Mr Schenk's death at the present time. You must not surmise anything from our conversation. Neither must you repeat it to anyone. Everything discussed here must remain confidential.' He listened to the agent's unconvincing assurances, before adding, 'If you say anything about this, to anyone, I'll arrest you for obstructing a police investigation. It's a very serious offence, carrying a prison sentence of up to three years.' He paused, giving Hughes the opportunity to signal he understood the gravity of the threat. 'If you hear from Ms Lacemaker, tell her to contact me, and let me know immediately she's been in touch.' This time, he remembered to leave a business card before he walked out.

SIX

'Should we even be talking about this, dude?' Dwayne Doud shoved the remains of a KitKat into his mouth. 'I let your girl in and then I was outta there. Kenny was still in his bedroom. I didn't see nuttin'.'

'She's not my girl, these days.' Graham Hughes giggled nervously. 'The cops are on her tail. She's going down for Kenny's murder.'

'The Feds?'

'Yeah, the po-leese.' Hughes's grotesque parody of an American accent caused Doud to scowl. 'They were here, asking for my help.'

Doud's expression became even more pained. 'Did they ask about me?'

'Nah. You're in the clear. They know Hermione did it. She could get crazy when she was pissed off – which was more often than not, by the way – but I didn't think she would ever behave like that.'

'Women're a mystery at the best of times.' Doud wondered how much one of the celebrity news websites would pay for the juicy titbit the agent had dropped into his lap. Nothing, if he wasn't first with the news. 'Look, man, gotta go. Things're pretty crazy here right now. There's a whole bunch of TV crews outside. Everyone's been told not to speak to the press.'

'I need to meet with Rick,' Hughes said quickly, before Doud could hang up.

'No chance, man. Rick's gone into, like, lockdown. Kenny was our God, and now he's, like, gone. It's like the end of the world 'n' shit. Everything's on hold until we can work out what the hell's gonna happen next.'

We? The idea anyone cared what Dwayne thought was laughable. 'I only need five minutes,' Hughes pleaded. 'The part Hermione was up for? I've got someone else who'd be great for it. Really fantastic.'

'Not happening, bro. But if you hear from Hermione, tell her to call Rick. He wants to talk to her.'

'If he wants to talk to her, he needs to talk to me.'

'Get hold of Hermione and he'll give you your five minutes.'

There was a click and Hughes was left listening to dead air. Catching Humphrey Bogart staring down on him, the agent flipped him the finger. 'Fuck off, Bogey,' he snapped. 'Don't give me shit as well.'

'Hermione Lacemaker's flight should be landing in Nice in about twenty minutes. Shall I alert the French police you want her picked up?'

'No, I'll deal with it. I want to keep it low key for now, until we know precisely what's going on.'

'It isn't standard protocol.' Deirdre Smith was less than impressed. 'I've tracked her movements through Border Force's computer system. My bosses can see what I'm up to, you know.'

'Don't worry,' Carlyle tried to sound reassuring, 'there won't be any comeback. If there is, I'll take any flak.'

'Damn right you will. I could get the sack.'

'You won't get the sack.' Carlyle was irked by the IT analyst's attitude. A couple of years earlier, he had given Deirdre's feckless son a free pass on a drugs offence. All he was doing now was calling in the favour.

Deirdre seemed set on working herself up into a state of some agitation. 'You shouldn't be dragging me into this,' she complained. 'Spying on private citizens isn't part of my job description.'

It's 99.9 per cent of your bloody job description. And, a minute ago, you were going to shop Hermione Lacemaker to the French police. 'I'll drop you an email,' Carlyle promised, 'make it all official.'

'You need to fill out a form.' Deirdre spewed out a line of letters and numbers.

'Sure.'

'And make sure you date it yesterday.'

'Will do,' Carlyle replied cheerily. 'Always a pleasure doing business with Border Force.' Laughing off her abusive response, he moved on to his next call.

'Carew Forensic Services.'

'Hey, Dudley, it's John Carlyle, how're you doing?'

'Inspector Carlyle!' Dudley Carew cried. 'To what do we owe this nugatory pleasure?'

Nugatory? Nonplussed, Carlyle forgot to mention his promotion. 'I was looking to speak to your lovely daughter.'

'Gloria's in Germany.' Dudley didn't sound best pleased about it. 'She's gone to take part in a White Hat hacking competition. White Hat hackers being the good guys.'

'I knew that,' Carlyle lied.

'She'll be back in a week.'

'Hm. Maybe you could help me out.'

Silence.

'I suppose,' Dudley said eventually, 'this is the point where I remind you – once again – that CFS is *not* a charity and the Metropolitan Police Force does *not* meet the criteria required to be considered a potential pro bono client.'

'Metropolitan Police *Service*,' Carlyle corrected him, 'we stopped being a force a while ago.'

'Bloody political correctness,' Dudley complained. 'You're the police. You're supposed to use force to keep the criminals and undesirables in order.'

It was a point of view with which Carlyle had considerable sympathy. 'I was wanting to track someone down and—'

'Staggered – teeth knocked out?'

'Sorry?'

'*The Times* Cryptic Crossword,' Dudley replied. 'My brain's not in gear this morning. Give me a hand and I'll listen to your plea.'

'Teeth knocked out . . . erm . . . gobsmacked?' He spelled it.

'It fits.' Dudley called out a succession of further clues until it became painfully clear Carlyle's first answer had been a lucky guess. 'You're hopeless at this.'

'I never said I was any good.'

'What's the name?'

'Huh?' Caught up on the crossword, Carlyle had momentarily forgotten the original purpose of his call.

'The name of the bloke you're trying to track down on the QT.'

'I'm not—' Carlyle abandoned the lie. 'It's a woman, Hermione Lacemaker.' Dudley's reaction indicated the name meant nothing to him. 'She's in Nice. I want to find out where she's staying.'

Dudley let out a harsh guffaw. 'You want me to hack every hotel and lettings service in Nice?'

'White Hat hacking.' Carlyle belatedly wondered if what he was asking was even remotely possible.

'Yeah, right,' Dudley grumbled. 'Gimme a couple of hours. I'll send you a text.'

***

'Who the hell's Superintendent Susan Moran?' Virginia Thompson was having an awful day. The mayor had chewed her out for failing to get to grips with the wave of moped crime in the capital, *The Times* had written a mischievous story claiming London now had a higher murder rate than New York, and the Royal Family was complaining, again, about their security detail. Worse than all of the above combined, her son had flunked his mock A-level exams. At this rate, the skunk-smoking waster was heading for some Mickey Mouse course at Oxford Brookes University, rather than PPE at the real thing.

Drumming her fingers on the desk, the commissioner listened to her special adviser, a consultant called Bruce Allen, run through the highlights of the superintendent's reasonably successful but overwhelmingly unspectacular career.

'And now she wants to sue the Met for sexual harassment because Gina Sweetman criticised her . . . appearance when they were getting drunk on some course?'

Allen tried not to smile. 'The assistant commissioner isn't contesting what happened. She admits she was intoxicated at the time. And she has repeatedly apologised to her colleague.'

'So why isn't that the end of the matter?' Knowing worse was yet to come, Thompson eyed the adviser warily.

'Two words.' Allen's tone was almost wistful. 'Abigail Slater.'

Thompson groaned. 'What's she got to do with all of this?'

'Slater and Moran live in the same apartment building. They're members of a book club for the female residents.'

'Abigail Slater reading a bloody book, ha-ha. I don't believe it.'

'It seems to function more as a networking thing,' Allen continued. 'Other members include a Labour MP, a couple of businesswomen and a former Olympic rower. It has its own WhatsApp group.'

Thompson held up a hand, requesting silence. Allen had

come from MI5 where he had doubtless learned many different tricks. If Moran's phone had been hacked, she didn't want to know. 'Moran tells Slater her tale of woe at the bloody book club and Slater decides to turn it into a money-making exercise?'

'That's about the long and short of it.'

'Pushing for a lucrative out-of-court settlement, no doubt.'

'Terry Brunel is also named in the particulars. He's the contractor who—'

'I know who Terry is.' Thompson suddenly saw the whole mess lurch closer to her personally.

'Of course you do.' Allen's smile was unsettling. Thompson was sure he was winding her up. 'Was he there when Gina lost it?'

'Brunel was a separate but related incident. I need to see the details of the claim. I've got a meeting with Anna Clarkson this afternoon. She seems on top of it.'

'Good.' Clarkson, the Met's head of Legal Services, was as pragmatic as she was hard. This might be a mess but, with her in charge, there was little chance things could get too much worse. 'We need to do some damage limitation.'

'Gina Sweetman will go through the usual disciplinary procedures. The charge is gross misconduct. There's a chance she could get sacked . . .' Allen paused '. . . but it won't happen if you put in a good word for her.'

'I suppose I'll have to,' Thompson sighed, 'as long as she agrees to go into rehab.'

'She already has.' Allen named an eye-wateringly expensive clinic in the Yorkshire Dales. 'The NPCC are paying for it.'

'That'll be another story if the press gets hold of it,' Thompson grumbled. 'The National Police Chiefs' Council wasn't set up to dry out drunks.'

'The assistant commissioner is up to date with her dues,' Allen noted. 'Plus, I think you'll find she isn't categorised as a drunk but, rather, as a colleague suffering from an alcohol-related condition.'

'She always liked the sauce too much.' Thompson struggled to empathise. 'Very unprofessional.'

'It's simply one more thing to manage. No one ever said this place ran itself.'

'No,' Thompson agreed, 'but sometimes I do wonder whether I should've stayed in Northumbria. The worst we ever had up there was a bit of sheep rustling.'

'Well, now you're the first ever female commissioner of the Metropolitan Police. Managing stuff like this will cement your place in the history books . . . if we handle it properly. This is a good prompt for setting up a once-in-a-generation review into sexual harassment in the Met to establish a world-leading code of conduct for all staff, especially those in senior positions.'

Leaning back in her chair, Thompson contemplated the London panorama through the window. 'One senior female officer mocking another for having cosmetic surgery isn't what most people understand as sexual harassment.'

'A commission allows us to get ahead of this.'

'A commission, now, is it? A minute ago, it was a review.'

'A commission of review,' Allen continued evenly, 'led by a senior officer from outside London and staffed by solid citizens from around the Met.'

Thompson raised an eyebrow. 'Presumably you have people in mind?'

Allen handed over a list.

The commissioner scanned the names without enthusiasm. Most were wearily familiar, mediocre time-servers to a man and woman. Near the bottom, however, was one Thompson hadn't expected. 'John Carlyle?' she asked. 'Really?'

Walking out of Nice airport, Carlyle was confronted by pleasant sunshine. Finding the back of the taxi queue, he checked his phone. Annoyingly, there was no message from Dudley Carew. He was in the middle of deleting a stream of junk emails when *Joaquin* flashed up on the screen. Feeling more than a little guilty at fleeing his post, the commander decided attack was the best form of defence. 'Have you sorted the colour scheme for my office?'

'Huh? Oh.' The PA took a moment to gather his thoughts. 'I'll send you a picture. See what you think. Facilities say you need to decide by the end of the week or they won't do it.'

'I'll leave it to you,' Carlyle grunted. 'Did you need something?'

'The commissioner wants to see you.'

'The commissioner?' Carlyle had only met the woman once, when he'd attended a Policing in the Community event, along with his wife, Helen, and about five hundred other guests. They'd shaken hands and exchanged a couple of pleasantries. Helen had been less than impressed with the woman; Carlyle hadn't felt the need to take a view, either way.

'In person.'

'That's going to be difficult.' Carlyle relayed his current location, roughly 640 miles south of Scotland Yard.

'You're in France?' Joaquin sounded dismayed rather than surprised. 'The commissioner will want to know.'

'I'll explain later. Do me a favour, book out the rest of the week as holiday.'

'Leave has to be agreed at least one month in advance,' said Joaquin, sternly, 'unless there are circumstances that—'

'Just fiddle the bloody form,' Carlyle hissed. 'Tell the commissioner I've had to deal with a family issue. Book in a meeting for next week, if she still wants to see me then. She can always give me a call if it's urgent.' He looked forlornly at the empty taxi rank. He counted at least eight fares in the line before him. It was going to be a long wait. 'What does she want, anyway?'

'Mr Allen didn't say.'

Bruce Allen's involvement guaranteed it wouldn't be anything good. Carlyle knew the commissioner's special adviser by reputation: a superannuated ex-spook with reported links to various dodgy right-wing groups. All in all, a man best avoided. 'See if you can find out what it's about.' Joaquin promised he would try his best. 'I'll see you next week.'

A text from Dudley Carew arrived as he finally slid into the back of a white Merc. *Hermione Lacemaker registered at La Perouse under Nicola Gray (her real name), along with an Ella Donovan.*

'La Per-ooze hotel.' Carlyle cringed at his pronunciation, but it was good enough to get a nod of acknowledgement from the taxi driver, an Arab-looking woman in a Rolling Stones tour T-shirt.

'No far,' she promised, as they pulled away from the kerb.

'What the hell are you doing in Nice?'

Carlyle liked her lack of deference for his rank. Back in the day he'd been pretty much the same. Sitting on his hotel bed, chugging an eight-euro bottle of Heineken, he recounted his pursuit of Hermione Lacemaker.

'Why didn't you get the French police to pick her up?' O'Sullivan asked. 'There was no need for you to go down there yourself.'

'I fancied a trip.'

'I always knew you management types had too much time on your hands.'

'I was a proper cop once.'

'Once.'

'You don't sound too convinced.'

'Oh, I am.' The inspector's tone softened. 'I've been asking round. Everyone says you were a good cop.'

Carlyle winced at the use of the past tense.

'A hard-nosed bastard, who didn't take any shit and went his own way.'

That was more like it.

'Liked to pick and choose his cases. Always happy to stick his nose in other people's business.'

Enough feedback, thanks.

'Like you're doing with *my* case, now.'

'I didn't choose this case, it chose me. Don't worry, though. If there's any glory to be had at the end of it, it's yours.'

'Not necessarily. Assistant Commissioner Sweetman bowled up to the Schenk press conference and basically ran the show. All the journalists think it's her case now.'

'What's her interest in Schenk?'

'Maybe the case chose her,' O'Sullivan said sarkily.

'Very funny.' If Carlyle liked swanning in and out of other people's cases, he didn't like other people swanning in and out of his. 'Let's worry about Sweetman later. The immediate priority has to be Hermione Lacemaker.'

O'Sullivan agreed.

'We don't actually know what happened with Schenk yet. There's no need to drag Hermione through the mud if it turns out Schenk had a heart attack.'

'The media have already got her name,' O'Sullivan pointed out. 'They're going crazy.'

Carlyle thought back to his conversation with Graham Hughes. The agent seemed exactly the kind of sleazebag who would throw his former client under a bus for a few quid. Carlyle regretted not giving the little scrote a couple of slaps.

'I can't imagine it's going to take them long to track her down.'

'I've got a head start.' Carlyle finished his beer. 'If I can have a quiet chat with Hermione, before the media descend on her, it'll make things easier later.'

'She should've stayed in London and got lawyered up,' was O'Sullivan's verdict.

'Yeah.' Abigail Slater's card was still in his pocket. Carlyle hated the woman but there was no doubt she was good at her job. Innocent or not, the actor would need good advice. Padding into the bathroom, he put O'Sullivan on speakerphone, listening to her update on the investigation while he had a piss and freshened up.

'We're not going to know the cause of death for a few days. Schenk's body's been taken to Horseferry Road, but they've got a serious staff shortage. Something to do with Brexit.'

'Eh?' Carlyle wondered how Westminster public mortuary could be so dependent on foreign staff.

'Most of them were Polish, and half have gone home. Autopsies are taking up to three weeks. Schenk's been pushed to the front of the queue but we're still going to have to wait a while.'

'Let me speak to Hermione,' Carlyle repeated, 'and we can take it from there. There's no point in getting an arrest warrant – with all the attendant hoopla – if it turns out it was a cardiac arrest.'

'She still smacked him on the head with the coffee pot.'

'Yeah?' Carlyle thought back to the heavy silver pot sitting on the breakfast table. 'A rather unwieldy weapon.'

'It was definitely used on Schenk's skull,' O'Sullivan confirmed. 'We've got five different sets of prints on it. Schenk, two members of hotel staff and two sets unknown. Presumably one belongs to Ms Lacemaker.'

Carlyle thought back to Dudley Carew's text. 'Nicola Gray.'

'Huh?'

'That's her real name.'

'Doesn't matter,' O'Sullivan grunted, 'if everyone knows her as Hermione Lacemaker.'

'You'd better check Nicola Gray doesn't have a record.'

'Unlikely.'

'I know, but still. It would be embarrassing if she had previous and we'd missed it.'

O'Sullivan conceded the point. 'It would help if you could get her prints while you're out there.'

Carlyle gave a weary sigh. 'Leave it to me.'

'You don't ask, you don't get.'

'Right.' Four sets of prints, plus those of Kenny Schenk. Even if the coffee pot did turn out to be a murder weapon, any lawyer worth their salt – like Abigail Slater, for example – would make mincemeat of any attempt to pin the film producer's death on the actor. Carlyle realised he was wasting his time in Nice: if the woman had two brain cells to rub together, she'd tell him to do one.

'From what I've read,' O'Sullivan said, 'Hermione's a nice middle-class girl, went to Bedales and Oxford, loves children and animals. The kind of person who likes to help the police with their enquiries.'

'Not if they think they could be facing a murder charge.'

'The girl's not stupid. She got a first in English literature. Did a dissertation on *Macbeth* and Queer Theory.'

'What, pray tell, is Queer Theory?' Carlyle wandered back into the bedroom.

'If it comes to it, she can always claim self-defence.'

'Is that what you're gonna tell the CPS?'

'The CPS,' O'Sullivan proclaimed, 'won't touch this with a barge pole.'

'They might go for manslaughter,' Carlyle mused. 'They love cases that get them in front of the cameras. Plus, they wouldn't want to risk the backlash of letting another pretty white girl cheat justice. Not after the kid at Cambridge who stabbed her boyfriend twenty times while off her face and was only sent to some drug rehab place.'

56

O'Sullivan knew the case. 'I think she was at Oxford. And she only stabbed the guy a dozen times.'

'Still, how many black kids get off their heads on heroin, kill their partners, avoid prison and get sent off for counselling?'

'Fact of life,' O'Sullivan noted wearily. 'When're you going to talk to Lacemaker?'

'I need to find her first. She's supposed to be here, in the hotel, but no sign yet.'

'While you look for her, I'll let the local police know you're in town, as a courtesy.'

'Thanks.'

'And warn them about the imminent arrival of the British press.'

SEVEN

Carlyle spoke to a solicitous clerk, whose English, although heavily accented, was better than his own schoolboy French. The woman raised an eyebrow when he flashed a Met warrant card but did not question his authority. After giving a short monologue on protecting the privacy of guests, she consented to call Ms Gray's suite with the news 'an important English policeman' was present in Reception and would like a word.

Message sent, Carlyle retreated to one of the lobby's very comfortable chairs. After ten minutes, an elegant, dark-haired woman emerged from the lifts and looked around.

Getting to his feet, the commander approached her. 'Hermione?'

The woman shook her head. 'I'm Ella Donovan. A friend. Who are you?'

Carlyle handed over his warrant card and took a step back while Donovan studied it. 'I need to speak with Hermione.'

Donovan returned the ID. 'What makes you think she's here?'

'Are you saying she's not?' With little or no leverage, Carlyle kept his irritation in check.

'You've got no authority here.'

'I'm here unofficially. I thought it was more important to try to deal with this thing quickly before it gets out of control.'

'It's already out of control.' The woman folded her arms. 'Have you seen Twitter?'

Right on cue, two dishevelled middle-aged blokes appeared in the foyer, speaking in English. Journalists. Carlyle watched them walk up to the desk.

'I'm looking for Hermione Lacemaker,' one told the clerk, talking slowly and loudly, the very caricature of the Englishman abroad. 'Which room is she in?'

The clerk's eyes drifted towards Carlyle, but she remained mute.

'Hermione Lacemaker,' the second reporter repeated, dropping two fifty-euro notes on the desk, 'the famous actress. *Kwel chambre*?'

'Gentlemen.' Adopting a thick French accent, Ella Donovan sauntered over to the desk. 'How may I help you?' Before they could reply, she spoke quickly to the clerk in a language that sounded to Carlyle like Russian. Nodding, the clerk disappeared into the office behind the desk.

'We're looking for the English actress Hermione Lacemaker.' The first reporter didn't bother with any introductions. 'She's staying here, in your hotel.'

Donovan gave them a big smile. 'I am sorry, but we are not able to give out any information about guests. As I told to the other gentlemen, it is against company policy.'

'The other gentlemen?' The hacks looked at each other in dismay.

Biting his lip, Carlyle pretended to study his phone.

'The three other English gentlemen. They were here an hour or so ago.'

There was some unhappy mumbling from the new arrivals as they reviewed this most unfortunate development.

'What did you tell them?' the second journalist asked Donovan.

'Nothing.' *No-theeng.* 'We take the confidentiality of our guests very seriously.'

'The other, erm, gentlemen,' the first hack said, 'where did they go?'

'I don' know.' Donovan thrust a thumb towards the entrance. 'They said something about dinner.'

Relaxing slightly, the second reporter fished out a couple more fifties, dropping them next to the first pair on the desk. Ella considered the pile of notes but said nothing. The mime was repeated twice more before Ella stepped forward and scooped up the cash. 'Hermione Lacemaker was booked in here,' she whispered, 'but it was only a decoy. Celebrities do this all the time. They book one hotel but stay somewhere else.'

Groaning, the reporter reached for his cash only for Donovan to shove it into her jacket pocket. 'But I know where she's really staying.'

Cue a murmur of delight from the hacks.

'My friend at the Luminy says Ms Lacemaker arrived there three hours ago.'

Hack number one pulled out a pen and a receipt from Duty Free at Heathrow. 'Spell it for me, love, if you don't mind.'

Donovan obliged. 'She's registered under the name Gloria Grahame.'

'Graham.'

'With an *e*, like the actor.'

'Yeah, right.' The hack clearly had no idea who Gloria Grahame was.

'I think it's supposed to be some kind of joke.'

'A joke, yeah, very good.' The hack was already heading for the door, his mate in tow.

Donovan followed them, keen to see them off the premises. 'You didn't get any of this from me, though.'

'No, no,' burbled hack number one. 'We never betray our sources.'

Carlyle stifled a laugh.

'This Luminy hotel,' his colleague enquired, 'how do we get there?'

'It is up in the hills, about thirty kilometres.' Donovan pulled a leaflet for a car-hire firm from a stand near the entrance. 'It won't take long to drive there at this time of the evening.' She handed over the leaflet to hack number two. 'The rental office is round the corner from here. If you tell them the hotel sent you, you'll get a discount.'

'Righty-ho, much obliged.' Saluting Donovan with the leaflet, the reporter led his colleague back out onto the street.

'*Bonne chance.*' Donovan gave them a cheery wave. 'Good luck.'

She retreated inside to a one-man round of applause from the commander. 'That was fast thinking.'

Donovan gave a small bow. 'All those improv classes finally came in useful.'

'You're an actr—, erm, actor, too?'

'Couldn't you tell?' Donovan gave him an exaggerated pained expression. 'I'm not sure about the French accent, though.'

'It was good enough for those clowns.'

'I speak French . . . Spanish, Italian and Russian.' Donovan looked at the clerk, who had reappeared behind the desk. 'Daria will say nothing if anyone else turns up looking for Hermione.' Donovan tendered the money the hacks had left. After a little persuasion, the receptionist pocketed the notes.

'Two down, one to go.' Donovan turned her attention to the commander. 'Why should I trust you?'

Carlyle dropped Abigail Slater's business card on the desk. 'Whatever happened with Kenny Schenk, Hermione's gonna need a lawyer. This woman's very hard-nosed, exactly the kind of person you want on your side in a situation like this. Google her. Google *me*, if you want. Hermione can give Ms Slater a call and she'll confirm I'm who I say I am, not some nutter, or a reporter.'

'Same thing.' Donovan stared at the card for several seconds before picking it up. 'Wait here.' She floated towards the lifts. 'I'll be back.'

Carlyle was on his second whisky in the hotel bar when Donovan reappeared.

'You took your time.' The booze helpfully took the edge off his irritation.

'Hermione's been talking to the lawyer.' Ushering him across the lobby and into one of the lifts, Donovan pressed the button for the sixth floor. 'Ms Slater seems a very forceful operator.'

'That's one way of putting it.'

'She said you're a bit of a tosser.'

'I've been called worse.'

'"He can be an annoying little shit," were her precise words.'

'I get the picture.'

'But she thinks you're trustworthy.'

Well, well, Carlyle thought. Looks like I've got a secret admirer.

'Ms Slater says Hermione can talk to you, as long as she listens in to the conversation.'

'First, we need to establish some rules of engagement.' Slater was no less irritating for being present only via the speaker on Hermione Lacemaker's iPhone. 'You know how important it is for everyone to be on the same page.'

'It's always good to be on the right page.' Sitting in a rather stiff chair, Carlyle scanned the spacious suite, trying not to feel too jealous. His own room, two floors below, was barely bigger than the coffee-table on which the phone sat. In the background, the Mediterranean vista contrasted sharply with his view of the hotel's rubbish bins.

'My client will give you a full and unabridged account of what happened during her meeting with Mr Schenk.'

Carlyle looked at Lacemaker, sitting next to Donovan on a sofa opposite, daintily sipping from a can of Diet Coke. 'I've retained Abigail,' the actor confirmed, 'to represent me in this matter.'

'Everything Hermione says at the present time is strictly off the record,' Slater chipped in. 'You will not make any recording of the conversation or take any written notes. In due course, I will accompany her to a police station in London where she will provide a formal statement.'

'Understood.' Carlyle was perfectly happy to keep their meeting secret. Evidence gleaned here couldn't be used in an English court anyway.

'No charges,' Slater continued, 'will be brought against Hermione in relation to this matter.'

'You know I cannot give any guarantee at this stage of the proceedings.'

'My client is not to be charged with any alleged offence,' Slater insisted.

'But—'

Slater talked straight over him. 'Once you've heard her story, you will see that no charges *should* be brought. Whatever the immediate causes of Mr Schenk's demise, the man was, indisputably, the author of his own misfortune. Hermione is simply the latest victim of the man's vile, predatory behaviour.'

I've heard lots of stories in my time, Carlyle reflected. Most of them end up being shown, at best, as only a partial version of the truth. Plus, Lacemaker was a professional thesp, able to spin him a line at the drop of a hat. However, this was no time to quibble. He consented to Slater's ground rules. If he needed to arrest Hermione Lacemaker later, he would have no qualms about going back on his word.

'Then we have an agreement,' Slater purred. 'Hermione, over to you.'

Lacemaker placed the Coke can carefully on the coffee-table. Sitting back, she made good eye contact with the commander before launching into her quickly rehearsed monologue. 'My agent arranged the meeting for me to discuss a part in one of Kenny's – Mr Schenk's – upcoming film projects. I turned up at the hotel at the appointed time and was let into Mr Schenk's suite by one of his assistants.'

Name? Carlyle said nothing. Let the girl tell her story. Questions could come later.

'The assistant left, and I helped myself to a coffee. Then Mr Schenk appeared. It looked like he'd rolled straight out of bed. He was wearing a bathrobe and wanted breakfast.' A practised pause. 'There was some small-talk and then he got down to brass tacks.' Another pause. A little cough. 'It was, like, how much d'ya want the part? He went to grab me, and I smacked him over the head with the coffee pot.' Lacemaker got to her feet and folded her arms. 'That's it. He was rolling around on the floor cursing and groaning when I left. He definitely wasn't dead. And he wasn't dying, either, only bashed up a bit.'

'Are you sure he wasn't seriously hurt?'

'He was getting off on the whole thing.' She waved a hand at the phone on the table. 'You can take a look for yourself. There are some photos on there to prove it.'

'You can look,' Slater chimed in, 'but no copies. And nothing is to be used outside this meeting.'

Carlyle reiterated his consent. Once he'd seen the images, the lawyer said, 'The next step is to get Hermione home. We'll have a meeting, then come to the police station to make a statement.'

'What about the media?' Lacemaker asked. 'They're already downstairs and they'll be all over the airport.'

Slater didn't miss a beat. 'I'm sure the commander can sort something out. I would fly down and bring you back personally, but I've got a most important engagement that can't be moved.

I'll see you in my office tomorrow morning – let's say eight. If we need to change the venue or there's any other problem, I'll let you know.'

She hung up.

Lacemaker looked at Carlyle expectantly. 'What's the plan, then?'

The commander didn't have a clue.

Ella Donovan came to his rescue. 'Pietro can help us out,' she burbled. 'His jet's at Mandelieu.'

'Pietro's Ella's new boyfriend,' Lacemaker explained. 'He's a health-supplements entrepreneur with his own private jet.'

'He's not my boyfriend,' her friend corrected her. 'I've only known him a day.' She gave Carlyle a smile that was, frankly, rather unsettling. 'And a night.'

'But he's smitten,' Lacemaker insisted.

'For sure he's smitten. I mean, *come on*, who wouldn't be?' Donovan started typing a message to her new beau. 'We were going to fly to Istanbul, but I'm sure Pietro'll be happy to take us to London instead.'

The commander had travelled on a private plane only once before, transporting a convicted fraudster from Manchester to an appeal hearing in London on a jet provided by the crook's lawyer. The cabin crew consisted of a solitary grumpy granny and he wasn't even offered a cup of coffee. By the time they'd landed at Luton and fought their way through the north London traffic to the court, it would have been quicker to take the train. To add to Carlyle's annoyance, the appeal was successful.

'Second time lucky.' Carlyle climbed aboard Pietro the pill salesman's plane at a small airport outside Cannes. While Hermione Lacemaker and Ella Donovan made themselves immediately at home, Carlyle, not the greatest fan of flying to begin with, tried not to think about taking to the skies in such a tiny aircraft.

This time, the inflight service lived up to expectations. A couple of glasses of excellent whisky helped take the edge off his anxiety. Carlyle was contemplating asking the stewardess for a third when a smiling Pietro came and sat in the seat opposite. A handsome boy, with a shock of black hair, he radiated health, wealth and self-confidence. 'You,' he purred, in heavily accented English, 'are Hermione's father?'

'No.' Carlyle pointed at the two women at the front of the plane, necking champagne like it was going out of fashion, 'that was Ella's idea of a joke. I'm, erm, a friend of the Lacemaker family,' he assured his host. 'It was very kind of you to give me a lift.'

'No problem.' Pietro's smile waned as he studied his guest. 'But you look very pale. How are you feeling?'

I'd feel better with another drink, Carlyle thought. He weighed the empty tumbler in his hand. It was heavy, crystal. 'Same as always, I suppose.'

The look of concern on Pietro's face grew. 'I wonder, are you getting enough vitamins in your diet?'

Carlyle had no idea.

'It's a big problem, you know? Almost seventy per cent of European men are deficient in one or more of the main vitamin groups. Thirty-four per cent are seriously deficient in three or more.'

'Interesting.'

'When you get older it becomes more of a worry, and having a stressful job adds to the problem.' Pietro looked at him like a physician fearing the diagnosis was bad. 'What is it you do?'

'Consultant.' Carlyle didn't miss a beat. 'Not too much stress.'

'And do you exercise?'

Once in a blue moon. 'A couple of times a week,' Carlyle fibbed. He tried to think of the last time he'd been to his gym in Covent Garden. It certainly wasn't in the last month, maybe even two.

'You need to stay active and take responsibility for your health.' Pietro jumped from his seat. 'I have something that might help.' Stepping into the galley at the back of the plane, he returned moments later carrying a large plastic tub of pills with a label bearing the legend 'ALPHA MALE'. Underneath, it said, 'Extreme multi-vitamin formula'. 'This is our bestseller.' He handed it to Carlyle. 'I want you to try it and let me know how you get on.'

'Thank you.' Carlyle looked at the instructions, which recommended taking two pills in the morning and two at night, with meals. 'It's very kind of you.'

'My pleasure.' Pietro gave him a pat on the arm. 'We sold more than a hundred and thirty million euros of this product last year. It's the market leader.'

'Must be good.'

'It's *very* good,' the businessman confirmed. 'Whatever your fitness goals, this is the ideal daily supplement.'

I don't have any fitness goals, Carlyle thought dolefully, unless you count staying alive.

'There's vitamin D, to help with calcium levels, selenium, which fights stress, and vitamin B5, to counter fatigue.'

'I'll give it a go.'

Pietro seemed delighted with his response. 'If you like them, I can get you a special deal through our UK supplier. They'll put together a special programme utilising our Typhoon Rage protein formula range. It'll make you feel like a new man.'

'Thank you.' Carlyle gave silent thanks to the stewardess, who had appeared with a fresh drink, saving him from further small-talk about vitamins. As Pietro retreated to canoodle with his girlfriend, he took a couple of pills from the tub and washed them down with the Scotch.

'Self-medicating?' Lacemaker dropped into the seat vacated by Pietro.

'I don't particularly like flying,' Carlyle confessed.

'And I don't particularly like playing gooseberry.' Lacemaker contemplated the loved-up couple. 'You wouldn't think they'd only just met, would you?'

'I wonder,' Carlyle whispered conspiratorially, 'what she sees in the multi-millionaire vitamin king with his own private jet?'

'I give it about a week,' Lacemaker murmured. 'Ella gets through them at a rate of knots.'

'And what about you?'

'I'm taking a break from dating.'

'I did that thirty-odd years ago.'

She gave him a sideways glance.

'When I got married,' Carlyle added hastily.

'You don't have to make an effort after that?'

'You still have to make an effort, but it's different.' He tried to explain it. 'It's like you don't have to watch your step the whole time.'

'I know what you mean. The whole dating thing is such hard work.'

'I don't remember it being much fun,' Carlyle agreed.

She looked at his hands. 'Where's your ring?'

He wiggled the fingers of his free hand. 'Don't wear one. Never have. Not into jewellery.'

She rolled her eyes. 'A man who doesn't wear a wedding ring,' she teased, 'is usually trying it on.'

'My wife doesn't wear one either.'

'Weird.'

'Not to us.'

'And what does she do, Mrs Carlyle?'

'She's not called Mrs Carlyle, either. Helen kept her own name when we got married.'

'Didn't that annoy you?'

'Not at all. Helen runs a medical charity. She's responsible for

68

hundreds of people. It's a far bigger job than mine. Why should she change her name because we got married?' Lacemaker clearly didn't get it, so he moved on. 'Anyway, thanks for agreeing to come back.'

'Why would I go on the run?' Lacemaker reasoned. 'I've done nothing.'

Carlyle didn't express a view. 'When we get back to London, Abigail Slater'll make sure you're properly looked after.' He couldn't believe he was talking up the ambulance-chasing lawyer, but continued, 'When you're ready, she'll accompany you to the police station to make a formal statement. If the press show up, you can go in through the back entrance. We'll make the whole thing as painless as possible.'

'Good. I've got a lot on my plate when I get back. I need to find a new agent for a start.'

Carlyle feigned ignorance.

'Graham's history. He isn't able to get me in front of the right people at this stage of my career.'

Carlyle wondered who the 'right people' might be. 'He did get you a meeting with Kenny Schenk.'

'Only so Kenny could try and . . . you know.'

'Yes, well, there is that.' The commander's blushes were saved by the pilot announcing that their descent into Biggin Hill was about to begin. Fastening his seatbelt, he turned his attention to the leaden skies outside.

EIGHT

Outside the airport terminal, Carlyle stared at the tub of vitamins at his feet. He was happy to be back on the ground but annoyed with himself for taking a call from the commissioner's special adviser.

'Where are you?' Bruce Allen demanded.

'I'm on leave.'

'Not according to your calendar.'

'It's my PA.' Carlyle sighed. 'He's hopeless.' He felt a prick of remorse for dumping on Joaquin, but it quickly passed.

'I need to see you tomorrow.'

'I'm still on leave,' Carlyle insisted.

'Come and see me as soon as you get back. I've got a job for you. Or, rather, the commissioner has.' He hung up. Carlyle watched Slater usher Hermione Lacemaker into the back of a black limousine. As he approached the car, the lawyer gave him one of her trademark insincere smiles.

'I'm sorry, Commander, I'd offer you a lift, but I need to speak with my client in private.'

'No problem.' Carlyle scanned the empty taxi rank on the far side of the road wondering how he was going to get back to London. Ella Donovan and Pietro had already buggered off and Biggin Hill seemed pretty much deserted. The airport was only twelve miles from London but, as far as the commander was concerned, that put it in the middle of bloody nowhere. Even if he could find a cab, the size of the likely fare made his stomach churn.

The lawyer was oblivious to his concerns. 'I'm told Inspector O'Sullivan is formally in charge of the Kenny Schenk investigation,' she said. 'Karen's an excellent officer.'

'You know her?' Carlyle wondered if he was about to be outflanked by the Sisterhood.

Slater ignored the question. 'I'll liaise with the inspector about the arrangements for Hermione to give a formal statement. In the meantime, I'd be grateful if you could make the inspector aware of our agreement. I think it's better if she hears about it directly from you.'

That would be a tricky conversation. Carlyle watched the car drive away and was googling a local taxi service when a battered Volvo pulled up at the kerb. The window buzzed down and Karen O'Sullivan gave him a cheery smile.

'You came all the way out here?' Carlyle made no effort to hide his surprise as he climbed in.

'I've IDed him.' O'Sullivan was exultant.

'Who?'

'Travis.'

'The man with no head, right.' Carlyle pulled on his seatbelt as she moved away from the kerb. 'How?'

'His shoes.'

Carlyle recalled the double monks.

'They were bespoke, specially made by a guy in Shoreditch. The owner's name was written inside.'

'Good spot.' Carlyle admitted he would never have thought to look inside the dead man's shoes. 'Who is he?'

'Richard Jobson.'

'Like the singer?'

To his consternation, O'Sullivan had never heard of the Skids.

'This Richard Jobson's a property developer. And get this – his company bought Paddington Green police station to turn it into flats.'

'The killing'll be something to do with the deal,' Carlyle decided.

'Maybe. It's hardly the only controversial deal he's done, though.' She mentioned a tower block on the river, near Blackfriars. There was a row about him buying the site on the cheap.

'We're making good progress. Got an address for Mr Jobson?'

'He has the penthouse apartment in the Blackfriars block.'

'Next of kin?'

'He's on wife number three.'

'All right.' The commander settled back into his seat. 'Let's go and pay her a visit.'

The journey back into the city gave him plenty of time to fill in the inspector on his French adventure.

'I can't believe you promised Lacemaker immunity,' O'Sullivan groused.

'I didn't do any deal,' Carlyle insisted.

The inspector was sceptical. 'I wouldn't trust Abigail Slater an inch.'

'I wouldn't trust her a hundredth of an inch but we've not got much choice on this occasion.'

'The famous John Carlyle pragmatism.'

'You've got to be realistic. Slater got Hermione to speak to me.'

'I don't understand how she signed her up as a client so quickly.'

'Slater already represents Schenk's ex-PA. She was in a meeting with Rick Ford when the news of Kenny Schenk's death broke. Maybe Ford let it slip.'

'I spoke to him.' O'Sullivan was unimpressed. 'He gave me bugger-all. I don't know about Schenk, but Ford's certainly a piece of work. He was in the station for over an hour, and I don't think his lawyer let him say more than three words. All the time he sat there with an irritating smirk on his face as he looked down his nose at me.'

Carlyle tried to sound sympathetic. 'I know the type.'

'Film-making,' O'Sullivan decreed, 'is one of those businesses where everyone's bent, one way or another.'

'In the old-fashioned sense of the word.'

'Yes, yes,' the inspector stammered. 'Don't get me wrong, I wasn't making any kind of homophobic comment. Or any kind of inappropriate comment for that matter.'

Carlyle held up a hand. 'I was only pulling your leg.'

'The film industry's not the kind of thing I'd want my daughter to go into.'

'Your kids are how old?'

'The boy's eight, the girl ten.'

'Nice ages. We're through that phase. Our daughter's at Imperial now.'

'Imperial?' O'Sullivan was suitably impressed. 'You must be very proud.'

'I'm really chuffed,' Carlyle admitted. 'Alice has done very well.'

'One good thing about ending up with a proper degree – she won't be chasing stardom. Not in the movies, anyway.'

'To be fair, Hermione Lacemaker seems pretty sensible.'

'You don't think she killed Kenny Schenk?'

'I didn't say that.' Carlyle watched a sign for Central London flash past. 'I'll believe what the autopsy tells me.'

'The mortuary's finally sorted out its staffing problems,' said O'Sullivan. 'We've got Mr Schenk booked in for tomorrow afternoon, if you want to come and watch.'

Squeamish at the best of times, Carlyle had no intention of watching the film producer being cut up. 'I'd love to,' he fibbed, 'but I've got a rather important meeting I need to attend. Let me know how it goes.'

Named after its architect, the Simpson Building was a fifty-three-storey glass tower, whose design – according to the marketing brochure – was inspired by a 1950s Japanese vase. A lift took forty seconds to take them to the top floor where a maid showed them into a reception room with predictably amazing views over the city.

Emma Jobson kept them waiting long enough to make the most of the experience without being obviously rude. 'Which one of you is in charge?' The woman was everything you would expect of a trophy wife, a tall, thirty-something blonde, with only the slightest hint of condescension in her tone.

After O'Sullivan had made the introductions, Carlyle stepped up to the plate. 'I'm afraid we've got some bad news.'

'Oh, yes?' The woman's expression suggested nothing a couple of cops could say would have much impact on her rarefied existence.

'It's about your husband.' O'Sullivan gamely took up the baton. 'We're afraid he's been killed.'

'What?' The woman let out a nervous laugh, just as an elderly man walked into the room. 'You hear that, darling? Apparently, you're dead.'

'Nice place.' The two men had retreated into Robson's study while O'Sullivan spoke with Emma in the reception room.

'It's on the market for ninety million.' Robson made it sound like he was selling a council semi in Acton.

Carlyle coughed. 'Nine zero?'

'Some Russian was gonna buy it, but the deal fell through.' Jobson poured a couple of inches of single malt into a tumbler and offered it to the commander. After a moment's hesitation, Carlyle accepted. 'Last heard of, he was in a Siberian prison.'

'Unlucky.' Carlyle took a sip of the whisky and made an appreciative *moue*.

'Those are the breaks. But it's like the Wild West over there.' Jobson poured a second drink for himself. 'Anyway, I thought I'd move in for a while. It's still on the market, if you're interested.'

'Interested,' Carlyle laughed, 'but lacking in funds.'

'I couldn't afford it myself.' Jobson chuckled. 'Don't tell Emma, though.'

'Sorry if we gave your wife a shock earlier.'

'No need to apologise. Emma's a tough girl.'

Carlyle recalled what O'Sullivan had said. 'Wife number three, huh?'

Jobson gave a rueful smile. 'Wife number one died almost twenty years ago now. Wife number two, well, she was a bit of a mistake. Emma's been great, though. We get on well, considering the age gap.'

Which must be pushing forty years. Carlyle said nothing.

'You married?'

'Just the once.'

'Divorced?'

'No, we're still going.'

'Good for you.' Jobson lifted his glass in a toast. 'Cheers.'

'Cheers.'

'I'll dine out on this story for years. Tell me, though, why did you think I was dead?'

Carlyle explained about Travis and the double monks.

'I have so much stuff,' Jobson admitted. 'Emma throws a lot of it out. Most of it goes to local charity shops. Maybe they can tell you who bought the shoes.'

'Maybe.' Carlyle was doubtful but it was worth a try.

'It's a lot of effort, killing someone by blowing off their head.'

'I know. It seems personal.' Finishing his drink, Carlyle accepted the offer of a refill. 'Just don't tell anyone. Drinking on duty's very old-school.'

'Your secret's safe with me, Commander.'

Halfway through his second whisky, he asked, 'I don't suppose you have any idea why someone should end up murdered in Paddington Green?'

'It wasn't me.' Jobson laughed. 'Maybe it was one of those bloody squatters.'

'We don't think so.' Carlyle was careful to limit what he said. 'We're wondering if it might be something to do with the building itself. Its past history . . . or maybe its future.'

'How d'you mean?'

'There must've been some competition for the place?'

'It's a good site, but not worth dying for. We were able to snap it up before it went to auction, which was just as well – the auction process is a complete and utter shambles. It's still got to get through the council, but we'll end up with around eight hundred flats, including social housing and various other community facilities. We'll make good money out of it, but we'll earn it. The whole project'll take the best part of twenty years.' Jobson drank some of his Scotch. 'In fact, most likely, I'll be dead before it's finished.'

Carlyle probed a little further. 'There wasn't anyone who was pissed off about you getting the site?'

'There're always people who're pissed off in my game.' Jobson chuckled. 'It's just the way it is.' The conversation petered out, and Carlyle was pleased when O'Sullivan stuck her head round the door, suggesting it was time to go.

'Have you been drinking?' she asked, as the lift took them back to *terra firma*.

Carlyle ignored the question. 'Looks like we're back to square one with Travis.'

'Not necessarily. Emma gave the shoes to a charity shop down the road about a month ago. Some donkey thing – she's a big animal lover. Maybe they can tell us who bought the shoes.'

The whisky-fuelled commander was keen to press on. 'Let's pay them a visit.'

'Not so fast.' They reached the ground floor and O'Sullivan led him through the palatial reception area. 'It's closed for today.'

'Already?'

'It's a charity shop. They don't exactly open twenty-four/ seven.'

'Hm.' Carlyle stepped outside to be hit by a gust of wind. 'I suppose that's as far as we can take it now.'

Happy to call it a day, O'Sullivan headed back to her car. Carlyle opted for a bracing walk by the river. Back at Charing Cross, Joaquin was nowhere to be seen. In his stead, a stout woman was eating a sausage roll and reading a celebrity magazine.

'The commander's not in,' she announced, not looking up from her reading.

'I am the commander.'

'Oh.' Wiping a crumb from her chin, she made no effort to hide her dismay at his arrival.

'Who are you?'

'Aditi. HR sent me.'

'Is Joaquin sick?'

'He's been moved.'

'Moved?'

The woman looked at him as if he was stupid. 'They've changed the work rotas,' she explained. 'There's a new policy that means only British passport holders can work for senior management. Good idea, if you ask me. It's ridiculous, all these foreigners, coming over here and taking our jobs.'

'Where's Joaquin now?' Carlyle demanded.

'I wouldn't know.' The woman put down the remains of her

77

sausage roll and turned the page of the magazine. 'And I've got to go soon. Doctor's appointment.'

'Fine.' Carlyle couldn't have cared less.

Aditi waved at his office. 'And the decorators'll be back in tomorrow. They reckon it'll take the rest of the week to repaint your office.'

Carlyle spied a decent excuse for staying with the Schenk case. 'What colour's it gonna be?' he asked.

The woman had no idea. 'I can ask, if you want.'

'Doesn't matter. Don't worry about it.'

Schlepping over to Scotland Yard, Carlyle presented himself in front of Bruce Allen's PA, a woman who might've been a clone of Aditi, except she was white.

'Mr Allen's on a call.' She pointed to a tatty sofa. 'He might be a while.'

Carlyle took a seat and played on his phone until Allen stuck his head round the door. 'Commander,' he said brightly, 'I was beginning to think you were a figment of my imagination.'

Entering the special adviser's office, Carlyle got straight to the point. 'You've moved my PA.'

'I've changed the rotas. You should've seen the email.'

'I've been away.'

'That shouldn't stop you reading your emails.'

'Surely the rota's a matter for HR?'

Allen offered a condescending smile. 'Working for the commissioner, I have the broadest possible remit. Simply put, I can stick my nose in where I like. Which is just as well, given the number of things that need changing here. In this case, it seemed inappropriate to have foreign nationals working for senior staff. Given the amount of confidential and highly sensitive material crossing your desk, I'm surprised – and more than a little disappointed – that an experienced officer like you hadn't thought of it before.'

'I want Joaquin back.' Carlyle was surprised by the vehemence in his voice.

'I'm afraid it's not possible. Anyway, you told me he was hopeless.'

'I didn't say I wanted him sacked,' Carlyle spluttered.

'He hasn't been sacked, just moved to less sensitive duties.'

'I want him back.'

'You've got to see the big picture. People don't want so many non-UK nationals working in Police HQ. My changes have gone down well – the feedback so far has been positive so why would I backtrack? It would set a bad precedent.'

'That's your problem. I want Joaquin back by tomorrow or I will ensure he – and everyone else you're discriminating against – gets proper legal advice. I can think of several lawyers who would happily take on a case like this, pro bono.' Abigail Slater, for one, would jump at the opportunity to launch a class action against the Met.

Allen blanched at this naked challenge to his dubious authority. 'You would be bringing the organisation into disrepute,' he blustered. 'It would be gross misconduct.'

'All I want is my PA back.' Carlyle folded his arms. 'I don't want to drag the Met through the mud.'

Allen drummed his fingers on the desk. 'I'll see what I can do, but it'll be the exception that proves the rule.'

'Thank you.'

'I must say, though, Commander, your views are very much in the minority.'

'Par for the course,' Carlyle replied.

'I'm very disappointed to get such a negative reaction to one of my initiatives from a senior officer such as yourself.'

'This is about Joaquin,' Carlyle insisted. 'I'm not making a wider point.'

'Hm.' Allen brought his hands together, as if in prayer. 'I've heard people say a few things about you, but no one's claimed you were one for sentiment.'

'Maybe I'm getting old,' Carlyle responded. 'Less uptight, more minded to live and let live.'

'It's better for all concerned if these people went back to their own countries.' Carlyle kept his mouth shut, but Allen could read his face. 'You may not like it, but you need to get into line on this. In everything I do, I operate with the full knowledge and blessing of the commissioner. We've known each other for a very long time. I know what she wants, and she knows I'll deliver. Other than your dear self, no one's complained about this move. And nor should they. We're talking about national security here. This is a British police service, paid for by British taxpayers, for the protection of British citizens. It simply cannot be staffed with foreigners.'

Carlyle started to protest, but Allen guillotined the debate. 'I haven't got much time, so let's finally get down to more pressing matters. What do you know about Assistant Commissioner Gina Sweetman?'

Carlyle played dumb. 'Nothing.'

'Never worked with her?'

'No.'

'Paths never crossed while climbing the ladder? Never worked out of the same station, before coming here, anything like that?'

Carlyle couldn't rule out the possibility. 'I don't think so.'

'Never fucked her on some management team-building course?'

'Want to get to the point?'

'The assistant commissioner is about to make history ... as the most senior officer in the Met ever to face a sexual harassment charge. It is, ahem, *alleged* that she abused a senior colleague for having cosmetic surgery, breast enhancements to be precise.' Allen let out a girlish giggle. 'You can read about it on the *Mail* website, just search for *cop boob job*.'

Carlyle pulled up the story on his phone and read with a mixture of bemusement and dismay.

'Sweetman's trying to call in favours all over the place, hoping to save her skin.'

'What's all this got to do with me?'

'The assistant commissioner will get the chance to put her side of the story when she goes in front of the disciplinary panel. The commissioner, meanwhile, wants to use the sorry affair as a catalyst for a root-and-branch review of ethical standards at all levels of the Met. To that end, we're launching a commission into standards and behaviours.'

'An ethics committee?' Carlyle still couldn't see where this was going. 'Sounds good,' he lied.

'The commission will be led by the former chief constable of Dorset, Paul Wheelan . . . and you're going to be on it.'

Not on your nelly, was Carlyle's immediate reaction. 'I'm far too busy.'

'Not from what I've seen.' Allen smirked. 'The number of meetings you miss is extraordinary. According to your PA – your *new* PA – your attendance rate is in single figures. I can't get my head round what you actually do all day.'

'I could say the same about you.'

'If you don't sign up for the commission, you may very well find yourself under investigation – for gross idleness and whatever else may come up.'

Carlyle felt his head begin to swim. 'I've got a job to do,' he said. 'Try to railroad me on this and I'll take it to the commissioner.'

It was the weakest of threats and they both knew it. 'Knock yourself out.' Allen pointed at the door. 'The commissioner owes you nothing. She couldn't pick you out of a line-up.'

The dystopian vision of retirement flooded Carlyle's brain as he made his way back downstairs. Mercifully, Aditi was nowhere to be seen. Slumping behind his desk, the commander wondered how he might rescue himself from Bruce Allen's commission.

Serious illness?

Jury service?

Secondment to Interpol?

Alien abduction?

When nothing credible came to mind, he was pleased to be distracted by his phone starting to ring.

'Carlyle.'

'Commander, I was beginning to wonder what had happened to you.'

It took him a moment to recognise the voice. 'My apologies for not getting back to you sooner. Things've been a bit frantic over the last few days.'

'No need to apologise,' Vicky Dalby-Cummins purred. 'I read all about Kenny Schenk – such a disgusting carry-on.'

'It is all rather distasteful,' Carlyle agreed.

'People like him deserve all they get, in my opinion. The world has changed. Serial sex pests need to be stopped in their tracks.'

'Hm.' Given the woman's business empire included one of London's biggest brothels, the commander was unsure her outrage carried much moral weight.

'But, look, I didn't call you to chat about that. How about lunch? There are various things we still need to discuss.'

'This is where Harry was shot.'

Carlyle peered across the desk. 'In the chair you're sitting in?'

'No, no. I changed everything when I moved in.' Well refreshed, Dalby-Cummins gave a gleeful shudder. 'Harry's taste was sadly lacking. And the blood stains would never have come out.'

Carlyle tried to show he was paying attention. 'You changed the name of the place, too.'

'Yes. I think the Chapel has a nice ring to it.'

For a knocking shop, Carlyle thought.

'We spent almost a million on the refurb. Life moves on.'

'Not everyone would be so sanguine about the violent death of their husband.'

'I'm not everyone.'

'And then, to top it all, you go into business with his killer.'

Dalby-Cummins raised an eyebrow. 'If you knew Vernon Holder was responsible for Harry's death, why didn't you arrest him?'

'Knowing is one thing, proving it is another.'

A smile danced around the corners of her mouth. 'Can you keep a secret?'

Carlyle thought about the two bottles of wine they'd drunk over lunch. His share had amounted to no more than a glass and a half. 'Sure.'

'Vernon isn't enjoying his retirement in the Caribbean. He's dead.'

Carlyle had not expected such candour. 'And why would you tell me that?' he asked.

'Because,' she smirked, 'knowing is one thing, proving it is another. Sandro – the guy you met at the hotel – killed Vernon in an abattoir with a stun gun. He died like a pig. Appropriate, don't you think?'

'You got your revenge for Harry.'

'I did, but that wasn't really the point. I've got big plans, but Vernon didn't want to know. He was too old, too lazy. And he was too much of a sexist pig to simply sit back and let me make him money.'

'Where is he now?'

'Depends on whether you believe in Heaven and Hell, I suppose.'

Carlyle rephrased the question. 'Where's the body?'

'Gone. Sandro fed him to my pigs. The pigs were turned into sausages. Prime British meat. One hundred per cent organic. Sold across Europe. Bits of Vernon probably ended up in Romania, Poland, the Baltic states. For all practical purposes, there is no trace of him left. Not one single atom. The man might as well never have existed.'

Feeling a little sick, Carlyle shifted in his chair. 'In my experience, you can always find something.'

Dalby-Cummins's expression darkened. 'Would that be a good use of scarce police resources? The old bastard got what he deserved. I delivered justice. I didn't thwart it.'

'I'm not sure Vernon's missus would agree.'

'Mrs Holder couldn't care less. Unlike Vernon, she did retire to the sun. Got herself a thirty-year-old toy-boy. By all accounts she's as happy as a pig in shit, so to speak.'

'I still don't understand why you're telling me this.'

'I want you to feel I'm being straight with you, right from the outset.'

Yeah, right.

'Because I want you to come and work for me.'

'What?' Carlyle recoiled in his seat.

'I want to offer you a job.'

'I have a job,' he pointed out.

'Not much of one, from what I hear.' She smiled. 'Dom sends his regards, by the way.' With a CV that included stints as a cop, a drug dealer and an art dealer, Dominic Silver was a controversial figure in law-enforcement circles, as well as being Carlyle's oldest mate. 'I spoke to him last week. I think he's getting bored on his boat. He's talking about buying a place in Cyprus. His wife's keen,

84

and you know how Eva wears the trousers in their relationship. They might be back in London next month. Dom'll give you call.'

'Good to know.' Carlyle wondered why Dom couldn't just send him a text.

'I've known Dom a long time. Not as long as you, of course, but I reckon I must be one of his oldest clients. One of his oldest *surviving* clients, at any rate.'

'You won't get at me through Dom. Lots of people have tried but it never works.'

She gave him a hurt look. 'I'm not trying to get at you, Commander. And I certainly wouldn't want to cause Dom any embarrassment.'

'There's nothing to be embarrassed about. Plus, if I'd ever wanted a new job, I'd have worked for Dom.'

'That might've been the case back in the day, when you were chasing your career and Dom needed the help. Now, the world's a very different place – he's a semi-retired gallery owner and your career is pretty much over.'

'Don't feel the need to sugar the pill.'

'Come on, where's your famous thick skin? It's not a criticism. We all reach the end of the road, sooner or later. Your story's hardly unique. After a long career as a no-nonsense copper, the brass kick you upstairs for a couple of years to beef up your pension before they put you out to pasture. You must be bored as hell. And depressed at the prospect of what's to come. I'm giving you the chance to take back control of your life. Collect your pension, then come and do some consultancy work for me. It'll be fun – and you'll make a fortune.'

'I'm fine where I am,' Carlyle insisted.

'Really? If you love all those meetings so much, how come you manage to miss so many of them? And what about this new commission on standards and behaviours? Do you want to waste a year of your life in a pointless talking shop?'

The woman was annoyingly well informed. 'The commission's members have yet to be confirmed. Anyway, it's only scheduled to take a few months.'

'These things always start off being scheduled to last for a few months and end up running for years. Claim your pension now – they'd love to get rid of you – and work with me. I can guarantee it'd be interesting.'

'Interesting and bent, no doubt.'

'Not necessarily.' Dalby-Cummins laughed. 'It depends on how you conduct yourself.'

There was an extended pause before Carlyle asked, 'What would the job involve?'

'People management, mainly.'

'Not my strong point,' Carlyle admitted.

'These people would appreciate your no-nonsense approach and straight-up honesty.'

'Such as?'

'First up would be Terry Brunel.'

'Don't know him.'

'Terry's a builder. He's on the Met's Approved Contractor list. One of his firms has won a contract to refurbish a bunch of police stations.'

'The ones that aren't closing.'

'Presumably, although you never know.'

Carlyle had to admit she was right. It would surprise no one if the Met spent a fortune tarting up stations, only to close them soon after.

'Anyway, I've been looking for a new business partner, post-Vernon, and Terry's my number-one choice. However, so far, he's not been very responsive to my overtures.'

'Why don't you feed him to the pigs?'

'I don't keep any, these days. Anyway, I want to work *with* Terry, at least in the beginning, not take him out of the game.'

'And I would strong-arm him into agreeing a deal?'

'Having a senior ex-policeman on the books would signal I'm a serious player. Bringing in someone like yourself is the next stage of professionalising and modernising the business, making it more legitimate.'

'There are plenty of ex-cops out there who're desperate for work. Take your pick.'

'You're my number-one choice.'

'Like Terry.'

'Seriously. Dom speaks very highly of you and I trust his judgement completely.'

Carlyle cursed his mate for putting him in the woman's sights.

'Think about it. You'll be very well paid.' She mentioned a sum large enough to cause Carlyle to take a sharp breath. 'A game-changing amount. Enough to get Alice on the London property ladder, for example.'

'Leave my daughter out of this.' Carlyle feigned indignation, but it was a tempting offer. There was no way on God's earth Alice would ever be able to afford a place inside the M25 unless he could come up with a large wedge of cash from somewhere. The possibility she might be forced to leave the city to find a home depressed him profoundly.

'Enough to buy her a nice flat in a not-too-bad neighbour-hood,' Dalby-Cummins persisted. 'Camden, say, or maybe even a shoebox in Notting Hill.'

He couldn't.

Not after all this time.

Not after saying no to Dom Silver so many times.

Could he?

'If it's not enough, I can increase the offer, throw in a discre-tionary bonus, assuming we get a deal with Terry.'

'It's not about the money.' Carlyle was trying to convince himself as much as his host.

'I can offer you more than cash.'

'Like what?' They were negotiating now: he could feel the ground begin to fall away beneath him.

'Like Bruce Allen, the commissioner's special adviser, I can give you his head on a plate.'

Carlyle played it cool. 'If I retire, Allen's no longer my problem.'

'Even so, you'd leg him over if you got the chance, wouldn't you?'

Carlyle did not demur.

'Dom says you like your revenge however it comes, hot or cold. Well, so do I. Take it from me, Bruce is a particularly nasty piece of work. I would certainly never get into bed with him – literally or metaphorically. I think it's to Virginia's great discredit she put him on the payroll.'

It took Carlyle a beat to realise that 'Virginia' was Virginia Thompson, the commissioner.

'I shudder to think what he's got on her.'

'What've you got on him?' Carlyle asked.

'One thing at a time,' Dalby-Cummins counselled. 'Join me and we'll deal with both Brunel *and* Bruce Allen.' She flashed him a winning smile. 'You can't say fairer than that, can you?'

NINE

'This is ridiculous.' Gina Sweetman gulped her Pinot Grigio. 'I can't believe it's happening.' Reaching for the bottle, she refilled her glass to the brim. 'I mean, the ungrateful bitch, what's she playing at?'

Eleanor Hicks looked on in dismay. 'Maybe you should slow down a bit.'

'Whaddya mean?' The assistant commissioner tossed more of the wine down her throat.

'Your drinking,' Hicks pointed out, 'is a contributory factor in all of this.'

'This is supposed to be a case-management chat,' Sweetman snapped, 'not an AA meeting.'

Hicks moved on. 'We're waiting for a date for your disciplinary hearing. The composition of the panel has been determined.' She ran through a list of names. 'You need to say if you object to any of them, for any reason.'

'Don't know 'em.'

'That's not so surprising,' the lawyer ventured. 'The Met'll want to play it pretty straight. By the book.'

'Which means what?'

'Which means,' Hicks took a deep breath, 'you could be sacked.'

'Be serious.' Sweetman's dismissive tone contained a thread of fear.

'These are very serious charges, Gina. Which, basically, we're not contesting.'

'They haven't even suspended me.'

'They wanted to.'

'Yes, but they couldn't, could they? Not without handing me a claim for abuse of process.'

'They're still serious charges.'

'I know, but, come on,' Sweetman necked more wine, 'the punishment has to fit the crime.'

'The fact you apologised to Susan counts in your favour. On the other hand, your seniority could be a negative. Your excellent career record will probably be overshadowed by the sense you should've known better.'

'Thirty bloody years and not a problem before now.'

'You've had a few complaints,' Hicks pointed out gently. Six being the exact number.

'Nothing that led to an official hearing – well, only the one and that was dismissed. Case not proven.'

'The victim withdrew his complaint.'

'The little shit finally saw sense. He was never a bloody victim in the first place. The thing was—'

The lawyer hastily stopped her client. 'I don't need to know.'

'My career's unblemished.'

Not any more. 'It's fair to assume the Met will want to set an example. They're worried – rightly – about the publicity. The press will call for your head.' Hicks paused. 'And then there's the embarrassment for you and your family.'

For the first time in the conversation, Sweetman looked abashed. 'The mood at home is pretty shitty,' she muttered, 'as you can imagine.'

'It's gonna get worse before it gets better.'

'Whatever happens, I've gotta keep my job. I'm the bread-winner, Dave earns next to nothing and we've got another three years before the kids are off our hands. If I were to get sacked, I'd have to pull them out of their schools and send them to the local comp.' She slammed a palm on the table. 'That isn't happening. The place is a fucking dump. If one of the kids gets a GCSE, they hold a party. It's had more kids run off to join Islamic State than any other school in the borough.'

Hicks tried to offer a crumb of comfort. 'Even in the worst-case scenario, you'd probably keep your pension.'

Sweetman gave a dismissive toss of her head. 'You don't have any kids, do you? The pension wouldn't cover one term's school fees – not when you add in all the extras. My son's signed up for a three-week trip to Nepal. And my daughter . . .'

'Let's hope it doesn't come to that,' was as much comfort as Hicks could offer. 'We need to gather all the testimonials we can. Fight it all the way. Throw ourselves on the mercy of the panel.' Sweetman looked like she'd rather cut off her own arm. 'The good news is Superintendent Moran's civil case – where's she's claiming damages against you and Terence Brunel – will be put on hold until after the Met hearing. Assuming you keep your job, any damages will be covered out of the service's professional liability insurance.'

'And if I don't?'

'It's not my place to give you financial advice,' Hicks replied, 'but you should take a look at your current assets. Start saving cash if you're not already. And put everything you can in your husband's name.'

'This is ridiculous.' Susan Moran gulped down the last of her coffee. 'I can't believe we need to go through all of this. The whole thing is so clear-cut. I mean, I'm the victim here.'

Carolyn Fairbairn agreed. 'But there's a process that has to be followed.'

'I know.' The superintendent folded her arms. 'But I need

closure. I can't believe Gina is fighting this.'

'She's fighting to save her job,' the lawyer pointed out. 'I don't suppose she feels she's got much choice.'

'She should've thought about that before she attacked me in such a vile and personal way.' Moran rolled her shoulders, trying to dissipate the tension in her body. 'How's it looking?'

'Things are moving slowly.'

Moran felt her angst levels edging back up. 'I can't believe she's been allowed to keep working.'

'A suspension could be considered pre-judging the issue. It could also have delayed the disciplinary hearing.'

'Is there a date yet?'

'No. It might not be for several months.' Before Moran could complain further, the lawyer added, 'It all depends on the availability of the panel members. Getting people senior enough to sit in judgment on an assistant commissioner into the same place at the same time is very tricky. Once we get a date, the hearing will probably run for three days, maybe a week.' She paused. 'You'll have to give evidence.'

'I'm up for it.'

'The basic facts about what happened on the night in question are not in dispute. But there'll be some questioning about your professional relationship with Gina, and also your own career.'

'I'm not the one on trial here.'

'No, but you've been in court enough times, you know what it's like. You make a complaint, you put yourself in the firing line, too.'

Moran looked askance. 'Are you saying I shouldn't do it?'

'All I'm saying is you need to approach this in the right way. When you go in there, you need to be cool, professional – as detached as possible.'

'But they'll want to know how I felt. My upset. The effect it's had on me.'

'I'm not just thinking about the hearing. That'll pretty much take care of itself. Afterwards, though, you don't want this following you around for ever.'

'It's a bit late,' the superintendent complained. 'I get it all the time.'

'We'll need to raise that,' Fairbairn agreed. 'You don't want to be hounded out of your job over this.'

'No.' Moran sounded less than sure.

'You're an experienced police officer with many years of public service ahead of you. You want to come out of this whole process as well as you possibly can, given the circumstances.'

'Gina was right,' Moran started fiddling with her phone. 'She said I would always be known as the woman who'd had the boob job.'

'Yes, well . . .' Fairbairn caught herself glancing at her client's chest. If it wasn't for all the hoopla, you wouldn't have known the woman had had enhancements. 'It'll be worse for Gina – she might very well get the sack over this.'

'D'ya think?' Moran brightened at the prospect.

'The panel'll decide on dismissal, or some lesser punishment, an official warning, or maybe a reprimand.'

Moran's face darkened again. 'Surely she'll get more than a slap on the wrist.'

'It's hard to say. Ellie Hicks, her lawyer, is very pragmatic. She'll be focused on damage limitation. Up to now, Gina has had a blemish-free career, pretty much. Ellie will be busy rounding up anyone who'll put in a good word for her client, in a bid to try to save her job.'

'Gina's a drunk.'

'Drink was clearly a factor in this incident,' Fairbairn agreed. 'But they might try to turn it into a positive, make her a victim, too.'

'But *I'm* the victim here,' Moran spat.

'Yes, but if Gina agrees to get help – maybe goes into a clinic for a while – the defence can outline a path to redemption. The panel might like that, although it won't play well in the press. The media'll want blood. From a PR point of view, the Met'll be praying Gina resigns.'

'She won't,' Moran predicted. 'The job means everything to her. I know Gina – she'll go down fighting, trying to throw as much muck around as she can.'

'The next best thing would be a speedy sacking. But if they don't show due process the Met'll run the risk of the whole thing getting played out again in an employment tribunal.'

'I thought police officers couldn't take their case to an outside court.'

'It's a grey area.'

'I thought the disciplinary panel had judicial immunity.'

'There was a ruling not so long ago. Some obese constable in Hampshire resigned to avoid a fitness test, then sued for disability discrimination.'

'If every overweight cop decided to sue, the police would be bankrupted overnight.'

'He lost the case. The point, though, is he was allowed to proceed with it. Gina could point to that if she wanted to take the Met to court.'

Moran stared into her cup. 'They're gonna let her off, so they don't get sued?'

'I'm not saying that. The panel's got a tricky job in determining the right punishment to fit the crime. How do they show they're taking the problem of harassment seriously while not making Gina a scapegoat? With the press all over it, they'll want to get it right.'

'Where does all this leave me?'

'It leaves you needing to be detached and professional,' Fairbairn repeated. 'You've got to remember this hearing isn't about you. It's about Gina. Don't make it personal.'

'It *is* personal,' Moran hissed. 'She slagged off my tits.'

'I don't want you to overplay the victim card. Keep sight of the longer game. Whatever the panel decides will be a win for us. More importantly, it will be a platform going into the civil case. Again, there are different things to consider. The panel's ultimate sanction – dismissal – would strengthen our civil claim the most. But, from a practical point of view, sacking Gina would strip her of the Met's insurance cover, potentially reducing her ability to pay any awarded damages.'

'I was wondering about that.' Moran's eyes narrowed. 'How much were you thinking of going for?'

Fairbairn gave a number.

'Wow.'

'We will be claiming against Mr Brunel as well, and he would appear to have substantial assets. Not that we're doing this as a money-making exercise.'

'Perish the thought.'

'But at the end of this process you could be looking at a very large settlement.'

Moran did some calculations in her head. 'Maybe I could retire.'

'I thought you wanted to stay on the job?'

'Theoretically speaking, it could be a possibility, depending on what we get.'

'There's a long way to go yet.' Fairbairn rose from her chair. 'Look, I need to run. I'll give you a call when we get a date for the panel and we can take it from there.'

'Sure.' Moran started googling property for sale in Vale do Lobo on her phone. 'That would be great.'

The call came from a doctor in A and E at the Royal Free. 'We've got a woman here with some nasty injuries. She had your business card in her pocket.'

Laura Taylor. Carlyle said he would be there directly and went off to find O'Sullivan. 'Reuben Barnwell's beaten her up again. I'm gonna have him.'

The inspector poured cold water on his machismo. 'You mean you're going to arrest him.'

'I'm gonna arrest him,' Carlyle growled, 'and then I'm gonna wring his bloody neck.'

'Maybe you should take some back-up, in case he doesn't come quietly.'

'Good idea.' Carlyle was already heading for the door. 'Let's go.'

'I wasn't thinking of me,' already late for picking up her kids, O'Sullivan did not follow him, 'but I did have someone in mind.'

Having been evicted from Paddington Green, the squatters had moved on to an office building on Haverstock Hill only a few blocks from the hospital. Carlyle, accompanied by Sergeant Francesca Angelini, found Laura Taylor sitting on a trolley in a gloomy corridor.

'I fell down some stairs,' Taylor called, as the cops approached.

'Never heard that before,' the commander scoffed.

'It's true.' Taylor looked around, as if hoping for someone to rescue her. 'It was my own fault.'

'The doctor says you were pretty badly hurt,' said Angelini. 'They're gonna have to keep you here for a while.'

'I want to go home.'

'Back to the squat?' Carlyle asked.

'It wasn't Reuben, if that's what you're thinking. You're just trying to fit him up.'

Angelini smiled. 'I wouldn't let him.'

'You're the good cop, eh? And he's the bad cop.'

'We're just trying to work out what happened,' Angelini said

96

soothingly. 'It's quite rare for a fit young woman to come in presenting injuries of this sort.'

'I told you what happened.' Taylor glared at Carlyle. 'Reuben wasn't even there.'

A nurse arrived, pushing a wheelchair, to say they'd found a bed in the Tigana Ward. She made it sound as if Taylor had won the lottery.

'I want to leave,' Taylor protested. 'You can't keep me here.'

'You need to rest,' the nurse advised. 'We can keep you under observation and see how things are in the morning.'

'Don't worry,' Carlyle put in. 'Now you've explained what happened, we won't take it any further.'

Angelini gave him a funny look.

'You'll leave Reuben alone?' Taylor asked.

'We have more than enough on our plate as it is,' Carlyle assured her. 'If you're not making a complaint, I'll leave it here.'

'I'm one hundred per cent not making a complaint.' Taylor allowed the nurse to help her into the wheelchair.

Angelini watched the girl disappear down the corridor. 'Looks like we came all the way up here for nothing.'

'I wouldn't say that.' Carlyle turned and set off in the opposite direction. 'Let's go and see the man of the hour.'

Angelini followed him. 'But you said—'

'Don't you ever lie to members of the public, Sergeant?'

'Well, no, actually.'

'Then you're a better officer than I am.' Spying a sign for the exit, Carlyle lengthened his stride. 'Now let's go and arrest this little shit.'

The welcome at the squat consisted of four guys with sporadic facial hair and poor personal hygiene. They circled Carlyle and Angelini as they stood in what had been the reception area of an insurance company. A banner proclaiming a *Safe Space for Progressives* hung from the mezzanine above.

'Which one is Barnwell?' Angelini hissed.

'He's not here. Presumably he's upstairs.' Carlyle noticed the sergeant had already adopted a fighting stance. 'I can handle this.'

Angelini looked unconvinced.

'No problem, trust me.' Carlyle stepped forward in the manner of an explorer greeting a remote jungle tribe. 'You must be the progressives, huh?'

Three of the men offered nothing more than ill-concealed hostility. The fourth, however, had supplemented his armoury with a heavy steel chain of the kind used to lock up bikes.

'Whadda you want, copper?' asked the guy with the chain.

'Where's Reuben?' He waited for the chorus of fuck-offs to subside, then said, 'We just want to talk to him.'

'Talk to me about what?' The man himself appeared at the top of the stairs.

'It's the wanker from Paddington Green,' said one of his comrades.

'He tried to stitch me up.' Barnwell began making his way down the stairs. 'But Laura sorted him out.'

'And she's now in hospital,' Carlyle pointed out.

Barnwell was unperturbed. 'She had an accident.'

'We can discuss it at the station.' Carlyle took a step forward and was rewarded with a fist in the face. He staggered backwards, holding his nose, listening to the sound of all hell breaking loose around him.

'Are you all right?' Angelini handed him a paper napkin from her pocket.

'Just a lucky shot.' Carlyle wiped the blood from his nose, gingerly shook his head, then did a double-take. Barnwell was face down on the floor, his hands cuffed behind his back. The guy wielding the chain was slumped on the stairs, holding his crotch and groaning loudly. The remaining members of the welcoming committee had fled. 'What happened?'

'I sorted them out.' Angelini hauled Barnwell to his feet and pushed him towards the door.

Carlyle was conscious of faces looking down on them from above. 'But—'

'I'll explain later,' Angelini said briskly. 'Let's get out of here.'

TEN

The dingy shopping centre in Elephant and Castle looked like it belonged more in Kabul than the middle of London. The place seemed to consist of nothing but charity shops, pound stores and rental outlets. O'Sullivan was a couple of minutes late, delayed by a call from Francesca Angelini. 'Some of the squatters were a bit hostile, I hear.'

'That's one way of putting it.' Carlyle wasn't keen on going into too much detail. 'Angelini knows how to look after herself, though.'

'And you, by the sound of it.'

Carlyle had to admit it was true.

'Carol's quite something,' O'Sullivan laughed. 'I'm surprised you haven't come across her before.'

'Carol?'

'Her nickname, after Carol Danvers, the comic-book superhero.'

Carlyle was none the wiser.

'Carol's got a black belt in taekwondo. On her first day at Charing Cross, one of the other sergeants touched her up. She gave him a broken wrist and two broken fingers. He got a trip to A and E, she got the nickname.'

'Laura Taylor could learn a thing or two.'

'Carol's unique . . . luckily for you.'

'I just hope she keeps her mouth shut. I don't want to be a laughing stock back at the station.'

'She's all action, no talk.'

'Sounds like my kind of cop.'

They came to a unit with a badly painted sign proclaiming *For the Love of Donkeys.* 'This is it,' O'Sullivan announced.

'Emma Jobson's a big animal lover,' Carlyle recalled.

'Right.'

Inside, it was like any other charity shop, dominated by the musty smell of second-hand clothes and paperback books. Resisting the temptation to browse, Carlyle followed O'Sullivan to the till where an old bloke was pricing up some recently donated items. As soon as he heard the word 'police', he looked around nervously. 'We don't want any trouble. I only do this as a volunteer, you know.'

O'Sullivan reassured him he had nothing to fear. 'We're just looking for information about a pair of shoes you sold recently.'

The man's eyes narrowed as concern was replaced by suspicion. 'Shoes?'

'A pair with buckles, like these.' The inspector held up a picture on her phone. A couple of customers had picked up on what was happening and were hovering on the outskirts of the conversation. Carlyle shooed them away.

'Ah, yes. I remember those. Nice shoes. Too big for me.'

'We'd like to know who bought them.'

'Hum. Well, wouldn't it be a matter of client confidentiality?'

O'Sullivan looked at Carlyle. 'Let's worry about that in a minute,' the commander suggested. 'First, can you confirm they were sold? Then, would you have a record of who you sold them to? If someone just walked in and paid cash, well, the whole conversation is academic.'

The man thought about it for a few moments. 'You'd better speak to Devon.' Leaving the till, he went to a door at the back of the shop. Opening it, he stood at the top of the stairs and yelled, 'Dev, can you come up here, please?'

While they waited, Carlyle drifted over to the book section, his eyes alighting on a recent Jo Nesbo. Pulling it from the shelf, he studied the blurb: *A young Norwegian murdered . . . nothing will stop Harry Hole from finding out the truth. The hunt for a serial killer is on, but the murderer will talk only to Harry . . .*

Had he read it? Hard to tell. The price was only three quid, but it would annoy him if he took it home to find another copy on his bookshelf. He was still undecided when a young woman in dungarees and outsized glasses appeared from the basement.

'The police would like a word,' the old man explained, shuffling back to the till to serve a customer clutching a *Lethal Weapon* box set.

O'Sullivan explained who they were and what they wanted.

Devon remembered the shoes. 'We sold them on eBay a couple of weeks ago. I took them to the post office myself.'

'So,' Carlyle asked, 'you've got the buyer's name and address?'

'Sure.' Showing a delightful lack of concern for data-protection laws, Devon headed back to the stairs. 'Gimme a minute.'

'You like that stuff?' O'Sullivan inspected the back cover of Carlyle's paperback purchase. 'The usual violence against women. Misogyny dressed up as popular entertainment.'

Carlyle wasn't sure if she was genuinely outraged or simply pulling his leg. Maybe it was a bit of both.

'And, as for the policing side of things, completely unrealistic.'

'It's genre fiction,' he shrugged, 'suspension of disbelief and all that.'

She handed back the book without further comment. 'Want to check this place out?' They had a new name now, James Gillespie, and an address in north London.

'Sure.' Walking to the tube, he asked, 'Where are we on Kenny Schenk?'

'The autopsy was inconclusive,' O'Sullivan replied. 'The blows to the head shouldn't have been enough to kill him but it looks like they brought on a cardiac arrest. On the other hand, if his arteries hadn't been so blocked, the heart attack wouldn't have been fatal. Lots of things contributed to his death – you could make a case for saying too many hamburgers killed him, if you wanted to.'

'Messy.'

'Yeah. If Hermione Lacemaker had called for an ambulance, he would probably have survived, depending on how quickly the paramedics got there. As it was, Schenk lay there for almost an hour before he was found.'

'You think she left him to die?'

'I took her statement and it's perfectly credible. It fits with all the supporting evidence and the other statements we've collected. Obviously, she'd been coached by her lawyer, but I don't think there's much of a gloss you can put on it. The facts are the facts. It depends on the narrative you want to construct with them. You might disagree with Hermione's story, but you can't disprove it. She's the only one still alive who was there at the time. I don't see why she wouldn't call 999 if she'd thought he was at risk of dying. She'd already taught him a lesson and she's not a psycho. I'd be minded to accept her version of events.'

'As a woman?' Carlyle regretted the question before it was out of his mouth.

O'Sullivan gave him a pained look. 'As a cop. Hermione might've used more force than was strictly necessary, but she couldn't have known the man's heart was going to pack in.'

'No.' He was relieved to hear her take on the situation.

'Sweetman, though, sees it differently. Last I heard, she was talking about pushing for her to be charged with manslaughter.'

'What?' Carlyle's heart sank. 'But I promised—'

'Tell that to the assistant commissioner.'

'What's it got to do with her anyway?'

The inspector's tone grew noticeably cooler. 'What's it got to do with *you*, Commander?'

'I was—' His phone started to vibrate. He looked at the screen. 'Oh, fuck.' Getting to his feet, he hit receive.

'You guaranteed there'd be no charges.' Abigail Slater sounded like she wanted to kill someone herself. 'You gave me your fucking *word*.'

'It's out of my hands. Assistant Commissioner Sweetman's taken a personal interest in the case.'

'Get this nonsense stopped,' Slater growled. 'Otherwise you might find some of your dirty laundry being washed in public. Like Vicky Dalby-Cummins, for example.'

How in God's name did Slater know about Harry's widow? Suddenly, a year of sitting on an ethics committee didn't seem like such a bad gig at all. Dismissed by Slater, he brought O'Sullivan up to speed. 'Hermione's lawyer's heard about what Sweetman's up to and she's massively pissed off.'

The inspector was sympathetic. 'It's hardly your fault.'

'Yeah, but it is my problem.' As Carlyle smacked the phone in the palm of his hand it rang again. *Sweetman*. 'Speak of the devil.' He hit receive.

'We need to talk,' the assistant commissioner said brusquely. 'Now.'

The Montevideo Arms was a cavernous public house near Scotland Yard. 'You know the great thing about this place?' Coat buttoned up to her chin to conceal her uniform, Gina Sweetman started on a Pornstar Martini with practised gusto. 'They've got this great app where you order your drinks and they bring them to the table.' She jerked a thumb in the direction of the hassled

East European girls serving a steadily swelling group of customers. 'Saves you having to go to the bar.'

Carlyle would have preferred to be checking James Gillespie's address with O'Sullivan. He eyed the door, like a convict weighing up a jailbreak. 'You drink a lot during the day?'

The assistant commissioner tapped the empty pitcher on the table. 'It helps me get through the afternoons. All those bloody meetings.'

Carlyle offered a sympathetic tut.

'You don't like meetings either, I hear.'

'It's not why I became a cop.'

'Didn't stop you taking the commander's job, though, did it?' There was an underlying belligerence in the woman's tone that reminded Carlyle of his mother, another woman who could start a fight in an empty room.

'Don't you fancy one?'

'I'm good, thanks.'

'Don't be such a bloody Calvinist,' Sweetman spluttered. 'You Scots are all the same – either blind drunk or preachily teetotal.'

I was born in Fulham. Carlyle let it slide. 'What's your interest in the Kenny Schenk case?'

'What do you think? There's a high-profile perpetrator in our sights and I need some credit in the bank before my hearing on the Moran thing.'

'You won't get a conviction,' he predicted.

'That's the CPS's problem. It's right we try to bring the matter to court. Hermione Lacemaker may have fluttered her eyelashes and made you swoon but it doesn't mean she gets a free ride. When the woman walked into that hotel room, Kenny Schenk was alive. When she walked out, he was dead ... or dying. Lacemaker's not the victim here. There's another narrative, one that sees her as an over-privileged member of the metropolitan elite getting away with murder because she's young, pretty and middle-class. That's the narrative I'm pursuing. Kenny Schenk was a self-made man, came from nothing. An ordinary guy.'

'An ordinary sex pest.'

'You're so quick to judge, Commander. Whatever he was – or wasn't – he didn't deserve to die on the floor of a hotel room. Ms Lacemaker doesn't deserve a free pass because she's your wet dream.'

Gritting his teeth, Carlyle asked, 'If she walks after a trial, or even before a trial, how does that help you?'

'I don't need to worry about the trial. I need the quick win of the arrest to send me into my hearing in good standing. Right now, I reckon it's maybe sixty–forty against me getting the sack. Reasonable odds, but they could be better. A bit of good publicity can push them more in my favour.'

'I told Lacemaker's lawyer she wouldn't be arrested.'

'It's my call.' Sweetman ran a finger around the rim of her glass. 'And, by the way, if I were to decide your little trip to Nice represented a case of misconduct, I could put you up in front of a disciplinary panel yourself.'

Carlyle sensed a bluff. 'Knock yourself out. Do you know how many times I've been up on charges over the years?'

'Not as many as you should've been.'

'Sorry?'

'I'm not the only one who's fallen foul of changing mores on sexual harassment, am I?'

'Hardly,' Carlyle scoffed. 'I've been accused of most things in my time, but never that.'

'Oh?' Sweetman raised an eyebrow so high it almost disappeared under her fringe. 'What about the thing with your sergeant?'

Carlyle gave her a blank look.

'Umar Sligo.' She sniggered. 'The Charing Cross flasher.'

'It was hardly my fault.'

'Allowing your sergeant to terrorise his co-workers by

sending them unsolicited pictures of his genitals hardly says much for your management skills, does it?'

'The complaints about his behaviour went through the official channels and were investigated properly. Sergeant Sligo resigned before his disciplinary hearing.' Carlyle resisted the temptation to ask the assistant commissioner to consider the same course of action. 'In the end, the matter was resolved to the satisfaction of all parties.'

'Not *all* parties. There was a young sergeant who wasn't happy your pal got off scot-free.'

Carlyle tried to think whom Sweetman might be referring to. Umar had chanced his arm with so many colleagues that Carlyle had never been able to keep track. 'He wasn't my pal. And he hardly got off unscathed, given he lost his job.'

'Still, she wasn't happy.'

'Umar getting murdered, not so long after he left the force, should've given her some form of closure.'

'She still feels there should've been action against those who covered up Sligo's appalling abusive behaviour and let him get away with it for so long.'

'There was no cover-up. This was all years ago. You're rewriting history.'

'Sergeant Sligo only flourished thanks to the cosy boys' club at Charing Cross.'

'Bollocks.'

'Lots of these old cases are coming out now. With predators like Kenny Schenk being thrust into the spotlight, who knows who'll be next? Lots of old cases are being reviewed in the light of the new realities. This woman – a well-respected and much-liked officer – might decide she's kept silent for too long. She's already publicly fighting one battle. She might as well fight two.'

Shit. The name hit him like a half-brick to the back of the head. 'Moran?'

'Well done. You got there in the end.' Sweetman gave a short burst of mocking applause. 'When she was a sergeant, Susan Moran spent almost a year at Charing Cross. Umar Sligo took a shine to her and, well, you can imagine what happened next.'

Yes, Carlyle thought ruefully, I can.

'In fact, it was during this time, I believe, that Suse began developing the self-image issues that led to her unfortunate decision to undergo surgery. In that sense, you could argue the only reason *I'm* up on a charge is because of *your* dereliction of duty.'

You could, if you were a totally unhinged lush. Carlyle glared at the assistant commissioner. 'What do you want?'

'I hear Bruce Allen has dragooned you onto his standards and behaviours commission . . . I can get you off it.'

Carlyle folded his arms, trying not to appear surprised by – or too interested in – her proposed bargain.

'Well, not me. David Langdon can get you off it.'

'Who's he?'

'David is deputy chief constable on Humberside. Not for much longer, though. He's about to be sacked for fiddling his expenses.'

'Not clever.'

'Especially not while you're shagging the clinically depressed mother of a teenage boy who choked on his own vomit while drunk in a cell in Goole.'

Carlyle tried to place Goole on a map, without success.

'It was a scandal. Then again, they don't have much else to get worked up about up there. For the poor deputy chief constable, it promises to be a downbeat end to a rather mediocre career.' Sweetman radiated *Schadenfreude*. 'It rather puts my issues into perspective, don't you think?'

Carlyle made no comment.

'Anyway,' she continued, 'it would appear the deputy chief constable was supposed to be one of the members of the panel for my disciplinary hearing. Now they need to find someone to replace him – I want you to take it on.'

'Me?' This time, there was no hiding his astonishment.

'Who better to get me off than a maverick who is genetically incapable of toeing the party line?' Before he could protest, she added, 'It's a great deal, a week or so throwing out Superintendent Moran's spiteful complaint, against a year, or more, debating police standards.'

Carlyle could not deny the merits of the woman's argument.

'I'll speak to Bruce – the bastard owes me a few favours. You speak to Thompson.'

'The commissioner?' Carlyle spluttered. 'Are you mad? She'll never give me the time of day.'

'Tell her it was a big mistake not having anyone from the Met on the disciplinary panel in the first place – what do a bunch of provincial plods know about the stress we're under, anyway? Make sure she understands you're doing her a big favour by making sure the punishment fits the crime *and* bomb-proofing the process at the same time.'

'Can't you tell her yourself?'

'It's better coming from a respected third party,' she looked myopically down her nose at him, 'or as close to one as I can get.'

'Don't feel the need to butter me up.'

'I thought you didn't like that kind of thing.'

'I don't, but—'

'You like honesty. I'm being honest. You wouldn't have been my first choice, but needs must.'

'What if I can't get you off?'

'Natural justice says I should get off.'

Carlyle said nothing.

Sensing his desire to leave, she moved on. 'There's one other thing.'

'Yes?'

'Reuben Barnwell.'

Carlyle kept his surprise in check. 'What about him?'

'Leave him alone. He's one of us.'

ELEVEN

Angelini caught up with a very unhappy Carlyle on the steps of the station.

'It explains why Barnwell was released so quickly,' the sergeant reflected.

'I can't believe there's a need to put someone undercover with a bunch of clowns like the Anti-Capitalist Rainbow Front,' the commander fumed. 'And the fact he's a cop doesn't allow him to beat up his girlfriend.'

'Don't worry about it.' Angelini sounded serene. 'I'll take care of it.'

Before he could ask her to explain, he felt a tap on his shoulder.

'I've been sent to the basement,' Joaquin made it sound like he was a kidnap victim, festering in a prison cell, 'processing traffic violations. Why did you move me?'

'Eh?' Carlyle watched helplessly as Angelini disappeared onto the Strand.

'If my work wasn't satisfactory, you should've told me.'

'Nothing wrong with your work.'

The Spaniard seemed less than convinced.

'I didn't do anything,' Carlyle insisted, shrinking slightly under the young man's sullen gaze. 'It was an, erm, bureaucratic error.' Now wasn't the time or the place to get into Bruce Allen's crazed attempts at ethnic cleansing among the higher echelons of the secretarial pool. 'An administrative cock-up.'

'Cock-up?'

'Someone made a mistake.'

Joaquin's expression softened slightly. 'You didn't complain about me?'

'It was me who wanted you in the first place.'

'You'll get it changed so I can come back, then?'

'Definitely.' Carlyle thought of Aditi, sitting upstairs, reading her celebrity magazines and booking her next doctor's appointment. 'I need to ditch – I mean, I'll need to speak to HR to *relocate* the woman they've given me now and then we can go back to the status quo ante.'

Joaquin looked at him blankly.

'We can go back to how it was.'

'How long's it gonna take to get her moved?' Joaquin had already seen enough traffic tickets to last him a lifetime.

'Soon.' Carlyle lowered his voice. 'In the meantime, what access do you have to the CMS?' The Central Management System allowed management at Carlyle's rank and above access to a range of restricted Met databases.

Joaquin shrugged. 'No one's changed my privileges since I got kicked out of your office, as far as I know.'

'In that case,' said Carlyle, 'there's something I need you to do for me.'

Another ageing A-lister had been accused of sexual assault by different women, over an extended timeframe. The entire film industry seemed to be grinding to a halt under an avalanche of accusations. 'Well, Kenny, you were certainly in tune with the zeitgeist.' Rick Ford scanned the *Variety* story and gave silent thanks for his low libido. That, and a thirty-year marriage to a South African woman, who would have chopped his balls off at the first sign of any bad behaviour, meant Ford had nothing to worry about on a personal level. Perendi Films, however, was another matter. Abigail Slater had already launched a claim on behalf of Hermione Lacemaker, to go with the one on behalf of Kenny's ex-assistant, Hayley Briggs. Doubtless more claims would follow. Ford had brought in an independent law firm to assess the scale of the problem and had come up with almost two dozen potential cases.

Ford cursed his dead partner. The harsh truth, though, was he had effectively facilitated his co-founder's disgraceful activities by doing both their jobs. As his wife put it: 'If the bastard had actually worked for a living, he wouldn't have had time or the energy to try to fuck everything that moved.' As a result, twenty years of hard work was gone, and equity that half a dozen private equity firms had been fighting over months ago was now worthless. The issue wasn't whether Perendi Films could be saved, rather it was a matter of trying to siphon off its remaining assets and close it down before the victims slapped their claims for compensation on the table. It never ceased to amaze him how people could claim, 'It wasn't about the money,' while trying to grab everything they could.

A knock at the door broke his train of thought. Throwing the magazine onto the table, he looked up to see Dwayne Doud stick his head round the door.

'Graham Hughes would like a word.'

Not wishing to be disturbed, Ford feigned ignorance. 'Who?'

'Hermione Lacemaker's agent.' Doud laughed harshly. 'At least, he will be if he manages to get her back.'

That's not very likely, Ford mused. The gossip was that the talented Ms Lacemaker was looking to sign with a large US talent group. Quite right, too. If the girl's career was to go anywhere she needed proper representation. Hopefully, her new agents would find her a nice role that involved filming in Latin America or somewhere else suitably remote for the next six or seven months. Long enough for Kenny Schenk to be dead and buried – literally and metaphorically – and any litigation against either the Schenk estate or, more importantly, the company to wither on the vine. Hopefully.

'I'm busy.' To emphasise the point, Ford retrieved the copy of *Variety* from his desk. Doud looked at the magazine as if it was some sort of ancient artefact. For a moment, Ford imagined jumping to his feet and smacking the gofer around the head with it. 'Tell him I'll ring him back.'

'He's here, in the office.'

'Well, he hasn't got an appointment, so he can fuck off.' Ford winced at his use of the F-word. It was a sign of just how much pressure he was under. Normally, such crude language would never fall from his lips.

'He says he wants to talk to you about Kenny.'

'Kenny,' Ford intoned, 'remains the subject of an ongoing police investigation. If Mr Hughes has any relevant information, he should inform the appropriate authorities.'

'He says it's for your eyes only,' Doud insisted.

'Oh, for Christ's sake.' Ford flung the magazine onto the desk with such fury it skidded off and landed on the floor. 'Show him in.'

Doud's head disappeared, and a few moments later, Graham Hughes shuffled into the room. Dressed in a battered leather jacket, torn jeans and a pair of garish hi-tops, he reminded Ford of his youngest son. The agent's face, however, indicated a party lifestyle that was fast catching up with him.

'Close the door behind you.'

'The last time we met was at the *Kingdom of Fear* premiere.' Hughes slumped into a chair in front of the desk.

'Yes.' Rick Ford winced at the memory of a movie that, on current projections, would turn a profit approximately three hundred years after his death.

'One of my clients was in it.' Hughes named the woman. 'She played Morag, the psychopath sister.'

Did Kenny try it on with her as well? Ford tried to put a face to the name.

'She's fine,' Hughes advised. 'She's spent the last eighteen months working on a children's TV series in Belfast. As far as I know, she never met Kenny.'

Jesus, the little hustler can read my thoughts. Hurriedly, Ford tried to clear his mind of anything incriminating or embarrassing. 'You had something to show me?'

Hughes tossed his phone on the desk. 'Take a look at these photos.'

Ford reluctantly picked up the phone. 'Urgh. Is this what I think it is?'

'Kenny Schenk breathing his last,' Hughes confirmed cheerily, 'as Hermione walked out on him.'

'Jeez.' Ford let the phone fall back on the desk. 'She photographed him dying?'

Hughes scooped up the phone and shoved it into his pocket. 'It would've been better if she'd videoed it, but Hermione never was much good with technology.' He scratched his nose. 'And I suppose she had more pressing things on her mind at the time.'

'How did you get these?'

'I installed a spy app on Hermione's phone while she was doing an audition.' Hughes sounded pleased with himself. 'I do it with all my clients – it's part of my full-service offer. I'm on the case twenty-four/seven trying to keep them out of trouble.'

'But they don't know about it?'

'The clue's in the name, *spy* app. Brilliant technology.'

'That can't be legal, surely?'

'It's the wrong question, Ricky.' Hughes patted the phone in his pocket. 'The question you *should* be asking is, what can I do with these pics and how much am I willing to pay for them?'

'You want to blackmail me?'

'No, no, no. I'm offering to provide you with valuable information, which will help you fend off any compo claims from Hermione and her lawyer. Plus, I can help you keep these pictures out of the public domain, help protect your reputation, along with that of Perendi Films.'

A bit late, Ford mused. 'Presumably Hermione could leak the pictures, if she wanted to.'

'Her lawyer won't let her, not at this stage of the game. The photos are still on her phone, but she hasn't done anything with them yet. There are only two copies, hers and mine. And – assuming we can reach an understanding – I can get both sets deleted.'

'What's your price?'

'You need to confirm Hermione's got the part she was supposed to discuss with Kenny. Give her a nice bump in salary, too. But only if she signs on for the project using me as her agent.'

Ford had no idea what role Hughes was referring to. It had to be more than a year since he'd had any meaningful work-related discussion with Kenny, who could have dangled anything in front of the girl to get her to do his bidding. All he could do was try to blag it. 'Let me get a pre-contract drawn up,' he said briskly, 'and Dwayne can bring it over to you this afternoon.'

The decorators had been and gone, leaving part of one wall covered with a sickly colour he couldn't name. The smell of paint making him gag, Carlyle stepped out of his office, closed the door and retreated behind his PA's desk. Beneath a well-thumbed celebrity magazine, he found a copy of a memo from Bruce Allen outlining the agenda for a meeting with Paul Wheelan, the head of the commission into standards and behaviours. Allen had scribbled in the margin: *Three-line whip. No excuses accepted.*

Stapled to the back was a note outlining the remit of the

commission and its goals. Carlyle scanned it for a couple of seconds, then filed the whole thing in the recycling bin. If he was to avoid spending the next year with his head stuck up his backside, it seemed he would need to get into bed with either Gina Sweetman or Victoria Dalby-Cummins.

The lush or the crook. Not much of a choice, but a choice he had to make. Now.

'It's Carlyle, you've got a deal.'

'Good.'

'Not the deal you proposed, but one that gets you what you want.'

There was a pause. Then, 'I'm listening.'

'I'll speak to Terry Brunel, as long as you get Bruce Allen off my back.' Carlyle outlined his disinclination to take part in the commission. 'I want him out of my face and – if possible – out of the Met. Permanently.'

'Permanently, like Vernon?'

Carlyle had a sudden vision of Vernon Holder being fed to the pigs. It was enough to make the most committed carnivore consider turning vegetarian. 'I want Allen out of my face,' he repeated. 'And no longer working for the commissioner. I don't understand why he's even here.'

'Consultants get everywhere. They're like cockroaches.'

'Do we have an understanding?'

Another pause. Then a nod. 'I'll deal with Mr Allen – once you get Terry to see sense.'

'Good.' Carlyle felt sure this was the better option. Vicky Dalby-Cummins might be a crook, but she was a *sober* crook. The commander had a high degree of confidence she would deliver. Plus, her price was far more reasonable than trying to nobble the assistant commissioner's dismissal hearing.

'When will you talk to Terry?'

The door opened and a pair of paint-splattered workmen

walked in. 'No time like the present.' Jumping to his feet, Carlyle nodded at each of the men in turn as he skipped out of the door. 'I'll let you know how I get on.'

Building Design Services, Terry Brunel's business, had its registered offices off Camden Square. After a ten-minute schlep from the tube station, Carlyle found the address, a dismal, single-storey light-industrial unit dating back to the 1960s. Inside, a workman pointed him towards a small office.

'You're not from the council, are you?' asked the receptionist.

'Erm, no.' Carlyle was slightly taken aback by her opening gambit.

'Well, Mr Brunel's not here,' the woman proclaimed. 'He's out.'

Carlyle jerked a thumb over his shoulder. 'It's not his Range Rover parked outside, then, is it? The one with the personalised number plate, TB101.'

'He's out,' the woman repeated.

Carlyle made a performance of showing her his ID. 'I've trekked all the way up here from Charing Cross,' he pointed out, making it sound like they were in Aberdeen, 'so, rest assured, it's important.'

The woman jerked open a desk drawer and pulled out a chocolate Digestive. Nibbling it, she considered the situation at some length, then clearly decided not to push her luck by obstructing the forces of law and order any further. 'If it's *urgent*, you'll find Terry in the pub.'

'Which one?' There had to be at least a dozen pubs within a two-minute walk.

'The Gerry Adams Arms.' She waved the half-eaten biscuit in the direction of the street. 'First left, across the road from the Irish Centre.'

Carlyle didn't know what his quarry looked like.

'He'll be the old guy sitting in the corner, drinking whiskey, reading the *Racing Post*, complaining about Arsenal.'

'Arsenal fans!' Carlyle quipped. 'Why are they all such moaners?'

The secretary couldn't explain it. 'They're all West Ham in my house.'

'Even worse,' Carlyle said, sotto voce, as he took his leave.

If the Montevideo Arms was a plastic facsimile of an old-style boozer, the Gerry Adams Arms was the real thing. Walking through its doors was like stepping back in time. Only the lack of sawdust on the floor and smoke in the air hinted you were still in the twenty-first century. A TV on one wall was showing a Gaelic football match, largely ignored by the smattering of punters spread around the bar. Terry Brunel was sitting in the corner, drinking whiskey, a rolled-up copy of the *Racing Post* on the table while he tapped at his phone.

Carlyle introduced himself.

Brunel seemed neither surprised by the cop's appearance nor curious at the reason for his visit. 'Denise told you I'd be here, did she?'

Carlyle didn't feel the need to confirm the source of his intel. 'Can I get you a drink?'

'Bushmills.' Brunel drained his glass and smacked it down on the greasy tabletop. 'Make it a double.'

How the hell could you be drinking Protestant whiskey in a pub named after Gerry Adams? Despite being a confirmed Jameson's man, Carlyle was happy enough to get a round in exchange for ten minutes of Brunel's time.

'Unusual name for a pub,' was his opening conversational gambit, as he placed a fresh drink in front of the businessman.

'They renamed it in his honour after he retired. It was either that or the Wenger Tavern. There was an online poll. I don't think either of them got many votes, but Adams won.'

'The will of the people,' Carlyle mused. 'Democracy in action.'

Brunel took a nip of his drink. 'I think they thought they were voting for *Tony* Adams.'

'An easy mistake to make.' Carlyle was tickled by the idea.

'Either way, I don't suppose you're here to pay homage to either of them.'

'No.' Carlyle outlined the reason for his visit.

'Susan Moran.' Brunel knocked back the rest of his drink in a single gulp. 'It's not my fault she couldn't take a joke. It was only a bit of banter.'

'Banter can be dangerous, these days.'

'Tell me about it. Moran's claiming damages for hurt feelings or summat.' A sense of outrage unleashed his inner Yorkshireman. 'She wants to cause Gina Sweetman maximum pain and I'm the collateral damage. The whole thing's a bloody joke.' Brunel slammed the shot glass down on the table so hard that a couple of nearby punters looked over to see what was going on.

Pulling his chair closer to the table, Carlyle kept his voice low. 'As I understand it, you could lose your police-station contract.'

Brunel's eyes narrowed. 'What's it to you?'

'Vicky Dalby-Cummins wanted me to have a word.'

'Another ball-breaker. You on her payroll?'

'No.'

'Why are you here, then, buying drinks and asking questions?'

'She can help you get out of this mess, and save me a problem at the same time. I'm on the committee with responsibility for the police-station-refurbishment programme, and the last thing I need is the whole thing going back out to tender because of a spat about a boob job.'

Brunel wasn't buying it. 'How come I've never seen you before?'

'Because going to meetings isn't my strong point. I've only made one in the last year.'

Brunel remained unconvinced. 'I don't remember seeing your name on any of the papers.'

Carlyle persisted with the lie. 'You can check with the assistant commissioner if you want.'

'Gotta keep well clear of her. My lawyer says we can't be seen coll-coll- . . .' He struggled to find the word.

'Colluding.'

'Aye, that's it. We can't be seen to be colluding or t'other side'll use it against us.'

'Happens all the time.'

'Bloody Gina's the one who got me into this in the first place. I wish she'd never mentioned it. I mean, I always thought Susan Moran had nice enough baps to start with. She always seemed to have a decent sense of humour, too. Certainly, we'd always got on.' Brunel scratched at a bald spot on the crown of his head. 'I've built this business up from nothing, you know. Decades of hard work.'

Carlyle downed his own whiskey. The Bushmills went down nicely, and he had an immediate taste for another. Brunel, however, face flushed, had clearly reached his limit for the afternoon.

'I employ two dozen staff, three or four times that many when you throw in contractors. And it's all gonna go down the pan because of one off-colour remark?' Brunel looked lost. 'It doesn't make sense.'

'I couldn't agree with you more. This thing, well, it wasn't anything to do with me. It had all been sorted and now it's threatening to come apart. That's why a deal with Vicky makes sense. It's a win–win. She can formally run the refurbishment contract while you pocket the profits.'

Brunel was less than enthused. 'My investors own most of the business,' he explained. 'I only own thirty per cent of BDS, these days. The rest is owned by a group of investors led by a guy called Gareth Mills.'

The name rang a vague bell in the commander's brain.

'He's one of the original Brexit Brat Pack – spent more than ten million quid of his own dosh to get us out of Europe.'

Carlyle rolled his eyes.

'They've made a movie about it. I'm going to the premiere.' Brunel suddenly seemed chipper at the prospect. 'I've known Gareth since he was a lad. I used to do a lot of work with his dad, Andy, when I first came down to London. We won a few contracts. A block of flats called Wessex House was our big breakthrough. Andy was able to do a deal with the planning committee. It's a difficult game, though. The competition can be a right bugger. A few years ago I got into trouble with another project in Archway and ran out of cash. Gareth rounded up a few mates and they bailed me out.'

'Taking seventy per cent of your business in the process.'

'Thirty per cent of something is better than a hundred per cent of nothing,' Brunel reasoned. 'Plus, they were able to put extra business my way – and they got me on the Met's Approved Contractor list.'

Encouraged by the guy's willingness to talk, Carlyle repaired to the bar for some more whiskey. On his return, he asked, 'It was Mills who got you in with the Met, then?'

'Nah.' Brunel took an appreciative sip of the Bushmills. 'That was another member of his little Brexit gang, Sir Christopher Sollerdiche.'

'Never heard of him.'

'He's banging that supermodel . . . Whazzername? I read about it in the *Daily Mail*. Lucky sod. Can't imagine his wife's very happy about it, though.'

'I suppose not.'

'Sir Christopher takes a very close interest in the business.

The bloke's always on my back. Not like Gareth. Gareth's very hands-off.'

Carlyle needed something to take back to Dalby-Cummins. 'If Vicky can get your investors onboard, might she be able to do a deal?'

'Maybe.' Brunel looked doubtful. 'Like I said, the cake's getting sliced pretty thin already.'

'But better a small slice than no slice at all.'

'My guys'll drive a *very* hard bargain. Even if she did take over my Approved Contractor status and become the acceptable face of BDS, she'd still be no more than the hired help.'

'I'm not sure Vicky would accept that.'

'Neither am I.' Brunel held up his empty glass. 'One for the road?'

'Sure.' The commander sighed. 'Why not?'

Carolyn Fairbairn cursed her rotten luck. It was incredibly unfortunate that the report into allegations of sexual harassment against Simon Scott QC had been delivered on her watch. One of the best-known lawyers in London, Scott was one of the founders of Morpheus Chambers, not to mention Fairbairn's boss. The alleged victim, an associate tenant, claimed Scott had subjected her to a campaign of verbal and physical abuse over a period of six months, almost five years ago.

'How do you want to proceed?' Charlotte James, one of the pupils, had a look of youthful indignation on her face, which reminded Fairbairn of her own daughter.

'Well . . .' As chair of Morpheus's women's forum, Fairbairn felt hopelessly conflicted. She knew, from personal experience, Scott was guilty as sin. On the other hand, were he to be sacked, Morpheus might collapse.

'We've got to get rid of him.' James couldn't contain her righteous exuberance. 'It's a no-brainer.'

Playing for time, Fairbairn looked slowly round the table. Given the importance of the meeting, it was a disappointing turnout. Three of her senior female colleagues were absent for different reasons, not all of which Fairbairn necessarily considered valid.

'This forum cannot make that decision,' Jeanne Ademeo piped up. Ademeo was a no-nonsense junior counsel, probably the closest to a reliable ally Fairbairn could count on. 'There are proper procedures to be gone through. We should let People and Behaviours do their job.' People and Behaviours was what Morpheus called its personnel department.

'These procedures will not be able to address the institutional failings in our organisation,' another barrister piped up. Murmurs of agreement from round the table made Fairbairn's heart sink even deeper. 'Institutional failings' was a catch-all term for abuse, covering everything and nothing, the boundless sins of the hegemony of the patriarchy, which forum members railed against at great length.

'Morpheus Chambers has a charter,' an emboldened James pointed out. 'Which I've read very carefully.'

You're probably the only one, Fairbairn thought.

'Among other things, we're committed to gender equality and a zero-tolerance policy towards inappropriate behaviour in our working environment.'

More voices of agreement.

'This group, the women's forum, is the means of enforcing that,' James insisted. 'Simon is guilty – he needs to go.'

'The report's not so unequivocal.' Fairbairn tapped the copy sitting on the table in front of her. Six months in the making, at a cost of more than a hundred and twenty thousand pounds, it was, if she was being brutally honest, nothing more than sixty-seven pages of hearsay, speculation and filler. 'It finds the complaint against Simon as "highly credible" but, at the end of the day, it's he-said-she-said.'

'Our glorious leader,' James squealed, 'the chair of the ACSAI no less, gets a free pass?' ACSAI stood for Accelerated Child Sexual Abuse Inquiry. At the time, Scott's appointment had seemed rather random. Now, if Morpheus's dirty laundry came out in public, it would appear negligent in the extreme.

'He can sexually assault a co-worker in a lift,' James spluttered, 'invite her for a threesome, quiz her on her sex life and . . . and we're going to ignore it?'

'I think we've taken this as far as we can, for now.' Fairbairn needed to wrap up this meeting as quickly as possible and get back to work. One of her clients, Susan Moran, had invited herself to a preliminary hearing on her civil case and would be waiting downstairs. Moran was turning into one of those impossibly needy souls who had to look over your shoulder the whole time. Thank God it was almost the weekend. The family bolthole in Norfolk beckoned. She started collecting her papers. 'I propose we share the report with the head of People and Behaviours and get their input before determining how to proceed.'

'Miranda's still on maternity leave,' someone pointed out.

'I'll call her.'

'What about the "no calls at home" policy?' asked another.

'I think we can allow an exception to the policy in this case. Miranda's been off for more than six months now. I'm sure she'll appreciate the intellectual stimulation.' Ignoring the grumbles from around the table, Fairbairn took her leave. 'I'll share her thoughts in due course.' Going down the stairs, she was intercepted by a pensive Simon Scott.

'What's the verdict?' Scott asked, his voice low.

'No verdict.' Fairbairn sighed. 'It has to go to People and Behaviours.'

Scott looked momentarily surprised. 'Is Miranda back already?'

'She's still on leave, but with two nannies, an au pair and a housekeeper, I'm sure she can find the time to take a look at the report.'

'That's what happens when you marry a partner in an investment bank that made more than twenty *billion* dollars last year. The woman certainly married well.'

'Simon, for God's sake.'

'You know what I mean. Feminist at work, little bourgeois housewife at home.'

There was nothing bourgeois about Miranda's domestic situation. Fairbairn recalled her tongue hanging out after reading a spread devoted to her colleague's home in the property-porn section of a Sunday newspaper. Fourteen thousand square feet of gleaming modernism in NW3. Much to their chagrin, Fairbairn and her husband – also a lawyer – had struggled to get their hands on a semi in less fashionable Dartmouth Park, a shoebox mortgaged to the hilt.

'Likes to flit between the nineteenth and twenty-first centuries when it suits her,' Scott sniped. 'And she's not the only one around here like that, is she?' As Fairbairn shushed him, he pushed back his shoulders and moved up a step, the better to look down on her. 'I'm relying on you, Carolyn, as the voice of reason around here. This report, it's all crap. And, still, it's hanging over me. The gossip in the firm has been about nothing else for months. It's leaking out, too.' He named an industry website. 'Some of the comments are very close to the mark.'

'We must follow due process.' Fed up at being caught in the middle of the row, Fairbairn cursed Miranda and her luxurious maternity leave.

'If you'd followed due process,' Scott insisted, 'this witch-hunt would've ended long before now . . . There's not one shred of evidence.'

I think you did it, Fairbairn thought glumly, but I can't prove it.

'If you try to sack me – drive me out of my own firm – I'll sue your arse off.' He chuckled rakishly. 'Am I allowed to say "arse" in this context?'

Fairbairn ignored the question. 'Gotta go.'

'Ah, yes.' Scott smiled. 'I saw the boob-job cop downstairs. To be honest, they weren't as big as I was expecting.'

Fairbairn groaned. 'Deep down, you want to be sacked, Simon, don't you?'

'I'm unsackable and you know it.' He moved further up the stairs. 'I've got child-abuse hearings all next week. Let's see if we can get our internal thing sorted out after that.'

Fairbairn made no promises. Instead, she asked, 'How's the inquiry going?'

'About as fast as your witch-hunt, which is the way the government wants it – a problem kicked down the road is a problem solved, as far as they're concerned.'

'Ha, good point.' Fairbairn headed down the stairs. 'See you later.'

'Knock 'em dead, kid. Give my best to your client.'

'We're gonna be late.' Catching sight of her lawyer, Susan Moran started to fret. 'The traffic's terrible.'

'We can get the tube.'

'I don't think so.' Moran touched the collar of her uniform, under her overcoat. 'It's a nightmare on public transport. The idea you might not be on duty doesn't compute with most people. They see the uniform and they think they can boss you about because,' she adopted a whiny voice, '"We pay your salary." I had one guy, not so long ago, thought he could get me to clean up litter at Holborn station. The stupid sod got pretty arsy when I told him it wasn't my job.'

'Driving it is, then.' Fairbairn reached into her bag and rummaged for her key. 'They can't start without us.' Outside, she was relieved to find her car had neither been vandalised nor given a ticket. Getting in, she took a pile of papers from the passenger seat and tossed them into the back, then opened the door for Moran.

'Nice car,' the superintendent declared, as she settled into the oxblood-leather seat.

'Gets me from A to B.' Fairbairn slipped the key into the ignition, then pulled on her seatbelt.

'I had a Porsche for a couple of years.' Moran wrestled her seatbelt into place. 'Got rid of it after I was caught speeding on the M1. When you had a bit of open road it was too tempting to put your foot down.'

'Uh-huh. Why don't you send them a message to say we're on our way?' Reaching for the key again, Fairbairn gave a flick of her wrist to start the engine.

Gagging at the stink, Patricia Snowden detoured round the pile of refuse sacks dumped beside a lamppost. 'Look, Mum, I've gotta go. I'll be late for picking Patrick up at nursery. Again . . . Yeah, I know it'll be the second time this week. Not good . . . No. They're perfectly nice about it, usually, but I don't want to push my luck.'

The stink seemed to be getting worse the further she moved away from the rubbish. Ending the call, Patricia started breathing through her mouth. On the far side of the road, a dog-walker was struggling with his charges. Funny-looking dogs . . . The thought was blown away by a huge roar, like the end of the world.

Next thing Patricia knew, she was sitting on the pavement. The stink of rubbish was gone, replaced by the acrid smell of burning. A worried-looking man was standing over her, asking if she was okay. At least, that's what she presumed he was saying: her hearing had gone.

I should call the nursery, Patricia thought, let them know I'm gonna be late again. She looked around for her phone, but it was nowhere to be seen.

TWELVE

'It wasn't me.' Gina Sweetman sounded positively giddy. Given the time of day, Carlyle imagined she might very well be drunk.

'What wasn't you?' On his way back to Camden tube station, feeling the effects of the Adams Arms' whiskey, he was in no mood to chat with the assistant commissioner.

'Susan Moran just got blown to bits.'

Carlyle came to an abrupt halt outside a hardware store. Across the road, a massive advertising hoarding carried a poster advertising *Brexit – The Movie*: a bunch of chinless wonders in Union Jack waistcoats waving champagne bottles, above the legend *The bad boys who changed the world*. The film was due to open later in the week.

'Last seen, her implants were flying somewhere over King's Cross. She was in a car with her lawyer and . . . boom.' Sweetman laughed out loud. 'The local glaziers are going to be making hay for weeks . . . and before you ask, I've got a watertight alibi.'

'Sitting in the Montevideo Arms with a hundred witnesses, no doubt.'

'How did you know?'

'Lucky guess. When did this happen?'

'About an hour ago. It's all over the TV. Three dead: Moran, her lawyer and some dog-walker. A couple of Labradoodles also got a one-way ticket to the big kennels in the sky. Dozens injured. They're saying it was the biggest bomb in London since the glory days of the IRA.'

'Moran was definitely one of the victims?'

'Oh, yes.' Sweetman's glee ticked up a notch. 'None of the names have been publicly released yet, but I know the senior officer at the scene – he's a good mate. I wanted to let you know.'

'Thanks.' Carlyle needed a little time to work through the significance of this latest development.

'And I wanted to make sure you understand it doesn't change our deal.' Sweetman sounded sober now, all business. 'I'm seeing Bruce Allen this afternoon – I'll get you off his stupid commission so you can sit on my panel. Be ready for his call.'

'Will the disciplinary hearing go ahead?'

'I would expect so. The Met intends to see this through to the bitter end. Looks like Susan Moran will be haunting me from beyond the grave.'

Feet up on his desk, Gareth Mills played with an embossed invitation to the premiere of *Brexit – The Movie*. A new five-thousand-pound tux from Savile Row hung in the corner in anticipation of his big night out. Mills was looking forward to grabbing a selfie with Benny Charleston, the actor who was playing him in the movie. He had wanted to play himself but the producers had had other ideas, even after Mills had agreed to underwrite the film's entire £40 million budget. Still, it could have been worse. Charleston was one of the hottest actors around and, more importantly, he could make an introduction to Hermione Lacemaker, a super-hot actress with a bit-part in the film.

'Are you still there, son?'

'Yeah.' Mills tore his thoughts from Hermione Lacemaker and stared at the speakerphone on his desk.

'I thought I'd lost you for a moment.'

'No, no,' Mills snapped. He liked Terry Brunel well enough, but the guy could get on his wick. 'I'm still here.'

'I had a visit from this cop,' Brunel repeated, unsure if Mills had been paying attention the first time around.

'Yes, yes. What did he want?'

'Vicky Dalby-Cummins sent him. She's the woman who wants to buy me out. Or, at least, buy into the business.'

'Harry Cummins's widow.'

'Right. She wants to get a slice of the Met work.'

Mills tossed the invitation onto the desk. 'And what would we get?'

'Credibility, I suppose.'

'But we are credible. You're an Approved Contractor. For God's sake, Sir Christopher bloody Sollerdiche himself got you on the list, remember? You can't possibly get any more credible than that.'

'Still, if the Moran thing doesn't go away, I could lose my accreditation.'

'Moran's been taken care of.'

'Whaddya mean?'

'Didn't you know? Moran got blown to kingdom come this afternoon by a bomb.'

'Blimey.'

'The explosion was so big I'm surprised you didn't hear it up your way.'

'I was in the Adams Arms, talking to Vicky Dalby-Cummins's cop.' Brunel recounted his conversation with Carlyle. 'I expect he'll pay you a visit, next.'

'A bent copper's nothing to worry about.' Mills snorted. 'Plus, he's given you a great alibi.'

'Don't be daft,' Brunel spluttered. 'No one would ever think I'd try to blow up Susan Moran.'

'Terry, the woman was suing you. You're bound to be a suspect.'

130

'But I was nowhere near where it happened.'

'Which is good.' Mills was becoming bored with the teasing. 'Just try to avoid touching up anyone else.'

'I didn't touch her up. I just—'

'Whatever. It doesn't matter now. Let's crack on with the police-station refurb work and then we can move on to the next thing. Sollerdiche has already got his eyes on the next bunch of contracts he wants to bid for.'

'What about Vicky?' Brunel asked. 'She's not going to give up. And she clearly has some decent police contacts. This guy today wasn't some junior plod, he's a commander.'

'What's his name again?'

'Carlyle.'

'And he was there in an unofficial capacity?' Mills thought about it for a moment. 'I wonder what she's got on him.'

'Want me to do a bit of digging?' Brunel offered.

'Sit tight,' Mills commanded. 'Get on with the day job. Leave the investigative work to me.'

'What are we gonna do?'

'What we're *not* gonna do is let her get her nose in the trough because you made a social faux pas.'

'But you liked Harry,' Brunel recalled.

'Doesn't mean I have to provide for his widow,' Mills replied, 'especially when she tries to do me over.'

Totò's was named in honour of Salvatore Schillaci, star of Italy's 1990 World Cup squad. The café had been opened by an Italian expat, who ran it for almost three decades before retiring to a village near Siena. Carlyle was surprised that the new owners hadn't changed the décor. A silent TV screen high in the far corner was showing highlights from some long-forgotten Serie A game from the 1980s.

'The Italians could do with someone like Schillaci now, huh?'

Karen O'Sullivan contemplated the football memorabilia that covered the walls as she sipped her black Americano with exaggerated care. 'They're in a complete mess.'

Carlyle deferred to her better judgement.

'I played for Chelsea Ladies for a couple of years. Even if I say so myself, I was pretty good.'

'You a Chelsea fan, then?' Carlyle asked warily.

'I liked playing, rather than watching. My dad used to go to Fulham – I went with him a few times when I was a kid, but never got into it.'

'I had a season ticket at the Cottage for years and years.' Carlyle toyed with his empty demitasse. 'Used to go with my old fella.'

'My dad was Italian,' O'Sullivan said. 'From Milan. He met my mum when she was there, working as an au pair. We always supported Italy in my house.'

'But you're a Londoner, right?'

'Born in the North Middlesex.'

'O'Sullivan's not a very Italian name.'

'It's my married name. It was just too much hassle to change it again after the divorce.'

'Hm.' Carlyle moved on. 'Did you find anything at Travis's address?'

'James Gillespie? Not a lot. Spoke to one of the neighbours who said they hadn't seen him for a while. We'll have to get a warrant before we can go in. I need to get on with it, but the kids've been sick and—'

'Don't worry about it. If Gillespie is, in fact, the man with no head, he isn't going anywhere.' Carlyle moved on to the second item on his agenda, Superintendent Susan Moran.

'Chief Inspector Tommy Mogrund's in charge of the investigation into the explosion.' O'Sullivan finished her coffee. 'I'm still focused on Kenny Schenk.'

Carlyle didn't know Mogrund.

'Tommy's a cockweasel who couldn't investigate his way out of a paper bag. He'll get bumped off it pretty sharpish, I'd have thought. A cop gets murdered, they're gonna put the A-team on it.'

'You'd hope so,' Carlyle agreed. 'What's the gossip?'

'Early days, but there's already a whole bunch of different theories. Moran's lawyer might've been the target. Her firm, Morpheus Chambers, does a lot of human-rights work, terror-related cases.'

'I got a call from Gina Sweetman within minutes of the explosion.'

'She must've been happy.'

'Delighted, especially as she has an alibi.'

'I never saw her as a possible suspect. I mean, Moran's death doesn't get the assistant commissioner off the hook. The panel will be under pressure to go for the harshest possible punishment, in deference to the memory of Susan Moran. Sweetman might find herself sacked as a way of honouring her traduced colleague.'

All the more reason I don't want to get co-opted onto the sodding panel, Carlyle reflected. 'Moran's civil claim'll fall by the wayside, though.'

'The estate might pursue it.'

'Unlikely.' Which means Terry Brunel gets off the hook, too. 'Fuck.'

'What?'

'Nothing.' The commander wasn't in the mood to explain how he'd given Brunel a great alibi for Moran's murder. 'Another self-inflicted problem.'

'Well, sorry to add to your burden, but there's something else . . .'

Carlyle groaned.

'Sweetman wants me to execute an arrest warrant on Hermione Lacemaker. I don't think it's a good idea, but she's insisting.'

'She told me.' Carlyle sighed. 'She thinks it'll get her some good PR ahead of her hearing.'

'What d'ya want me to do?' O'Sullivan asked. 'I thought you'd done a deal with Lacemaker's lawyer.'

'Play for time.' Carlyle had more to worry about right now than Abigail Slater. 'Schenk's autopsy was inconclusive. There's not enough evidence to charge Hermione with anything.'

'Sweetman says it's for the CPS to decide. She wants me to make the arrest tomorrow, once she's tipped off the press.'

Carlyle rubbed his temples. 'Do what you need to do. If Sweetman wants the arrest, make the arrest. It'll get sorted out in due course.' Once O'Sullivan left, he rang Abigail Slater. The call went straight to voicemail, but the lawyer rang back before he could order another coffee.

'It might be time for your client to take another little trip.' Carlyle explained the unfortunate turn of events.

Slater called him all the names under the sun. 'We had a deal,' she thundered. 'You're *supposed* to be a man of your word.'

'I am,' Carlyle insisted, 'but the assistant commissioner has other ideas. Get Hermione out of the way for a few days and it'll all sort itself out.'

'But Hermione's got a film premiere to attend.'

'Well, unless you want your client to be arrested right in front of the press, she should give it a miss.'

'More to the point, I'm going as her guest.'

Carlyle thought back to the billboard in Camden. 'The Brexit movie?'

'Yes. It doesn't sound very exciting, and it'll lose a shitload of money, but it'll be a good party. Loads of big names will be there.'

'In that case,' Carlyle smirked, 'you can take me along with you.'

'What?' Slater was bemused by the suggestion.

'It would be a disaster for Hermione to get nicked in the middle of Leicester Square, especially with all the media in attendance. And I wouldn't want you to go on your own.'

'You're not my idea of arm candy, no offence.'

'None taken. Trust me, I scrub up well. And I'll be on my best behaviour.'

'You're serious, aren't you?' Slater thought about it for a moment. 'Suppose I go along with your little plan, what's in it for me?'

'Beyond keeping your client out of jail?'

'Beyond that, yes.'

'I'll owe you a favour.'

'Not nearly good enough,' Slater snorted, 'but I'm sure I can come up with something.'

THIRTEEN

Catherine Sarah Dorothea Wellesley, a.k.a. Kitty Pakenham, Duchess of Wellington, wife of Field Marshal Arthur Wellesley, 1st Duke of Wellington, looked down from above the library fireplace, irritated, no doubt, that the St James's gentlemen's club that bore her name had never extended membership to women. Ignoring Kitty, Bruce Allen cradled a snifter of brandy as a series of familiar images appeared on the TV in the corner. The sound was muted – members didn't like the noise, particularly when the news was bad – but it didn't matter, for Allen knew the script by heart. After clinging to power for longer than expected, the prime minister looked ready to resign. Another miserable election loomed.

Dismissing the views of the BBC, Gareth Mills contemplated his gin and tonic. 'Interesting place.'

'My father was a member. He got me in when I was twenty-one. It's a bit stuffy but the location's good and it's handy for networking. Plus, it has a wonderful wine list.' Allen took a large mouthful of his drink and let it linger on his tongue. 'And the cognac's not bad, either.'

'I wouldn't have thought the company would be much to your taste.' Mills eyed a portrait of Edgar Carlton, much smaller than Kitty's, which hung on the wall behind the TV. The former prime minister was one of the club's most famous members from recent years. 'Too many liberal metropolitan elite moaners.'

'Politicians are all the same,' Allen grunted. 'At the end of the day, all you can do is try to stop them fucking things up too badly.'

'Same as with policemen.'

'Same as with policemen,' Allen agreed. 'Public service has never attracted the brightest and the best.'

'Doesn't stop you taking a civil-service salary,' Mills teased.

'A temporary posting, part of my portfolio of jobs.' Allen waved his snifter in the air for emphasis. 'The commissioner needs my help – who am I to refuse? Anyway, as we know, my current role is useful when it comes to leveraging business opportunities for the likes of BDS.'

'Does the commissioner know about your work for us?'

'All of my interests are properly organised, maintained and disclosed,' Allen parroted.

'I'll take that as a no.'

'The commissioner doesn't need to know about Building Design Services. She has nothing to do with the awarding of contracts. There's no conflict of interest.'

If you say so. Mills sucked his drink through a straw. 'About this guy Carlyle . . .'

'You're not the first person to ask about him.' Allen thought back to a brief, tetchy conversation with a less than sober Gina Sweetman. 'No one likes him but, somehow, he manages to sur- vive.' He finished his drink and signalled to a passing waiter for a refill. 'A bit like a cockroach, I suppose.'

Mills declined the offer of another drink. 'Commander Cockroach,' he chuckled, 'I like it.'

'Don't worry, I'll deal with him. If, as suspected, he's on the payroll of Victoria Dalby-Cummins, he'll be out of the service so fast his bony arse won't hit the door on the way out.'

'According to Terry Brunel, he was just doing her a favour, having a quiet word.'

'No one does anything for nothing in this world.'

'The cockroach must be doing it for a reason.'

'I know Vicky well enough. She wouldn't want to be in the man's debt. I'm sure his price must've been agreed in advance.'

'You've worked with her before?'

'I know *of* her.' Allen backtracked in the face of Mills's evident curiosity. 'She's been making a bit of a name for herself since she came to London.'

'Anyone working with Vernon Holder needs some pretty big *cojones*.'

Allen could only agree.

'What happened to Vernon?' Mills wondered. 'He seems to have disappeared.'

'He's got a place in the Caribbean. I think he's basically retired these days.'

'Lucky bugger.'

'Pah. Retirement's not all it's cracked up to be. You lose your appetite for the game, you might as well dig your own grave.'

'It's a point of view.'

'The game's the thing,' Allen insisted. 'Look at us, on the brink of acquiring a billion's-worth of the Met's unwanted brown-field sites inside the M25.' He waved his glass in the air again. 'We're gonna double our money, triple it. If that doesn't get you going, nothing will.'

'Sounds good,' Mills agreed.

'It's fucking great,' Allen chirped. A couple of annoyed looks from co-members caused him to lower his voice. 'Remember the feeling and compare it with the buzz when you're looking at all those zeroes in your bank account.'

'We still need to close the deal.'

'Relax. The Moran thing is going away. Things are looking up.'

'Boom.' Mills garnered more black looks from a couple of elderly members on their way to dinner. 'Talk about lucky.'

'Talk about random.' Allen kept his voice low. 'The biggest explosion in Central London since seven/seven and it turned out it was a fractured gas main. Half the bloody anti-terrorist squad turned up before anyone noticed the roadworks. Even then, they spent for ever chasing the bomb theory.'

'Unbelievable.'

'I know. Always go with the most obvious explanation, right? Some idiot workman was laying some cables and managed to fracture the pipe. How is that even possible? Then some bloke walking a bunch of dogs tosses a cigarette butt into the hole and the whole thing goes up. Poor old Moran happened to be sitting there in her lawyer's car at the time. You'd get shorter odds on winning the lottery. On the plus side, we can now claim to have put the first British dog in orbit. That's a key performance milestone reached for the National Space Programme.'

Mills looked at him blankly.

'It's a joke. One of the dog-walker's dogs was blown so far into the air that it was found three streets away. A diabetic poodle called Alfie.'

'You'd have thought someone would notice the smell.'

'It's London,' Allen reasoned. 'You get a nasty smell in your nostrils, you start walking a bit faster. No one in this damn city has an ounce of community spirit in their body. It's a modern-day Sodom and Gomorrah. About time we brought it to heel.'

'Yes.' Mills had absolutely no idea what Allen was rambling on about. The man's ability to talk nonsense was unparalleled, at least outside the House of Commons. According to Chris Sollerdiche, this was partly due to a bad case of syphilis, which Allen had contracted in his early twenties. Mills liked the explanation, although Sollerdiche was notorious for inventing scuttlebutt, the more malicious the better.

'You couldn't make it up.' Allen took a fresh drink from the returning waiter. 'But, look, we need to learn from this – you must keep your man under control.'

'Don't worry,' Mills promised as the waiter beat a hasty retreat. 'Terry won't repeat his mistake.'

'He'd better not. The idea we could lose billions – *billions* – because some moron comes over all Benny Hill is enough to do your head in.'

'Who's Benny Hill?' Mills asked.

'Never mind. Just keep Terry in check. I'll make sure the commissioner appoints a suitable and speedy replacement for Moran on the Building and Infrastructure sub-committee. We don't want any slippage on the timetable.'

'What about Dalby-Cummins?'

'I'll deal with Vicky,' Allen promised, 'and her little puppet, Commander Cockroach.'

The bouncer at the Chapel wasn't having any of it. 'Sorry, mate, my kid could've made something better on his laptop.'

'For fuck's sake.' Carlyle waved the warrant card in front of the guy's face one last time. 'Why would I be making any of this up?'

Folding his arms, the bouncer gave the commander a feeble smile. 'You'd be amazed at the stunts some people pull to avoid paying.'

No way was Carlyle coughing up forty-five quid to get through the door. 'Can't you ring your boss?'

The bouncer's expression changed slightly. 'You know Eric?'

'I meant Vicky.'

'Who?'

'Vicky. Victoria Dalby-Cummins. She owns this place.'

'Good for her. My boss is called Eric. He certainly doesn't own this place.'

Christ on a bike. Carlyle called Dalby-Cummins, only to get voicemail. Turning away from the smirking bouncer, he stalked up the street. Leaving a message, he crossed the road and took refuge in a busy juice bar. By the time he'd made his way through an insanely expensive Instant Energiser, his quarry called him back. 'Sorry, I don't know what's happening with my phone. I didn't see your call and the message has only just come through.'

Carlyle recounted his difficulty in gaining entrance to the club.

Dalby-Cummins offered a modicum of sympathy. 'The people on the door change all the time.'

'The guy was only doing his job,' Carlyle acknowledged grudgingly.

'Are you still there?'

'I'm across the road, in the juice bar.'

'Let me send someone down to collect you. Do me a favour, I'd love a Hangover Heaven, if you could grab one for me.'

'Sure.' Carlyle looked it up on the menu and winced at the price. At this rate, the juice bar was going to clean him out. It would have been cheaper to pay the entrance fee to get into the club. 'Gimme five minutes.'

Returning to the Chapel, juice in hand, he was met by a slender young woman called Karolina, who introduced herself as Dalby-Cummins's office manager. To his disappointment, the bouncer who had denied him entry was not around to see his triumphal return. In his place was a small, middle-aged guy, who looked far less intimidating.

Dalby-Cummins's office was at the top of the building. From behind a laptop, she greeted his arrival with a broad smile.

'How much do I owe you?'

Placing the Hangover Heaven on her desk, Carlyle waved away the offer as he took a seat. 'My pleasure.'

'Thank you.' With a pair of spectacles on her head, and minimal make-up, Dalby-Cummins projected the look of a marketing consultant.

He waited for her to try the drink and signal her approval, then said, 'I went to see Terry Brunel.'

Straw still in her mouth, Dalby-Cummins nodded. 'Did he blow up Susan Moran?'

'Looks like it was an accident, a gas leak.' O'Sullivan had told him the investigation had been quickly closed before anyone could ask how the cockweasel Tommy Mogrund could mistake a gas leak for a bomb.

'A bloody big accident.' Dalby-Cummins placed the juice back on the table. 'Extremely convenient for Terry.'

'And for his investors.' Carlyle held her eye. 'Why didn't you tell me about Gareth Mills and the others?'

Dalby-Cummins seemed slightly taken aback by his irritated tone, but she played it cool. 'Terry is the weakest link at Building Design Services. If we got him onboard, our hand would be much stronger when we approached the others.'

We? 'Well, the leverage of Moran's lawsuit is gone. Even if he was tempted – and when I spoke to him, he didn't seem very interested – Terry won't want to play ball now. Game over.'

'Hardly. This is only the beginning.'

That wasn't what Carlyle wanted to hear. 'I did what I said I would,' he pointed out. 'I kept my end of the deal.'

'The *deal* is you help me get into BDS and I help get Bruce Allen off your back.'

'It all seems one-way at the moment,' Carlyle grumbled.

'Don't worry, Commander. I'll do my bit, as long as you do yours.'

When you sup with the devil, you should use a long spoon. Carlyle's brain told him he should cut his losses, get up and leave. Instead, he asked, 'What's next?'

'Go and talk to Gareth Mills. Tell him I know all about the big deal he's got planned.'

'What deal? Refurbishing the police stations?'

142

'That's just a little taster. This is much bigger, different scale entirely.'

Carlyle waited for her to go on.

'Last year, the Met did a massive audit of all its property in London. Half the remaining police stations in London are going to be closed down and sold off. The sites are scattered all over the place, but the prime ones are in the West End and Chelsea. The Building and Infrastructure sub-committee has to decide whether to sell off the properties piecemeal or to go with a preferred bidder for the whole lot. If you sell things off bit by bit, you'll probably make more in the end but it's a hassle and it'll take for ever. Using BDS as a Trojan Horse, Mills and his pals want to buy the whole lot on the cheap without getting drawn into an auction.'

'That's not what you told me before.'

'You didn't need to know before,' Dalby-Cummins riposted, 'but now you're moving up the food chain, you need to see more of the big picture.'

The commander let it slide. 'If these guys have such deep pockets,' he asked, 'why do they need you?'

'If I don't get to play, I can scupper the deal.'

'How?'

'That's on a need-to-know basis and you don't currently need to know.'

Carlyle refused to be riled. Instead he changed tack. 'Is it worth the hassle?'

'If it gets preferred bidder status, BDS will pay about £180 million for the portfolio. Redeveloped, it could be worth ten times that.'

Carlyle let out a low whistle. 'Big numbers.'

'These boys are looking at a profit of more than a billion . . . *pounds*. Why risk that by refusing me a little nibble?' She waved a hand in the air. 'Even if I only ended up with five per cent of BDS, it would knock all of this into a cocked hat. I'll have made more than Harry could ever have dreamed of in a dozen lifetimes.'

'Is that what this is all about? Getting one over on your old man?'

'It's the game. People like you don't understand. You think in terms of "How much money do I need so I can stop and put my feet up?" People like me never want to stop. I don't need the money. It's just a way of keeping score. I'm not competing against Harry or even Vernon. I've already left them behind. I want to compete against the guys on the next rung up the ladder, people like Gareth Mills.'

'And Sir Christopher Sollerdiche?' Carlyle had checked out the guy online, large as life and twice as corpulent.

'He's quite a few rungs further up but maybe in time.'

The woman's words made sense. Kind of. Carlyle had to admire her competitive streak.

'Go and see Gareth Mills,' Dalby-Cummins instructed. 'Make him see it's in his interest to bring me in on his deal. Then I can sort out your Bruce Allen problem.'

FOURTEEN

Carlyle slipped into Leicester Square, heading for the TV lights illuminating the front of the Empire cinema. After a brief search, he found Abigail Slater standing next to one of the large posters advertising *Brexit – The Movie*.

'Where the hell have you been?' Wearing a flimsy dress under what he presumed was a fake fur coat, the lawyer was clearly suffering in the cold. 'I've been waiting for ages.'

'Sorry. Work got in the way.'

'At least you've managed to put a suit and tie on.' Grabbing him by the arm, she led him towards the entrance. 'Let's get a bloody drink.'

Inside, the foyer was rammed. Carlyle estimated around five hundred people, dressed to the nines, were happily necking the free champagne. Everyone seemed very pleased with themselves. Looking around, he saw various familiar faces, actors and celebrities of different sorts. Of Gareth Mills, however, there was no sign.

After three glasses of champagne, Slater felt able to discard her coat, leaving Carlyle a disconcerting view of her décolletage.

'How's Hermione getting on?' he asked, gamely trying to maintain eye contact.

'She's in Mumbai,' Slater helped herself to a fresh drink from a passing waiter, 'or will be in a couple of hours.'

'I'll let Inspector O'Sullivan know.'

'I spoke to the inspector this afternoon. She wasn't very happy about it, but I told her Hermione would be back soon enough, so there's no need for any international arrest warrant.' Slater glared at him over the top of her glass. 'You should keep your people under control.'

'O'Sullivan's okay. She just has Gina Sweetman on her case.' Carlyle related Sweetman's attempts to generate some good PR in the wake of her spat with Moran. 'The assistant commissioner's fighting for her job.'

'The whole thing's ridiculous,' was Slater's verdict. 'I mean, what's wrong with having a boob job?'

Blushing slightly, Carlyle stared at his drink.

'I've met Gina Sweetman a few times. Every time, the woman's been half-cut. The Met should've done something about her a long time ago.' Slater gave him a sly look. 'I can see my new client filing a claim for harassment and unlawful arrest.'

'Hermione hasn't been arrested,' Carlyle pointed out.

'She had to run off to bloody India when she should have been enjoying this wonderful gala event.'

'She doesn't have a very big part,' Carlyle pointed out, trying to downplay the scale of the injury.

'Size isn't everything.' Another giggle. 'Tonight's not about the film, it's about profile. Getting your picture in the paper.'

'I suppose.'

'Hermione's had an on–off thing with Benny Charleston for years. Tonight should've been all about are they together again or not? The answer, by the way, is "not". Benny's spent the last three months working on a movie in Canada, shacked up with a trans stuntwoman called Maddy. Hermione's very annoyed about it.'

'I can imagine,' Carlyle sympathised.

'But it doesn't mean she wouldn't have walked down the red carpet with him.'

'No.'

'Then, even more important than the publicity, is the net-working. This is an important industry event – who knows what contacts Hermione could've made this evening, if she hadn't been chased from the country by the unprofessional, unethical and no doubt illegal actions of the Metropolitan Police? I shudder to think of the roles up for grabs here that she'll miss out on. The damage done to her career, not to mention her bank balance, could be immense.'

'Leave me out of it,' Carlyle pleaded.

Slater's eyes narrowed. 'You're in it up to your neck.'

'Hardly.'

The lawyer was having none of it. 'Just get things sorted out before Hermione's home and we'll call it quits. Put Sweetman back in her box and I'll make it all go away.'

'How long's she going to be away?'

'No more than a week, ten days absolute max. Her new agent got her an advert over there, for a brand of Swedish whisky, plus she'll go and see a few studios. You never know, if Hollywood doesn't come up with some decent parts, Bollywood might.'

'She's got a new agent?' Carlyle thought back to his meeting with the sleazy Graham Hughes. 'Good for her.'

'The previous guy was second division, at best. And pimping her out to Kenny Schenk was the last straw.'

Finishing his drink, Carlyle looked around for somewhere to leave his empty glass. 'I suppose that sort of thing happens a lot.'

'All the time. You'd be amazed.' Slater put a hand on his arm, causing him to inch away. 'Well, I don't suppose *you* would, Commander, but you know what I mean. I suppose you've seen it all in your time, eh?'

'I've seen a lot of things,' Carlyle agreed, 'although I've never worked Vice. My wife wouldn't allow it.'

Slater studied his ring-free hands. 'Are you married?' The possibility seemed to amuse her. 'Or divorced?'

'Married. One daughter. She's at Imperial, studying some-thing I don't understand.'

'That's how it should be, don't you think? You want them to have left you in their wake by the time they hit twenty, at least.'

'I suppose so.' Carlyle hadn't really thought about it in those terms.

'My two are still at school, boarding, in Hampshire. Their father had the good grace to cover their school fees before he dropped down dead at fifty-four.'

'My condolences.' Carlyle adopted his standard bureaucratic tone. 'I'm sorry to hear that.'

'I'm not. The little shit was banging some teenager when it happened. Literally. He was fucking some poor girl – who'd been trafficked from Bulgaria, no less – up the arse when he had a massive stroke and collapsed on top of her. If I'd known what he was up to, I'd have killed the bugger myself.'

'What happened to the girl?'

'Oh, they deported her.' Slater's face brightened. 'It's good we're cracking down on the bloody immigrants at last, don't you think?'

Carlyle's reply was interrupted by the sound of screams from outside. His first thought: Terrorist attack.

Slater, however, was unmoved. 'Looks like Benny Charleston's arrived. We should get our seats before the rush.'

The film was dismal, with no obvious plot and a succession of characters who were as one-dimensional and unappealing as their real-life equivalents. As the end credits started to roll, Slater pulled him to his feet. 'Thank Christ that's over. Let's get a drink and I'll introduce you to a few people.'

The after-party was held in a private club above the cinema. While Slater fell into conversation with another lawyer, Carlyle stood around, holding his champagne flute, feeling awkward.

'Commander, I didn't expect to see you here.'

I suppose I could say the same. Carlyle mustered a smile. Even talking to Graham Hughes was better than looking like a lemon.

'If you're after Hermione, I hear she's off filming some advert abroad.' The agent wrinkled his nose in disgust. 'The kind of thing she wouldn't have touched with a bargepole if I'd proposed it.'

'I heard she'd dumped you.' Carlyle had no interest in sparing the man's feelings.

'These things happen. It's no big deal.' Hughes tried to sound blasé, but his annoyance was clear. 'I think we've seen peak Hermione, even if she gets off on the Schenk thing.'

Carlyle ignored the man's blatant fishing. 'And what about you?'

'I'll be fine.' Hughes reeled off a bunch of names. 'I've a good stable of talent – all keen, all hungry, all on the way up.'

'Maybe you should've sent one of them to see Kenny Schenk for breakfast.'

'Maybe I should,' Hughes agreed. 'It would've saved everyone a lot of trouble.'

'You might be right.'

'I'm always right.' Holding his glass above his head, Hughes waved at someone behind the commander. 'Ricky – over here. Come and give us an update.'

Heads turned as Rick Ford made his way through the crowd, a worried expression on his face. 'Are you on duty?'

Carlyle pointed his glass in the direction of Abigail Slater, who was now engaged in animated conversation with Benny Charleston. 'I came with my, erm, friend.'

'You're friends with Abigail?' Ford looked aghast. 'Isn't it a conflict of interest?'

'"Friends" is overstating it,' Carlyle backtracked. 'I'm filling in for a last-minute dropout.' He took a sip of his drink. 'How're things going, business-wise?'

'We're soldiering on as best we can.' Ford looked pained. 'New claims against Kenny are coming in every day.'

'Come on,' Hughes smacked Ford's arm, 'chin up. It'll all work out. We've got lots of films to make together.'

Ford seemed less than enamoured of that prospect. Before he could reply, however, Slater reappeared. 'I think it's time for dinner,' she pronounced, as Hughes and Ford took the opportunity to melt away into the crowd. 'I need some food to soak up some of the alcohol.'

'I wanted to meet Gareth Mills.' Carlyle looked around the room hopefully.

'You've missed him. Benny told me he got the hump and left when he heard Hermione wasn't here.'

'Bugger.'

'Benny gave me his phone number, though.' She grinned. 'I'll let you have it if you take me somewhere nice.'

Slater led him across the square to an expensive restaurant behind the National Gallery, a fusion place where the lighting was too low and the music too loud. The prices on the menu caused Carlyle some difficulty breathing. While searching for something appealing yet relatively inexpensive, he prayed the lawyer would pick up the tab after all.

Slater sensed his discomfort. 'Don't worry, this is my treat. I know being a cop, even a top cop, doesn't pay well.' Catching a passing waiter, she ordered a bottle of wine. Carlyle asked for some sparkling water.

Slater looked offended. 'You can't let me drink on my own. I'm halfway sozzled already.'

Carlyle said nothing. Never much of a wine drinker, the champagne had left him feeling slightly thick-headed.

'Why are you so interested in meeting Gareth Mills?' Slater asked. 'Has he been a naughty boy?'

'Not as far as I know.' Carlyle tried to keep his explanation truthful but uninformative. 'The Met is in the process of selling off various police stations. Mills is a potential buyer.'

'I saw that. Doesn't seem a great idea. Selling off the family silver is always a mistake in the long run.'

'I'm on the committee looking into the sale. I thought tonight might be a useful opportunity to make contact and get to know a bit about what he's up to.'

Slater's eyes narrowed. 'You're on a committee flogging off police stations? That doesn't sound like the guy who threw Francis McGowan off a roof.'

'I didn't throw Father McGowan off the roof,' Carlyle corrected her. 'He jumped. I tried to save him.'

'What an amusing man you are. However, as I recall, my client wasn't the jumping kind.'

'Your client was a child abuser. How could anyone know what was going on inside his head?'

Slater graciously conceded the point. 'Whatever happened back then, I'd never have imagined you'd turn into a bureaucrat.'

'Responsibilities of rank,' Carlyle pronounced.

'I never had you down as a commander, either. I couldn't believe it when I heard you got promoted. You always were an annoying plod.'

'Very kind of you to say so.'

'You've got to admit it looks very weird. I never heard of an inspector being kicked upstairs so far, so fast. It must be pretty unprecedented.'

'Plenty of people have pointed that out to me.'

'You must have some right dirt on someone.'

'I was the last man standing.'

'How very old-school. You'd have thought the job would go

to a woman these days, like Susan Moran, for instance.'

'You knew her?'

'I'd met her a few times at different events. Not as tough as Gina Sweetman, but a good cop.'

'Better than me?'

'Comparisons are invidious.' The waiter arrived with the wine. Slater took a sip and gave a nod of approval. 'Shall we order?'

The food was as insipid as it was expensive. Carlyle kept the conversation ticking over with a succession of relatively amusing anecdotes while Slater polished off the booze with minimal assistance. To his relief, she abstained from a second bottle, instead ordering a peppermint tea, while he had an espresso.

The bill arrived with the drinks. 'How are you going to resolve the Hermione situation?' Slater asked, as she tossed a black Amex card onto the table.

'I'll speak to Sweetman.'

'You're learning to play the game. Better late than never.' Slater shifted in her chair. A moment later, Carlyle was shocked to find a hand on his thigh. 'It's the game,' she purred, 'which keeps things interesting, don't you think?'

Christ, you must be *really* drunk. Pushing back his chair, Carlyle got to his feet. 'Thanks for an, erm, interesting evening,' he burbled, 'but I need to get going.' He quickly finished his coffee. 'I'll keep you informed.'

Slater started to speak but was interrupted by the waiter arriving with a credit-card reader. Taking his chance, Carlyle said, 'Good night,' and bolted for the door.

FIFTEEN

'Heavy night?'

'It was a bit late,' Carlyle admitted. 'When did you get back?'

'This morning.' Joaquin seemed pleased to have been restored to his former position. 'Aditi's gone on sick leave – having gastric-band surgery.'

'Blimey.'

'It's very common, these days.'

'Yeah.' Carlyle recalled that Bernie Gilmore, a muckraking journalist, had had the same procedure. 'I know a guy who had one put in.'

'Did it work?'

'He lost a lot of weight.' Carlyle didn't go on to explain that Gilmore had been murdered and strangled, post-mortem, with the band, which had been ripped from his stomach. 'Good to have you back.'

'Aditi's gonna be away for at least a fortnight.'

'But she's not coming back here?' It was as much a plea as a question.

Joaquin had no idea.

The smell of paint coming from his office reminded Carlyle that the decorators were still in situ. 'I think I'll go and get a coffee.'

'The commissioner and Mr Allen want to see you.'

Carlyle groaned.

'And I've got the information you asked for.' Joaquin handed him a green folder.

What information? Carlyle couldn't remember asking for anything.

'The stuff you asked for on the steps outside,' Joaquin reminded him.

'Oh, yes, thanks. Tell the commissioner's office I'm on my way over. I'll be up there in an hour.'

Joaquin raised an eyebrow. 'An hour?'

Carlyle waved the folder. 'I'll read this first.' He decamped to a café off Trafalgar Square, the better to scrutinise the file undisturbed. Joaquin had collated the personnel information on both Gina Sweetman and Bruce Allen. Carlyle noted the assistant commissioner had been on the job almost as long as he had himself. Allen, on the other hand, had been hired by the commissioner less than a year ago, on a consultancy contract.

'Doubtless costing a fortune,' Carlyle grumped, slurping his coffee.

Finding nothing of interest in the official documentation, he turned his attention to the compilation of media stories that padded out the file. The majority related to Sweetman and her spat with Moran, but what caught Carlyle's attention was a *Private Eye* story: '*The Electoral Commission has launched an investigation into spending by an outfit called Brexit Heroes. The men behind this shadowy organisation are thought to include propagandist-in-chief Bruce Allen and Brexit bagman Sir Christopher Sollerdiche.*' Sollerdiche was a mate of Gareth Mills and an investor in Terry Brunel's building business, bidding for the redundant cop shops.

Interesting.

Before he could determine the significance of the Allen–Sollerdiche connection, his phone started vibrating across the table.

'How's it going?'

'Same old, same old,' Karen O'Sullivan groaned, 'but I see you're having fun.'

'Eh?'

'There's a picture of you in the *Metro* this morning at the premiere of that Brexit movie,' O'Sullivan informed him cheerily. 'You're standing next to some woman, looking down her dress.'

He knew better than to protest his innocence. 'Why would they have a picture of me?'

'They didn't. They had a picture of Benny Charleston. You're in the background. They obviously forgot to airbrush you out.'

'Hm.' Carlyle was glad Helen wasn't around to see the offending image. He wondered if Alice had spotted it. Presumably not, or his daughter would have been in touch.

'Did you meet him?'

'Charleston? No. There were hundreds of people there. The film is crap, by the way. I wouldn't bother going to see it.'

O'Sullivan, not much of a cinema-goer, didn't care one way or the other. 'That wasn't why I was ringing. Sweetman's spitting mad about Hermione Lacemaker doing a runner.'

'She hasn't done a runner,' Carlyle insisted. 'She's gone to India to film a commercial for Swedish whisky.'

'Do they make whisky in Sweden?'

'They must do. Anyway, Hermione should be back in a week or so. I'll deal with the assistant commissioner. How's the investigation going?'

'Sweetman doesn't want me wasting any more time on it. We're to arrest Hermione Lacemaker, send a report to the CPS and let them decide what to do from there. She has a press release ready to go.'

'The woman's got a screw loose,' was Carlyle's verdict.

'Maybe, but we basically know what happened to Kenny Schenk. From here on, it's just a question of how people want to spin it. You could let Hermione Lacemaker walk, you could charge her with murder, or anything between.'

'I would be amazed if the CPS tried to take it to court.'

'Stranger things have happened.'

'Better we try to nip this in the bud.'

'That would be my thinking.'

'I'll deal with Sweetman,' he repeated. 'And I'll speak to Abigail Slater, too. If there has to be an arrest, we can do it when Hermione gets back. There's no need to turn this into an international incident.'

'I don't know – if Sweetman thought she could get more publicity that way, she might do it.'

'Leave it to me.' Finishing the call, Carlyle retrieved a discarded copy of the *Metro* from a nearby table. After some searching, he found the photo on page twelve. To his dismay, O'Sullivan's description was pretty accurate. On the plus side, it was impossible to identify the partially obscured Slater. Carlyle, however, was immediately recognisable and his gaze was not at eye level.

'Bollocks.' Dropping the paper into a bin, he headed for Scotland Yard.

Virginia Thompson and Bruce Allen sat side by side on a rather grubby orange sofa. Their conversation stopped abruptly as Carlyle walked through the door.

Pouting, the commissioner invited him to take a seat on the chair opposite.

'I was beginning to think you might've gone under a bus,' Allen quipped. 'Then I saw your picture in the paper, looking down Abigail Slater's dress.'

How did he know it was Slater? Carlyle retained his equanimity. 'How can I be of assistance?'

'What are you doing,' the commissioner enquired, 'getting involved with Gina Sweetman?'

156

'I have nothing to do with the assistant commissioner,' Carlyle insisted.

'Other than the fact you inserted yourself into the Kenny Schenk case,' Allen spluttered, 'and you want to get yourself onto Gina's disciplinary panel.'

Sweetman's obviously had a word with you, Carlyle thought. Having decided not to deal with the assistant commissioner, the commander had no intention of sitting on the disciplinary panel and this was his opportunity to talk his way out of it. 'The Schenk case is being handled by an Inspector O'Sullivan. Her investigation is ongoing but, as I understand it, the CPS is very unlikely to bring charges. The assistant commissioner wants to make an arrest regardless, in order to get some good publicity ahead of her hearing.'

'That's pretty cynical,' Allen observed, 'and leaves you open to accusations of bias.'

Which is exactly what I want. 'It's impossible not to have an opinion on Gina,' he said, hopefully digging a bit more of his own grave.

'I don't understand why you want to take on such a difficult job,' said Thompson. 'The hearing is going to be a total minefield.'

'I'm just trying to do my bit,' Carlyle replied, not looking her in the eye.

'A bit late for that,' Allen huffed.

Carlyle remained unruffled. 'One can always do more. The Sweetman hearing is one example . . . Another might be the Capital Projects Group.'

'Ha,' Allen interrupted. 'Now we're getting to it.'

'I know there's a vacancy on the Building and Infrastructure sub-committee,' Carlyle continued, 'after what happened to Superintendent Moran.'

'Poor Susan.' For a moment, Thompson seemed lost in

contemplation. 'The funeral's the day after tomorrow. I'm not looking forward to it, I can tell you.'

Carlyle doubted there could be much left to bury. 'I'd like to think I can help build on the superintendent's good work.'

Allen didn't like the idea one bit. 'There's a process for filling vacant posts on the committee,' he said coolly, 'which should be respected. You can't cherry-pick the job you want.'

'I haven't demanded anything.'

'It would be helpful,' Allen snarled, 'if you did what you're bloody well told.'

'Calm down, Bruce.' Thompson placed a hand lightly on her adviser's forearm. 'The commander's trying to be helpful.'

Allen took a breath, trying to regain his composure. 'I'm in the process of putting together a list of possible replacements for Moran on B and I, and I'm sure the other committee members will have their own views.'

'You could use those names for your standards and behaviours commission,' Carlyle suggested.

Allen looked like he wanted to jump up and punch him. 'The commission requires a different skill-set entirely,' he wailed.

'Which is not my skill-set.' Avoiding Allen's glare, Carlyle resumed his pitch to the commissioner. 'Leadership is the art of getting someone else to do something you want done because he wants to do it.'

'What?' The commissioner looked flummoxed.

'It's a quote from President Eisenhower,' Carlyle explained.

'Ah.' Thompson appeared none the wiser.

'B and I has some important decisions to make in the coming months, as the property sell-off programme gathers pace. The process needs to be transparent and professional. Any inkling we haven't got a good price, the press'll have a right go. At you.'

'You've certainly given the matter some thought.' Thompson seemed impressed.

'But your attendance record is terrible.' Allen played his trump card, 'You never turn up to *any* meetings, which is why we called you to this meeting in the first place. It's unacceptable.'

'The Capital Projects Group and the Building and Infrastructure sub-committee will be my absolute top priority,' Carlyle promised. 'From now on, there'll be no more distractions like Kenny Schenk.'

'And the Sweetman hearing?' Thompson asked.

'Maybe, as Bruce suggests, I might be seen as a little too controversial for that one.'

'You can't waltz in here and haggle with the commissioner,' Allen growled. 'This isn't a Turkish bazaar.'

'Although sometimes it feels like it.' Thompson turned to Carlyle. 'I very much appreciate your willingness to roll your sleeves up, Commander. I would appreciate it very much if you would sit on Gina Sweetman's panel and also take Moran's seat on Building and Infrastructure.' She offered a weak smile. 'That way you can take the blame if either – or indeed both – of them goes wrong.'

One–all, Carlyle decided, a score draw. He hadn't escaped sitting on Gina Sweetman's disciplinary panel but he had inserted himself into the police-station-sale process, potentially increasing his leverage over Gareth Mills and his usefulness to Vicky Dalby-Cummins. Dismissed by the commissioner, he made it into the hallway before Allen caught up with him. 'What the hell are you playing at?' the special adviser hissed.

'Just trying to make myself useful.' Not willing to wait for a lift, Carlyle headed for the stairs.

'I'll get this reversed.' Allen chased after him, clipping Carlyle's heel and causing them both to stumble.

Regaining his balance, the commander grabbed the collar of Allen's jacket and pushed him through a set of fire doors. 'I'm a commander in the Metropolitan Police Service,' he spat, 'and you're a parasite who's taking the commissioner for a ride.' Releasing his grip, he resisted the temptation to give the man a shove down the stairs.

'We'll see who has most clout.' Red in the face, Allen fussed with his coat. 'You might be fucking Abigail Slater, but don't get ideas above your station.'

Carlyle didn't bother to correct the misperception. 'It's not Slater you need to worry about,' he advised. 'If I were you, I'd be more worried about Vicky Dalby-Cummins.'

'I heard you were in her pocket, too.'

'I'm not in anyone's pocket,' Carlyle proclaimed, starting down the stairs, 'as you will find out.'

Drowning in bad news, Rick Ford waved his phone angrily in the air. 'What the hell happened?'

'Obviously someone leaked the Kenny photos,' Graham Hughes replied. 'It wasn't me.'

'But I thought you and me, we were the only people who had them.' He watched in dismay as Dwayne Doud bounced into the office without knocking. 'Get out.'

Doud beat a hasty retreat.

'You were the only person I gave the pictures to,' the agent insisted. 'It'll be Hermione's lawyer who's given them to Dead Celebrity News.'

'Kenny never considered himself a celebrity.' Ford scowled.

'Well, he is now. He's all over DCN.com, trending on Twitter and—'

'Yes, yes.' Ford threw his phone onto the desk. 'It's a total mess.'

'We still have a deal, right?'

'Are you kidding?' Ford spluttered. 'What deal?'

'Our deal.' Hughes pouted.

'Forget deals. I don't have a business any longer. Best-case scenario, Perendi Films gets sold to a hedge fund for a dollar, assuming our insurance cover holds.' Worst case, I go and live in Paraguay under an assumed name.

Hughes was determined to see the bright side. 'These pictures should help you. They show Kenny was the victim, rather than a pervert.'

Not a pervert? What was the kid smoking? 'He's lying there, with his dick in his hand, for Chrissakes. Those pictures make him look like the biggest pervert ever, even when he's fucking dead. Our only hope was to keep those damn images out of the public domain. *You* were supposed to keep them private.'

'I did, for a while. Bought you some time at least.'

'Yeah, like five frickin' minutes.' Ford ran a hand through his thinning hair. 'All right, look. The deal still stands. *If* we make any more movies, we will look seriously at your people for available roles.'

'Cool.' Hughes rubbed his hands together in glee.

'In the meantime, find out who leaked the damn photos.'

'What difference does it make?'

'Just find out.' Ford pointed to the door, signalling the meeting was over. 'And find out when Hermione is back in London. I want you to set up a meeting.'

Dwayne Doud watched Graham Hughes hustle out of the boss's office and head for the exit without even saying goodbye. Ungrateful sod. Doud angrily stabbed at the screen of his phone, refreshing the account page of his Bitcoin wallet. Getting the Dead Celebrity people to pay for the Schenk pictures in cryptocurrency had seemed like a good idea at the time but no payment had been made and he was beginning to fear he had hacked his boss's phone for nothing.

'Cheap bastards.' Doud flicked onto the DCN app. Kenny had already fallen out of the Top Ten stories chart. Old news.

Ancient history. The bloody pictures were worthless now. He cursed himself for not insisting on cash in advance.

'Dead Celebrity News?' Carlyle had never heard of it.

'If you were involved with this,' Abigail Slater hissed, 'I'll have your bloody badge.'

Carlyle basked in his innocence. 'I didn't even know the pictures existed. Did you?'

Slater claimed she did not.

Carlyle closed the web page. 'Be thankful they pixilated the images. You wouldn't want to be exposed to Kenny Schenk in all his glory.'

'They've given the whole scandal a new burst of life,' Slater complained.

'Unlike Kenny.'

'Your tastelessness is astounding, even for a cop.'

'The pictures don't change a thing.'

'Hermione's back in the spotlight. She was chased through Mumbai by a bunch of reporters today. It's very upsetting. She wants to come home ASAP but she's worried Sweetman'll try to snap some cuffs on her at the airport.'

'I'll deal with the assistant commissioner.'

'So you keep saying.'

'I'm off to see her now, as it happens.'

'You're heading for Scotland Yard?' Slater sounded slightly mollified at the prospect of action.

Carlyle had another destination in mind. 'Gina's more likely to be in the Montevideo Arms. It is lunchtime, after all.'

Gina Sweetman occupied the same table as before, although the pitcher of martinis had been replaced by a bottle of Sauvignon Blanc.

Declining the offer of a drink, Carlyle took a seat. 'I don't mind a drink, but not at lunchtime.'

'My husband reckons I'm a functioning alcoholic. Then again, he can talk.'

Carlyle offered neither advice nor sympathy. It wasn't his job to sort out the woman's problems.

Sweetman looked up from her glass. 'I hear you tried to dodge my panel but Thompson put you on it anyway.'

'News travels fast.'

'I spoke to Bruce.' Her eyes narrowed. 'Are you going to screw me?'

'I'll make sure you get a fair hearing.'

'You need to do better than that. Get me off or I'll start shouting about why you want to be on Capital Projects.'

'Sorry?'

'I know all about Vicky Dalby-Cummins. Are you banging her?'

Never underestimate a functioning alcoholic. Carlyle gritted his teeth.

'I was on the Building and Infrastructure sub-committee, too, remember. I know Terry Brunel well. In fact, if I hadn't told the stupid sod about Moran's fake tits, none of us would be in this mess.' Sweetman slurped her wine. 'Terry told me all about Dalby-Cummins trying to muscle in on the police-station sale.'

And you told Allen, Carlyle surmised. This woman was truly dangerous.

'Here's *our* deal. If I keep my job and you keep your little girlfriend's nose out of Terry's business, you'll be left alone, free to piss about and do whatever it is you do all day.'

Not an unattractive offer, Carlyle thought.

'You won't be hassled to take early retirement and there might even be one more promotion before you go, get your pension pot nicely topped up.'

'Let me think about it.'

The assistant commissioner's face fell. 'What's to think about?'

Outside, a taxi driver and a cyclist were shaping up for a fight in the middle of a gridlocked junction. A cacophony of angry car horns invited them to move on. Ducking between two stationary vans, Carlyle crossed the road, fretting about his conversation with Gina Sweetman. At moments like this he was acutely conscious of his wife's absence. Talking things through with Helen invariably illuminated the path best followed. Without her, he felt seriously exposed.

Waiting at a streetlight, he toyed with the idea of giving her a call. But Helen, in Africa for work, had her own problems to deal with. Ringing her up to complain about being played by a drunk assistant commissioner seemed more than a little wet. Instead, he called Carew Forensic Services.

After a couple of rings, his reward was a cheery 'Hi' from Gloria, Dudley's daughter.

'I thought you were in France,' said Carlyle, surprised.

'It was Germany. I got back a bit earlier than planned last night.'

'The hacking competition didn't go too well, then?' Carlyle was pleased he was able to remember the purpose of her trip.

'I think Dad's expectations were a bit too high,' Gloria said. 'Some of the kids were unbelievable. I was a bit out of my depth. I got binned after the first round.'

'Never mind,' Carlyle sympathised. 'Maybe next time.'

'I don't know if I'd do it again. The people running it seemed a bit dodgy, to be honest.' Gloria mentioned a couple of hackers although the names meant nothing to her caller. 'I don't know if they always stay on the right side of the line.'

Cyber-crime didn't interest Carlyle. It was all too abstract, too *clean*. For him, crime would always involve blood, snot and tears. 'It all seems a bit of a grey area to me.'

'Attacks are happening all the time. Serious stuff.'

'Hm. Is your dad around?'

'He's gone off to his Brexit Delivery Action Group meeting.'

Carlyle groaned.

'I know. He's the youngest one there by about twenty years. It's just a bunch of old duffers who go down the pub and get pissed. They're all convinced the Europeans are gonna invade to prevent us leaving.'

Carlyle raised an eyebrow. 'I thought we'd left?'

'Yes and no. Dad keeps getting wound up by the nonsense he reads in the *Telegraph*.'

'I thought he got it for the crossword.'

'If only. You could try his phone, but he's not very good at answering it.'

Carlyle had the same fault himself. 'Maybe you could help me.' He outlined how he was trying to track down Gareth Mills.

There was a pause before Gloria asked, 'Have you tried Google?'

Carlyle threw himself on her mercy. 'I'm useless when it comes to this sort of thing.'

'But you don't do anything about it.' Gloria tapped a few keys and clicked on a few links. After a while, she found herself looking at the annual report for something called Antigen Capital Partners. 'ACP,' she explained to Carlyle, 'is an investment company run by Gareth Mills. Most of the cash it manages comes from Sir Christopher Sollerdiche. They've had a couple of big successes, making a load of money out of care homes and cyber-security software.'

'Two things that obviously go together.'

'It's all about where they can make a return. ACP's got five funds. Looks like four of them have been very successful but the fifth is struggling. Commercial property. They got their timing wrong. Need to sit tight and hope it turns around.'

For example, by doing a sweet deal with the Met. 'One more thing,' Carlyle said. 'Can you see if you can find a connection between Mills and a guy called Bruce Allen?' He spelled the surname. 'Allen's a consultant working for my boss, the commissioner.'

'Virginia Thompson has hired her own consultant on the Met's payroll?' Gloria looked surprised. 'That seems pretty risky, given her problems with the IPCC.'

Carlyle invited her to explain.

'Before she came to London, Virginia Thompson was chief constable in Northumbria. She was referred to the Independent Police Complaints Commission by a think-tank called Open Government Research. OGR claimed Thompson had a conflict of interest on the basis that her husband was running a campaign group, which her officers were investigating for fraud and a bunch of other things, including racial discrimination and sexual harassment of female staff.'

'How do you know all this?' Carlyle asked, impressed.

'We did some work for the Ambassador's Group, Peter Thompson's company,' Gloria explained, adding, 'All our clients are confidential, though, so don't tell Dudley I told you.'

Carlyle promised he would stay schtum. 'Have you ever met Peter Thompson?'

'He was a creep, but he paid his bills. We don't work for them any more, much to Dad's dismay.'

Carlyle knew better than to put Gloria on the spot by asking precisely what work CFS had done for its well-heeled client. Instead he asked, 'What did the IPCC do?'

'Nothing. OGR wanted Virginia Thompson to be made to take a sabbatical but then she got the Met job and the whole thing kind of resolved itself. As far as I know, the investigation into the Ambassador's Group is ongoing, but it seems to be pretty dormant.'

Carlyle had one final question. 'Is there any connection between the Ambassador's Group and an outfit called Antigen Capital Partners?'

'ACP is a corporate sponsor of Ambassador's. They invited Dad to a drinks reception a while back. He was delighted.'

'I bet.'

'The main guy, Sir Christopher Sollerdiche, is a private sponsor as well. Dad says he basically bankrolls the whole thing.'

'Interesting.' Carlyle decided Sollerdiche might be worth a visit, once he had finally spoken to Mills.

'Helpful?'

'Very,' Carlyle confirmed.

'Who was the other guy you mentioned . . . Allen?'

'Leave Bruce Allen for now,' Carlyle advised, not wanting to push his luck too far. The special adviser had just slipped down the pecking order and could wait. 'You've given me more than enough.'

'I'm just too accommodating.' Gloria chuckled. 'Don't tell Dudley.'

SIXTEEN

Antigen Capital Partners had their offices in a modern building in Mayfair, directly across the road from the Saudi embassy.
Avoiding the armed police officers standing in front of the
embassy gates, Carlyle spent a couple of minutes watching
people come and go. It was getting late in the working day and
the pace of activity was slowing. Spotting a break in the traffic,
he jogged across the road and ducked through a set of revolv-
ing doors. Acknowledging the lone security guard, he walked
up to the first receptionist who made eye contact and showed
his police ID. A hushed telephone conversation resulted in him
being sent to the top floor. There he was met by a young flun-
key who didn't introduce himself. The kid showed Carlyle into a
meeting room and disappeared.

Stepping over to the window, Carlyle looked down on the
cops guarding the embassy. 'Tough gig.'

'What is?'

Carlyle turned to face an angular man dressed in a pair of
jeans and a green Lacoste polo shirt. The expression on the man's
face was deeply neutral. 'Commander Carlyle.' He stretched out
a hand. 'I'm Gareth Mills.'

'I was watching the colleagues across the road.' Carlyle shook
his host's hand. 'VIP protection's hard, unglamorous work. You
need to be focused, all the time.'

'I suppose.' Mills seemed less than interested. 'But it's the world we live in. The price of freedom is eternal vigilance, and so on.'

'Thank you for seeing me.'

'Terry Brunel said you might turn up.' The man's face remained unreadable.

'I tried to catch you at the movie premiere.'

'You were there?' Mills lowered himself into a chair and invited his guest to follow suit. There was no offer of hospitality. 'What did you think of the film?'

'It was interesting,' Carlyle lied. 'The behind-the-scenes story and all that.'

'I wouldn't describe it as factually accurate,' Mills scoffed. 'The Americans, once they get hold of things, well, reality goes right out the window. In the end, I couldn't believe I had such a small part. My character was barely on the screen for twenty minutes. Benny Charleston, the actor playing me, wasn't pleased about it, I can tell you. He gave his agent a right old earful.'

'I enjoyed the party.'

'To be honest, I got out as quickly as I could. The place was full of whining liberals, didn't you think?'

'I don't have a view. As a policeman, you never take sides.'

'Come on, Commander, the police *always* take sides.' Mills's face hardened. 'Take your little visit to see Terry Brunel, for example. You made it very clear which side you're on.'

'If I'd known you owned the business,' Carlyle pointed out, 'I'd have come straight here. In my experience, it's always better to start with the organ grinder, rather than the monkey.'

'I wouldn't call myself an organ grinder,' Mills replied, 'and I don't own BDS, not all of it, anyway. But I'm no fool, so, a word of advice, don't try to play games here.'

'I'm not playing games.' The statement was patently untrue. Then again, thanks to people like Mills, they were living in a

169

post-truth world, so he could say what the fuck he liked. 'I'm making some pretty routine enquiries.'

'In relation to what?'

'In relation to my ongoing investigations.'

'Very enlightening.' Mills snorted.

'There's nothing I'm obliged to disclose at this stage.'

'Should I speak to my lawyer?'

'I don't know. Have you done anything wrong?'

'In my entire life, I've never had so much as a parking ticket.'

'Well, then, you've got nothing to worry about, have you?'

'Other than having a senior policeman sitting in my office, making vague insinuations.'

'I'm not insinuating anything. I want to understand a bit more about your property business and its interest in the decommissioned police stations we're selling off.'

'What's it to you?'

'My interest's in making sure the taxpayer gets a good price for any assets that may be sold. You pay your taxes, don't you?'

'Of course.'

'Then I'm sure you'd want the Met to get the best deal on your behalf.'

'Don't be a smartarse, Commander.' Mills glared at Carlyle. 'I like to know about the people who walk in here – especially the ones who want to try to put me on the spot. And when it comes to you, it seems there's a lot to know.'

Go on, Carlyle thought, surprise me with your stunning insights.

'A journeyman cop, plodding along for decades, whose career suddenly takes off for no apparent reason.'

Carlyle had heard the critique so many times before that it no longer bothered him. 'Like someone once said, ninety per cent of success is simply turning up.'

'You've enjoyed a charmed life in the police service. I was

wondering why that might be. Then I see one of your guys, a serial sex pest called Umar Sligo, upped and went to work for a wannabe gangster called Harry Cummins. My sense is you took a piece of that deal, which was why you were able to get so close to the widow.'

It was a completely bogus narrative, based on a few random facts, but no less potentially damaging for that. 'Vicky,' Carlyle countered, 'isn't the one trying to make millions by buying police stations on the cheap.'

Mills threw back his head and let out a short, harsh bark. 'But she's trying to muscle in on it, isn't she? This is set to be the biggest property deal in London for the last five years, maybe even a decade. And your girlfriend thinks she can turn up and grab a slice of it? Not a chance. Vicky Dalby-Cummins can fuck right off. She's getting nothing from this.'

Carlyle paid no heed to the rant. 'What's Bruce Allen's role in all this?' he asked calmly.

'Bruce is a consultant. It's his job to offer advice, make connections and smooth things through.'

'I thought he worked for the commissioner.'

'He works for a lot of people.'

'How much will he get from you if this deal goes through?'

'Now *that* is none of your business.'

'However much it is,' Carlyle argued, 'he's got a clear conflict of interest.'

'I'd have thought if anyone was in danger of falling into the trap of having a conflict of interest it would be you, Commander.' Mills's eyes narrowed. 'I'd be very careful before I went around making any accusations. If your connections with Vicky Dalby-Cummins were to come to light, the commissioner would show you the door.'

Carlyle stiffened. 'I have no connections with Vicky, erm, Victoria.'

'That, I think, would be a difficult case to argue.' Mills jumped to his feet. 'Tell the little bitch to back off. Otherwise both of you are going to see your fortunes take a sharp turn for the worse.'

'Is that a threat?'

'I'd call it an informed prediction.' Opening the door, Mills pointed Carlyle towards the lifts. 'I don't expect to see you here again. This is my place of work and I don't like having to waste my time on crooks and beggars.'

It was getting dark outside. The lunchtime drinkers were long gone, and the Montevideo Arms was now in the hands of what could loosely be termed regulars. The post-work rush was still a little way off.

Failing to make it back to work after lunch was never a good sign. However, after three bottles of wine and a couple of G and Ts, Gina Sweetman knew it was better to go AWOL than turn up obviously off her face. A key part of being a functioning alcoholic was accepting when you couldn't fake sobriety to a high enough standard for your colleagues to feel able to turn a blind eye.

Finishing her latest drink, the assistant commissioner squinted at the words she'd spent the last hour and a half composing on her phone. The email was probably the longest thing she'd written in the last twenty years. It wasn't going to win the Booker Prize, but you could get the gist. From here on, any further redrafts would probably only make it worse. After letting her finger hover over the screen for a moment, she hit send. Gathering up her things, she went outside to find a cab.

Arriving at the Chapel, Carlyle took a call from Danny Hunter, the former military policeman. 'I spoke to a few of my old contacts. The V40 might be a red herring. Once you lot had moved out, the army used Paddington Green for a couple of urban-warfare training exercises. After one of them, a box of grenades was left behind.'

'Jesus Christ.' Standing on the pavement, Carlyle kicked an empty fag packet into the gutter. 'What if those Rainbow people got hold of them?'

'Eight were misplaced, of which six have since been recovered. Another is accounted for, i.e. it blew the victim's head off, leaving one to find.'

'Great.'

'This is all between us, you understand.'

Carlyle agreed reluctantly. 'I can see why the army would want to keep it quiet.'

'There's no point in making a song and dance about it.'

'Let's hope they find it. Meantime, we might have a name for the dead guy. James Gillespie.'

'Gillespie. I'll see if it raises any red flags.'

'Thanks. And let me know if they find the missing grenade.' Ending the call, he went inside to find Vicky Dalby-Cummins in a foul mood.

'Sandro's going to be deported. The bastards shopped him to the fucking immigration police. He's been taken to Yarl's Wood. I've got him a lawyer but it's a complete waste of time. They're gonna kick him out. It's like dealing with the bloody Nazis.'

Carlyle had no real interest in the fate of Dalby-Cummins's toy-boy, but he could still sympathise: Yarl's Wood detention centre was a dismal facility. He slid into a chair. 'Who shopped him?'

'Who do you think?' Dalby-Cummins slammed her palm down on the desk. 'Gareth Mills has a lot of political contacts. And Chris sodding Sollerdiche – he's bought and sold most of the cabinet in his time. A quiet word with one of his pals in the Home Office and the next thing you know Sandro's being bloody renditioned.'

'You should've told me about Mills and the rest of his little

173

gang before I went to see Terry Brunel. They're heavy hitters, a rather different kettle of fish from some north London builder.'

Dalby-Cummins brushed off the criticism. 'Talking to Terry was a first step.'

'Talking to Terry was a waste of time,' Carlyle pointed out. 'It put me on the back foot from the start.'

'And if you'd known about Mills and Co from the outset you'd have backed right off.'

'I'd at least have thought more carefully before making my first move.'

'You're so bloody negative.' She looked ready to leap across the desk and throttle him. 'No wonder crime in this country is out of control.'

That's a bit rich, Carlyle thought, coming from a crime boss. 'All I'm saying is that I think you should've trusted me a bit more. I can't help you if I don't get full disclosure.'

'Well, now you know everything.'

Carlyle didn't believe it for a second.

'And there can be no more excuses.'

'I don't make excuses,' Carlyle snapped. 'Never apologise, never explain is my motto.'

'Ha.' Dalby-Cummins's expression softened. 'Now we've got that sorted out, where do we go from here? You think we can still get in among these guys?'

'That's not the plan.'

'No? Then, pray tell, Commander, what is the plan?'

'The plan is to fuck them up good and proper and put them out of the game.'

'Not unattractive,' Dalby-Cummins agreed, 'but how does it help me get into the property deal?'

'It'll give you time to find a proper partner.' Carlyle hoped this sounded as if he'd thought things out. In reality, his brain was working a fraction of a second before his mouth.

'And who would that be?'

'How the hell should I know? I'm a simple cop. Do some research . . . If you want to become a respectable businessperson, you need to start doing business with the right kind of partner.' He jerked his thumb towards the door. 'You could start cleaning this place up, too.'

The response was cool. 'One thing at a time, Commander. I need to think of my cashflow.'

'Never let it be said I'd try to tell you how to run your business.'

Dalby-Cummins rolled her eyes. 'I'm beginning to see how you've managed to get such a reputation for being a wind-up merchant.'

'I'm trying to find a way forward,' Carlyle insisted. 'I'll get Brunel's bid kicked out – which it should be, after all – and then we'll run a proper, transparent bid process. If you come up with a winning bid, fair enough. If you don't, well, life goes on.'

Dalby-Cummins thought about it for a moment or two, then gave a nod of agreement. 'Deal.'

'And I'll see what I can do for Sandro.'

'If you can, great, but I wouldn't worry too much about it. If there's one thing I learned being married to Harry, it's that men are completely disposable and infinitely replaceable.'

'My wife would probably agree.' Carlyle was only half joking.

'One final thing. I'd still be happier if you were on the pay-roll. Gives me a bit more . . . confidence in the stability of our relationship.'

Thinking of Helen gave Carlyle an idea. 'Tell you what,' he said, 'why don't you make a donation to Avalon, the charity my wife runs?'

Dalby-Cummins said nothing.

'Make it a big one,' he said casually. 'I'm sure it'll be tax deductible.'

***

On his way out of the club, Carlyle felt a hand on his shoulder. Turning around, his surprise leached into dismay. 'What're you doing here?'

'I could ask you the same question, Commander.'

'Police business.'

'No need to be embarrassed.' Bruce Allen led him back into the building. 'Let's get a drink.' Taking a seat at an otherwise deserted bar, the special adviser ordered champagne. 'It's fortuitous we bumped into each other. I've got something for you.' He pulled a folded sheet of A4 paper from the inside pocket of his jacket and handed it to Carlyle. It was a copy of an email from Sweetman to Virginia Thompson, ccd to the Met's head of HR. In the subject line: *Sexual Harassment Complaint against Commander J. Carlyle.*

Carlyle forced himself to read the contents with extreme care. When he had finished, he let the paper fall on the table. 'I've never behaved in an inappropriate way.'

'Either way, this is still a bona fide complaint, containing serious allegations from a very senior officer.'

'Who is up on charges of her own.'

'From a very senior officer with a very long track record of service.' A bottle of champagne was placed in front of Allen, along with two glasses. He filled one and offered it to Carlyle.

'Not for me.'

'There is no way the commissioner could ignore this, even if she wanted to. There will need to be a full and proper investigation.' Tasting the champagne, Allen gave an appreciate nod. 'Unless you do what you should've done already and get Vicky Dalby-Cummins to back away from Gareth Mills's property deal.'

Carlyle jerked his thumb towards the ceiling. 'She's upstairs. Why don't you go and tell her yourself?'

'Vicky is not someone I can do business with,' was Allen's cryptic response. 'Beyond my recreational visits here, that is.'

'Why?' Carlyle tried to counter-attack. 'What's she got on you?'

'Do what I ask and maybe you'll keep your job.' Conversation over, Allen drained his glass and beckoned to a passing member of staff. 'Is Chloë in yet?'

'I saw her upstairs.'

'That's my cue to leave.' Grabbing the bottle, Allen slid off his stool. 'Let me know when it's done.'

SEVENTEEN

The decorators had left his office, but the smell of paint lingered. With some effort, Carlyle managed to open a window before turning back to face Laura Taylor. The young activist looked to be well on the way to recovery as she threw out a choice selection of curses and insults.

'You've disappeared him,' she squealed, 'taken him to Guantánamo or somewhere.'

'Eh?'

'Reuben's being held in of those black-ops sites you run with the CIA.'

'I don't think the Metropolitan Police run black ops,' Carlyle sounded wistful, 'with the CIA or anyone else.'

'Don't pretend you don't know where he is.'

'I have genuinely no idea.'

'When I got back to the squat, they said you'd arrested him. He hasn't been seen since.'

'Really.' Carlyle raised an eyebrow. 'And you think he's missing.'

'I *know* he's missing.'

'Maybe he's just . . .' Carlyle searched for the term '. . . ghosting you or something.'

'He wouldn't do that,' Taylor screamed. 'You've put him in jail.'

Some people just won't be helped. Carlyle's empathy was exhausted. He pointed at the door. 'If you want to file a missing-person report, it's downstairs, ground floor. Take a ticket and wait for someone to call your number.'

Once he'd got rid of Taylor, he tracked down Angelini.

'She won't be seeing Reuben again,' the sergeant explained. 'I said if he didn't fuck off, I'd blow his cover.'

'Simple, but effective.'

'To seal the deal,' Angelini grinned, 'I gave him a couple of slaps.'

'A taste of his own medicine,' Carlyle was impressed. 'I like it.'

'Bastard deserved it.'

Alex Morrow was waiting in his office when Carlyle returned. The union lawyer waved a copy of Gina Sweetman's email in the air. 'Technically, I can't represent you.' Dressed in a grubby T-shirt and a pair of jeans ripped at the knees, he offered a passable impression of a tramp. 'You're too senior. The Police Federation is only supposed to represent the rank and file.'

'I still pay my dues.' Carlyle hoped it was true. Morrow had bailed him out of various scrapes in the past and he didn't want to go into this latest battle with a new lawyer. Moreover, he was the partner of Carlyle's long-time colleague, Sergeant Alison Roche, which made him almost family.

Morrow scratched at his trademark day-old stubble, which had helped earn him the nickname Shaggy. 'Okay, well, let's just get on with it, then, and see what happens. If there's a problem, we can deal with it later. Is the email all you've seen?'

'So far.'

'And you got it from Bruce Allen?' Morrow looked pained. 'This is highly irregular. If nothing else, we can get them for failing to follow proper procedure.'

'I want to turn the tables on the blackmailing bastard.' Carlyle summarised Allen's attempts to force the sale of the disused police stations to Gareth Mills at a discounted price.

Morrow listened patiently, then asked, 'How do you know all this?'

'I got it from a whistleblower.' Carlyle knew that sounded evasive, but he wanted to keep Dalby-Cummins out of the picture for as long as possible.

'This is a bit out of my league, to be honest.' Morrow scratched his head. 'Shouldn't you take it to the commissioner?'

Carlyle shook his head. 'She's in it as well.'

Morrow raised an eyebrow. 'Are you saying there's a conspiracy?'

'Something like that. Thompson and Allen go back a long way. And Thompson's husband's got form, so he might very well be caught up in it as well.'

Morrow winced. 'Messy.'

'If I take this to the commissioner too soon, I think she'll try to bury it. We need to get things out in the open.'

'Let me think. I'll talk to Ali.' Carlyle was less than impressed with his response. 'She can speak to her uncle – her dad's brother. His wife is some big lawyer.'

'I thought you were supposed to be a big lawyer?'

'If this is the kind of massive organised fraud you're claiming, we can't fight it on our own.' Morrow got to his feet. 'Let me put out a few feelers.'

It wasn't exactly the call to arms Carlyle had been hoping for, but it was all he was going to get right now. He showed Morrow out. 'How's Ali getting on with the maternity leave?'

'It's all good. She sends her best.'

'Good luck with number two.'

'Second time round, it's a lot more relaxed.'

'I'm sure.' Having had only the one kid, Carlyle had no idea.

Morrow glanced at Joaquin, earwigging on their conversation from behind his computer. 'I'll be in touch.'

'Shouldn't lawyers dress properly?' Joaquin enquired, once Morrow had left.

'Don't judge a book and all that.'

'Eh?'

Carlyle couldn't be bothered to explain. 'Get on with some work, or it'll be back to the basement for you.' Before he could retreat to his office, Joaquin's phone started to ring.

The Spaniard answered it, then offered him the receiver. 'It's Inspector O'Sullivan. She says it's urgent.'

'What happened?'

O'Sullivan held up a familiar statuette in a transparent evidence bag. 'Looks like Hermione battered her agent to death with the Oscar.'

'Her ex-agent.'

'He certainly is now.'

Carlyle squinted at the blood-splattered statue. 'Is it real?'

'No.' O'Sullivan handed the statue to one of the forensics technicians who were busying themselves around the flat. 'At least, I assume not. Hermione's certainly never won one – never even been nominated.'

'Where is she now?'

'They took her to the station at Notting Hill.'

Carlyle frowned. 'I thought they'd closed it.'

'Not yet. It's on the list, but it's still open. Her lawyer's there, too.'

'Hm.' Now wasn't the best time to run into Abigail Slater.

'It was Slater who called me. I think she realises that this time her client's gonna have to face the music.'

'And the press.'

'And the press,' O'Sullivan agreed.

Carlyle watched as Graham Hughes was carefully lifted into a body-bag by a couple of paramedics. 'What precisely happened?'

'Hughes turned up at Lacemaker's flat to try to convince her to take him back as her agent. According to her, he was high on drink, or drugs, or both. He started getting aggressive. Fearing for her safety, she smacked him around the head a few times, he went down, hit his head on the side of the coffee-table and, bang, game over.'

'She must only recently have got back from India.'

'Yesterday.'

The commander had a thought. 'She didn't take any photographs, did she?'

'Not this time.'

'And she'll be going for a plea of self-defence? Again?'

'Kenny Schenk wasn't self-defence, as such. I mean, she didn't actually kill him, did she?'

'I suppose not.' Carlyle's phone started to buzz in his pocket. He checked the screen: Slater. He answered it with a sigh.

'Are you coming down here?' the lawyer demanded. 'It's a complete circus. The street is full of TV crews.' Carlyle put the call on speaker for O'Sullivan's benefit. 'We're never gonna be able to get out of here.'

'I don't think Hermione'll need to worry about that for a while.' Carlyle watched the paramedics manoeuvre the body out the room.

'Whaddya mean?' Slater shrieked. 'The poor girl is completely traumatised. Subjected to *another* brutal assault by – by the representatives of the patriarchy, she now has to deal with all *this*.'

Representatives of the patriarchy? Carlyle looked at O'Sullivan.

'It's simply not good enough,' the lawyer continued.

'We'll try to get things sorted out as quickly as possible,

but there'll be no running off to India this time. It looks like Hermione will be charged with . . .' Carlyle was about to say 'murder' but softened it to '. . . attacking Graham Hughes.'

'Charged?' Slater spluttered. 'Are you kidding me? This is criminal. Totally bloody criminal.'

Carlyle groaned. 'Look, Abigail—'

'I need to go back to my client. Get over here and sort this out. Now.'

'What're you gonna do?' O'Sullivan asked, once they had been cut off.

'I don't want to get in your way,' Carlyle stuffed the phone into his back pocket, 'but I suppose I'd better go and take a look.'

Arriving at Ladbroke Road, Carlyle counted four satellite trucks and nine TV crews, along with a handful of familiar faces among the gaggle of print reporters. Avoiding eye contact with any of the hacks, he made his way briskly into the police station. In an interview room on the top floor, he found Hermione Lacemaker reading from a pile of unbound A4 pages while Slater typed furiously on her phone.

'That's a hell of a statement,' Carlyle joked.

Lacemaker looked at him blankly. 'It's a script I'm considering.'

There's optimism for you, Carlyle thought.

'It's a reworking of *Silence of the Lambs*, set in outer space.'

'I see.'

'I thought it would be good for Hermione to focus on work while we're waiting for you to let us go.' Slater didn't look up from her phone.

'Female director, female crew,' Lacemaker explained.

Slater finished sending her message and gave Carlyle a wan smile. 'All-women productions are the future. As with so many industries, the film business is changing.'

The cultural discussion was cut short by the arrival of Karen O'Sullivan. Pointing at the window, the inspector addressed Slater: 'The press are gagging for you to go out and speak to them.'

'Nice try,' the lawyer laughed, 'but I'm not leaving this room until you confirm my client is free to go.'

'Not going to happen, I'm afraid.' O'Sullivan turned to the actor. 'Hermione Lacemaker, you are under arrest on suspicion of the murder of Graham Hughes.'

'Now hold on, you can't—'

Ignoring the lawyer's protests, O'Sullivan read Lacemaker her rights before ushering her out of the room to be formally processed.

'We had a deal,' Slater hissed.

Carlyle did not deny it. 'But now all bets are off. Hermione will be treated properly. You need to let the process play out.'

'Yes, yes, yes.' Slater rummaged in her bag and came up with a bright red lipstick. 'In the meantime, looks like I'd better talk to the press after all.'

Skulking out of a back door, Carlyle headed back to Charing Cross on foot, using the long walk to clear his head. Returning to his office, he was dismayed to find a stack of papers six inches thick on his desk.

'What are these?'

'Background reading for the Building and Infrastructure sub-committee.' Joaquin appeared in the doorway. 'You've got your first meeting tomorrow morning.'

'Isn't there an executive summary?' Carlyle pleaded.

'That *is* the executive summary.' Joaquin smirked. 'Details of all the property the Met is looking to sell, along with a list of the main bidders. It's interesting when you get into it.'

Carlyle's eyes narrowed. 'You've read it?'

'I took a look,' Joaquin admitted. 'Just to get an idea of what was going on.'

'Then why don't you write me up a one-page summary? No more than a dozen bullet points.'

After much grumbling, Joaquin removed the stack of papers, returning after an hour with a single sheet of A4. Carlyle absorbed the information that the number of front counters in London had already been cut from 161 to 92. The Met's latest 'public access engagement strategy', endorsed by the mayor's office, planned to reduce this number further, first to 73 and finally 32. Closing the front desk effectively meant closing the police station behind it, with the personnel being redeployed in larger stations, with a limit of one per borough.

Some of the stations – like Paddington Green – had already been sold. Most were still to be auctioned, along with various office buildings, warehouses and other properties acquired by the Met over 120 years. In total, there were almost 200 lots in the portfolio, spread randomly across the capital. According to the estate agent who had compiled the list, it could be worth anywhere between £700 million and £1.1 billion.

'That seems a big spread,' Carlyle muttered to himself. Joaquin had listed three potential buyers, of which Building Design Services, Terry Brunel's outfit, had been declared the preferred bidder, despite their offer being at the lower end of the range. A final decision was due to be taken in a fortnight. At the bottom Joaquin had asked the key question: *Why is BDS the best deal for the Police Service?*

'I suppose that covers it.' Drumming his fingers on the table, Carlyle wondered who might be able to help him better understand what was going on here. The obvious answer would be Dudley Carew, or Gloria, but he had drawn too often from that well recently. After some further thought, he reached for his phone and pulled up a less frequently used number.

'I must say, I was pretty surprised to get your call.' Francesca Culverhouse sipped her coffee. 'I didn't think we'd ever hear from you again.'

'I've always had a very professional relationship with the press.' Carlyle watched the outside traffic slide by. He had deliberately chosen to meet in a café far removed from any of his usual stamping grounds. Being caught in cahoots with the founder of the Investigation Unit, a bunch of old-school reporters who dug up stories that newspapers didn't have the resources – or the balls – to go after would put yet another nail in his professional coffin.

'Even the ones who were trying to bring you down?' Culverhouse smirked.

'Especially the ones who were trying to bring me down,' Carlyle replied. 'I'm not bent, so I've always had the luxury of being able to play things straight.' It was a gross simplification of the truth, verging on an outright lie, but offered a nice soundbite.

Culverhouse ratcheted up her amusement a notch. 'Bernie always said you were, quote unquote, a slippery little sod.'

'He should know.' Carlyle lifted his mug in silent tribute to the late Bernie Gilmore, muckraker *extraordinaire*. 'Found a decent replacement for him yet?'

'There are one or two youngsters who've got promise but it's such a slog, these days. Even if you publish a good story, the bad guys shout, "Fake news," and try to ignore it.'

'Which works pretty well, it seems to me.'

'Most of the time.' Culverhouse sighed. 'The idiot in the White House has a lot to answer for. When I started the Unit, I thought we could do some good work. And we have, but no one gives a flying fuck, these days, do they? I've been in this game, one way or another, for more than fifty years, and right now things are worse than they've ever been.'

'I might have a decent story for you.' Carlyle took a copy of Joaquin's synopsis of the Met property sale and handed it over.

Pulling a pair of spectacles from her pocket, the journalist considered it carefully. 'I've read about this.' Culverhouse placed the note on the table. 'It's not new. There are always grumblings about closing police stations.'

'The company set to buy the entire portfolio is called Building Design Services, BDS. It's run by a guy called Terry Brunel but the main owners are Gareth Mills and Sir Christopher Sollerdiche.'

A flicker of interest crossed Culverhouse's face. 'The Brexit clowns?'

'They're getting it for a low price. It seems complicated.'

'These things always are,' Culverhouse scoffed. 'The more complicated you make it, the harder it is for anyone on the outside to work out what's going on.'

'BDS is in bed with a guy called Bruce Allen. He's—'

Culverhouse held up a hand. 'Let me put you in touch with one of my bright young things. You can give them the details.'

'Won't you handle it?' Carlyle was miffed about being fobbed off with the help.

'I can't. I'm off on holiday next week – a trip to Iran – but the woman I have in mind is very good.' Culverhouse tapped the sheet of paper with her finger. 'Can I keep this?'

'Sure.'

'Anything else you can share with us, on a "no fingerprints" basis, obviously, would be helpful.'

'Okay, but there's only a couple of weeks until the deal gets agreed.'

'We'd better get on with it, then.' Rising to her feet, Culverhouse was happy to let Carlyle pick up the bill. 'We'll be in touch.'

Watching her leave, Carlyle fished some change from his pocket. To his relief, he came up with enough to cover two coffees and leave a reasonable tip. As he piled the coins on the table, his phone started to ring. Answering it, Carlyle found himself talking to a sergeant from Kentish Town called Paul Levin.

'Sorry to disturb you, Commander,' Levin sounded sheepish, 'but we've got a guy in custody up here and he's asking for you.'

The cells in Kentish Town were the same shade of green as his office back in Paddington. Leaning against the frame of the door, Carlyle folded his arms and contemplated the battered figure of Terry Brunel.

'Me and my big mouth.' Brunel winced. 'It's always getting me into trouble.'

Carlyle flicked his chin towards the ceiling. 'The boys upstairs say there was a mini-riot. The Gerry Adams Arms could be shut for weeks.'

'I don't think it was that bad,' Brunel argued. 'They had the Arsenal game on and—'

'And Arsenal were three down in twenty minutes.' Carlyle had lapped up the match report.

'Yeah, well, tempers were a bit frayed. There were a couple of Spurs fans in there, and they started giving it some and—'

Carlyle got the picture. 'Who hit you?'

'Who didn't hit me?' Brunel groaned. 'I dodged getting glassed and then someone smacked me across the back with a stool. I went down and stayed down until the cops arrived. They brought everyone back here, and the next thing I know, I'm being charged with GBH, affray and causing criminal damage.'

'There were thirty officers called to the scene,' Carlyle pointed out, 'a dozen arrests. All over a bloody football match.'

'I was the one trying to calm things down.'

'What if something important had happened while you were

188

behaving like a big kid? What if there'd been another terror attack? All those cops tied up having to deal with your nonsense.'

Brunel stared at the floor.

Carlyle checked the time on his phone and swore. True to form, he was going to miss his first sub-committee meeting. 'How d'ya manage to be such a shit magnet, Terry?'

'I wanna do a deal.' Brunel looked up, with a pleading expression. 'I'm an innocent man.'

'Tell it to the judge.'

'I can give you names.'

'I don't need names.' Carlyle wasn't sure what he *did* need. 'I know all about you and Mills and Allen.'

A feeble smile appeared from underneath Brunel's bruises. 'But you don't know about Peter Thompson, do you?'

Carlyle tried not to seem too interested in the commissioner's husband. 'I know about the Ambassador's Group.'

'Tip of the iceberg, mate. Get me out of here and I'll give you the whole story.'

Leaving Kentish Town, Carlyle ducked into a café on Fortess Road and ordered egg and chips. While he waited for his food, he reluctantly called Joaquin. The PA did not sound in any way surprised his boss had gone AWOL.

'Not enough people turned up to the meeting and they need to reschedule.'

Result, Carlyle thought.

'But it'll still go down as another unexplained absence on your performance sheet.'

'How can that be right?' Carlyle complained. 'If they cancelled the meeting, they cancelled the meeting.'

'If you'd turned up,' Joaquin countered, 'maybe they wouldn't have been forced to cancel.'

'Not necessarily.' Carlyle was slightly mollified by the arrival of his food. Smiling at the waitress, he began dousing his chips in ketchup.

Joaquin had no time for his excuses. 'They're trying to get a new time for later in the week. I'll let you know when it's confirmed. Will you be coming into the office later?'

Carlyle saw no need to commit himself. Ending the call, he attacked his meal, clearing his plate before his phone started to ring. The caller introduced herself as Emily Quartz. She sounded very young, not much older than his daughter, Alice.

'I work for the Investigation Unit. Francesca Culverhouse has asked me to take a look at your story.'

They've given me the bloody intern. 'It's not my story,' Carlyle nit-picked.

Quartz persevered in the face of his obvious lack of enthusiasm. 'I've begun to do a bit of digging and I think you might be on to something. I wondered if we might have a chat.'

'We're having a chat now.' He tried not to sound too annoyed about it.

'Face to face,' Quartz pressed, mistakenly hoping her cheeriness would eventually trump his ill-humour. 'You can't do all this stuff on the phone, I find.'

Carlyle forced himself to cut the young reporter some slack. 'Now is pretty good for me, as it happens.'

That clearly wasn't the answer Quartz had been expecting from a busy police officer. 'Um, I'm just heading off for a swim. What about in a couple of hours?'

EIGHTEEN

Sitting on a bench, Carlyle contemplated the semi-manicured lawns of Kenwood House. Waiting for Emily Quartz, he had spent the best part of an hour watching the world go by. The experience had left him feeling surprisingly mellow.

'I'm a member of the LPA – the Ladies' Pond Association.'

'Uh-huh.'

'My mum was a member for years and years.' The young woman now sitting next to him was extremely good-looking in a middle-class Home Counties kind of way. 'She got me into it.'

'Uh-huh.'

Sensing his lack of interest, the reporter moved on: 'Francesca told me you knew Bernie Gilmore.'

'Bernie and I went back a long way. He was a real character.'

'Is it true he was investigating you when he was killed?'

Carlyle gave her a sideways look. 'Bernie was investigating everyone all the time. It's what made him good at his job.'

'Interesting non-answer, Commander.'

Carlyle refused to be ruffled. 'I don't know what precisely Bernie was looking into when he died, but if there was anything involving me, I'd have been very relaxed about it. I've been in this game a long time. Early on, I took the view it was easier to be clean – and to *appear* clean. Otherwise, it's only a matter of time before you crash and burn.'

'Ah, yes, Dominic Silver.'

'What about Dom?' Carlyle edged away from his inquisitor, the better to read her expression.

'Francesca told me Mr Silver is a legend in the Metropolitan Police. Cop turned big-time drug dealer.' Quartz paused. 'And your best mate.'

'An acquaintance,' was as much as he was going to admit to this ingénue. 'Dom's an interesting guy. Been a successful art dealer for some time. He's got a gallery on Cork Street.'

'Which he bought with his drug money.'

'Not the matter in hand,' Carlyle said gruffly.

Quartz relented. 'I read the note you gave to Francesca about the sale of the police stations. How's it going on the sub-committee?'

'Early days.' Carlyle wasn't going to admit he hadn't yet attended a single meeting. 'You said you'd done some digging?'

'A bit.' Quartz ran him through some background on Building Design Services and the relationship between its owners and Bruce Allen, nothing he didn't know already.

'It's a clear conflict of interest, right? I mean, how can Bruce Allen be working for the Met and BDS at the same time?'

'Allen has a private company, BA Projects, through which he funnels all his income, for tax purposes.'

'He's a tax dodger as well?'

'Probably,' Quartz speculated. 'But no one's interested, these days. It's been done to death. Show me a man who *doesn't* fiddle his taxes and it might be a story.'

'Fair point.'

'The interesting thing about BA Projects, though, is its sole full-time employee is one Peter Thompson.'

'The commissioner's husband?'

'Exactly. The commissioner's other half is involved in a deal that could cost the Met hundreds of millions – quite a story, don't you think?'

Carlyle agreed it was.

'Does the commissioner know about all this, d'you think?'

Carlyle thought about it for a moment. 'Either she does,' he decided, 'or she should. Terry Brunel – the guy who founded BDS – knows about Mr Thompson, so it's not exactly top secret.'

'I'd better go and talk to him next.'

'Who, Terry? He's currently in the cells at Kentish Town nick.' Carlyle recounted the fracas at the Gerry Adams Arms and Brunel's subsequent willingness to do a deal.

'You'd better take me down there, then,' Quartz jumped to her feet, 'before he changes his mind.'

When Terry Brunel was brought up from the cells, Carlyle introduced Quartz. 'This is my, erm, assistant.'

Nodding at Brunel, the journalist tossed a notebook onto the interview-room table.

'When do I get out?' Brunel eyed the notebook. 'I'm not talking till you've kept your side of the bargain.'

'You're gonna have to trust me.'

'Fuck off, Commander. Don't take me for a mug.'

'Terry, come on. We have to trust each other.'

'No way.' Folding his arms, Brunel gave Quartz a sour look. 'Sorry, love, looks like he's brought you here for nothing.'

Carlyle tried to sound philosophical. 'If I walk out of here empty-handed, I can find out what I need to know from other sources. And you can go hang, so to speak.'

'But we had a deal,' Brunel complained.

'We still have a deal, but the terms need to be refined a little.' Carlyle pointed to the fisheye lens in the ceiling. 'That's been switched off. We're not being videoed. This conversation never happened.'

'And then I can go?'

'Then I will make a couple of calls,' Carlyle promised. 'And everything will be swept under the carpet. Just give the Gerry Adams Arms a wide berth for a while, at least until Arsenal next win the league.'

'Arsenal are never gonna win the title,' Brunel remarked dolefully, 'not in my lifetime anyway.'

'Exactly.' Carlyle chuckled.

'Let's get started.' Quartz pulled a biro from her bag. 'What is the connection between Peter Thompson and your bid for the Met's old police stations?'

Brunel looked at Carlyle. 'I thought you were asking the questions?'

'Delegation's a key skill when you reach my rank,' the commander advised.

'Mr Thompson,' Quartz repeated. 'How do you know him?'

Brunel gave a resigned shrug. 'I've only met him a couple of times. He's a mate of Bruce Allen's. Him and Allen are providing consulting services for the BDS bid through the Ambassador's Group.'

Head down, Quartz scribbled in her notebook. 'What kind of services?'

Brunel looked at Carlyle.

'Full disclosure, Terry,' the commander reminded him, 'or I leave you here to let justice run its course.'

'Inside information. Allen got us details of the other bids and Peter fed back what the commissioner was thinking.'

'How did you win with such a low bid?' Quartz asked.

'There were concerns the other bidders wouldn't be able to come through with the funding. We didn't want to announce a deal then see it fall apart because the winner couldn't get the financing. The BDS bid is pretty bomb-proof. Mills and Sollerdiche provide most of the money and Peter's organising the rest. Then we get planning permission, flip some of the sites to cover our costs and develop the others.'

'And make out like bandits.'

'And make out like bandits,' Brunel agreed, 'which is why your girlfriend wanted a nibble.'

'What girlfriend?' Quartz eyed Carlyle suspiciously.

'You're not banging this one, too?' Brunel laughed harshly in Carlyle's face. 'You dirty old dog.'

Quartz's cheeks went a shade of pink.

'Watch your mouth,' Carlyle said icily, 'or you can rot in here.' He turned to Quartz. 'Have you got all you need?'

'Enough to be going on with.'

'Meet me outside.' Once Quartz had left, he faced Brunel. 'Look, Terry. There's getting out of here, and there's *staying* out of here. From now on, your fucking mouth needs to stay shut . . . especially when it comes to Vicky. Whatever happens to this property sale, whatever happens to BDS, you're gonna suck it up and get on with the rest of your life. If I hear a peep from you, you'll be back behind bars faster than you can say, "Up the Gunners." Do you understand?'

'Yeah,' Brunel said unhappily.

'Good man.' Carlyle got out of his chair, reached across the table and gave him a pat on the cheek, friendly, if a little harder than was absolutely necessary. 'Sit tight. I'll have you out of here in no time.'

Sitting in the back of a taxi, heading towards the centre of the city, Quartz asked, 'Who's the girlfriend Brunel was talking about?'

'Terry was talking shit.'

She gave an irritated tut. 'I need full disclosure, if this relationship is going to work.'

Carlyle grumbled to himself as he deleted a string of junk emails. 'You've had full disclosure.'

Quartz was unconvinced. 'Francesca predicted you'd be

difficult. And what was all that stuff about me being your assistant?'

'What was I going to say? "This is some journo I've dragged in off the street to stitch up my boss"?'

'You hardly dragged me in off the street.'

'You know what I mean.' Carlyle finally looked up from the screen. 'How long till you publish?' He was keen for the story to land before Brunel walked. He was happy to get Brunel out, but he didn't want him talking to Mills before Quartz's piece blew the BDS bid for the police stations out of the water.

'Dunno. I'll need a second source.'

'Terry was your second source,' Carlyle insisted, 'after me.'

'You're not a source. You don't have any direct knowledge of Thompson. And you're unreliable.'

'Says who?' asked Carlyle, genuinely offended.

'Says Francesca . . . and I'm inclined to believe her.'

'I'm perfectly reliable.'

'At the very least, you're conflicted.'

'How?'

'There's a credibility issue,' Quartz insisted. 'This story'll need to be watertight or the Unit's lawyers'll never agree to us publishing. I need at least one more source.'

Carlyle thought about it for a moment. 'All right.' He sighed. 'Leave it to me.' Pulling up a number on his phone he hit call.

'If you need to take the call, go ahead.'

'It's all right.' Victoria Dalby-Cummins dropped the phone into her pocket. 'It's nothing that can't wait.'

Gareth Mills directed her gaze towards the well-stocked booze cabinet in the corner of his office. 'Can I get you a drink?'

'I'm good.' Dalby-Cummins sat up in her chair and gave her host some good eye contact. 'This needn't take long. I thought it might be better if we tried to sort things out face to face.

Dealing with middle-men doesn't seem to be getting us very far.'

A smile crept across Mills's face. 'You might want to choose your associates more carefully. The cop you sent – what a loser.'

'The guy might not look like much,' Dalby-Cummins conceded, 'but he can be helpful in getting your deal over the line.'

The smile dissolved. 'It's very kind of you to offer but we don't need any help. Things are moving along nicely.'

'It's not a done deal yet.'

'Is that a threat?'

'Simply an observation.'

'And if you don't get what you want, what are you gonna do? Feed me to the pigs, like you did with Vernon Holder?'

Now it was Dalby-Cummins's turn to smile. 'Total urban myth. Anyway, I stopped keeping pigs. They were all turned into sausages ages ago.'

'Just as well the health inspectors didn't get round to testing them.' Mills smirked.

'I had some myself. They were very nice.'

'I'm sure. Look, Vicky, maybe in the future there'll be deals we can work on together – I wouldn't rule it out. But, right now, there's nothing here for you.' Mills tapped the desk with the flat of his hand. 'This deal is in the bag. We don't need your help. You're trying to come to the party too late. Deal with it. Move on.'

'All right.' Dalby-Cummins rose to her feet. 'At least we've started a dialogue. Maybe next time.'

'Maybe next time.'

'And if you ever want to visit the Chapel, let me know. I'd be delighted for you to be our guest one evening.'

The last thing I need is another STD, Mills thought sourly. After showing his guest to the door, he poured himself a large tot of rum. Lifting his glass, he offered a toast to the London skyline. 'To the victors,' he breathed, 'the spoils.'

Leaving the offices of Antigen Capital Partners, Dalby-Cummins walked a block west at a casual pace. She had expected to be fobbed off by Gareth Mills and her irritation quickly dissipated. Ducking into a packed Starbucks near Park Lane, she spied a familiar figure sitting at a table near the back.

Sandro tracked her movement through the throng of patrons. He had been waiting for what seemed like hours. The chaos of the coffee shop almost had him pining for the relative peace of the detention centre. A bureaucratic blunder by some Home Office clerk had brought his release from custody. According to his lawyer, this was not uncommon. It would probably take the authorities up to a week to realise their mistake and as long again to come looking for him. By which time, Vicky had promised he would be safely out of the country. A farm in Ireland, part of Vicky's legitimate business empire, was to be his home for the next few months.

First, however, there was a job to do.

Slipping into the seat beside him, she gave him a peck on the cheek and dropped a hand between his legs, grinning as he began to stiffen. 'I'm gonna miss you in Ireland.'

'You can come visit,' Sandro said hopefully.

'Yeah, maybe.' Having revved him up, she removed her hand. 'But, first, business.'

'Did you get the deal?'

Dalby-Cummins shook her head. 'No deal.'

Sandro took the news in his stride. 'Okay, now I get rid of him.'

'Sssh. Not so loud.' Dalby-Cummins looked around, concerned, but the remark had been lost in the general hubbub. Taking his arm, she whispered in his ear. 'But, yes, now you get rid of him.'

***

'If I'm going to help you, I need full disclosure.' Alex Morrow's attempt to look assertive was undermined by his ensemble. In Carlyle's book, a Green Day T-shirt, torn jeans and red hi-tops did not a shit-hot lawyer make.

'Of course.'

The lawyer looked pained, like he'd recently eaten something which hadn't agreed with him. 'So why didn't you tell me the whole story?'

Carlyle didn't like the sound of that. 'What *whole* story?'

'It's not just Assistant Commissioner Sweetman's harassment claim.'

'It isn't?'

'Do you know a woman called Victoria Dalby-Cummins?'

Carlyle's heart sank. 'I know Vicky,' he confirmed. 'One of my former sergeants, Umar Sligo, worked for her husband, Harry Cummins. When Harry died, she took over the business.'

'Ever taken any money from her?'

'No.'

'Any hospitality?'

'I haven't taken anything – this is a stitch-up by that bastard Bruce Allen.' He let out a bitter laugh. 'The irony is, Allen's a client at Vicky's knocking shop, the Chapel.'

'Allen's not the one who's making the complaint,' Morrow whispered. 'It's Virginia Thompson.'

'The commissioner?' Carlyle spluttered. 'I'm being trolled by the fucking commissioner of the fucking Metropolitan Police?'

'I'd say this is a bit more serious than trolling. It's not every day you're on the wrong end of a complaint from the commissioner, on top of a separate one from an assistant commissioner. Looks like you're rewriting the record books here.'

'We'll deal with it.' Carlyle tried to sound dismissive and confident at the same time. 'They've got nothing, either of them.'

'Whether they have or not,' Morrow replied, 'they clearly

want to do you maximum harm. I'll do what I can, but I think you're going to need additional help.'

'Okay.'

'And in the meantime . . .'

'Yes?'

'Maybe stop calling her "Vicky".'

Nodding to the beat of the music coming from the twenty-grand speakers installed in the ceiling, Colin Holyoak leaned on the bar as he watched the barman mix a rum and Coke. Given the chance, the staff would water down the drinks. It was a pretty stupid thing to do when you were charging more than twenty quid for a shot, but some people couldn't see the big picture.

Taking the drink from the barman, Holyoak handed it to Gareth Mills. 'There you go.'

Mills took a sip and gave an appreciative nod. 'How's business?'

'There's a lot of punters from the US and the Middle East. We're doing well.'

'Glad to hear it,' Mills lifted his glass in salute. The XY Club was busy enough but he knew Holyoak was over-leveraged. A refinancing was on the cards, meaning there might be a killing to be made.

'Haven't seen you in a while.'

'Been busy.'

'I was beginning to think you might've taken your business elsewhere.'

'You know me, Col.' Mills watched a stripper take to the tiny stage at the far end of the bar and start her routine. 'I'm always loyal to my friends.'

'Glad to hear it.'

'Besides, you've got the best blow in London. And the best girls.'

'What do you fancy tonight?' Holyoak asked. 'The usual?'

'I was thinking,' Mills finished his drink and waved to the barman for another, 'maybe it's time for a change.'

'There's good news and bad news.'

Carlyle always took bad news first.

O'Sullivan obliged. 'We didn't find much at James Gillespie's place. Nothing, in fact.'

'We still think he's the man with no head?'

'It's a working hypothesis.'

Carlyle waited for the good news.

'Forensics lifted a fingerprint from the cell where Travis was found, belonging to a guy called Nick Dawson.' The inspector paused, waiting for the obvious question, which Carlyle quickly asked.

'Who's he?'

'A.k.a. Reuben Barnwell.'

Sandro followed Gareth Mills on the short journey from his office to Berkeley Square. Crossing the square, Mills ducked into a door next to a Bentley showroom. On closer inspection, this turned out to be a place called the XY Club. After handing over eighty pounds for a twenty-four-hour membership, Sandro was ushered into a large bar filled with businessmen, its piped techno music pumped up a couple of notches too loud. At the far end of the room, a stripper finished her act and shuffled off the stage to the general disinterest of the crowd. Mills was standing at the bar, talking to another guy. Keeping his distance, Sandro handed over ten pounds for a beer and waited for the two men to finish their conversation. After a few minutes, the men shook hands and Mills disappeared through a door next to the stage. Leaving his drink untouched, Sandro followed him.

Through the door was a corridor, leading to a flight of stairs.

On the floor above, Sandro found a similar corridor with four closed doors leading off the right side. The first two doors were locked. The third opened onto a dimly lit room. Standing by the side of a single bed, Mills had his trousers round his ankles and his dick in his hand. Her back to the door, a scantily dressed woman was searching the drawer of a bedside table.

Sandro could feel the music from downstairs vibrating through the thin soles of his shoes.

Mills appeared unconcerned about being caught with his trousers down. 'Got the coke?' he asked Sandro, as the woman turned around, clutching a selection of condoms.

'Who're you?' The woman scowled at Sandro.

Pretending not to understand, Sandro stepped into the room.

'You shouldn't be here,' the woman snapped. 'You're in the wrong place.' Ignoring her, Sandro pulled a blade from his pocket and jammed it under the man's jawbone. Arterial spray redecorated the wall before Mills, swooning, crumpled to the floor.

The woman looked on in mute horror. Sandro's gaze was drawn to the pool of urine gathering at her feet. Wiping the blade on the duvet, he shoved it back into his pocket. 'I'm gonna go now,' he said calmly. 'Count to a hundred and then you can leave, call the cops, whatever. You'll never see me again, so you can tell them what you like.'

The girl remained mute.

'Understand?'

Her mouth opened and out came a feeble croak he took as 'Yes.'

'Good. Don't worry.' He eyed the carpet, sticky and black. 'Be careful not to step in the mess.'

On his way back down, a black guy blocked his path. 'Who're you?'

Sandro answered with a head-butt that sent the man tumbling

202

to the bottom of the stairs. A couple of swift kicks to the ribs ensured he wouldn't be getting up in a hurry. Going through his pockets, Sandro came up with a thin wad of cash and a small plastic packet containing a fine white powder.

'Thanks.' Stuffing the cash into his pocket, Sandro took a bump of the coke before heading back through the bar and into the night. On the street, he began walking, a nice buzz developing in his brain. Looking down, he noticed blood on his shoes. Laughing, he picked up the pace.

'I presume you know what I cost?' Abigail Slater quoted an hourly rate that made Carlyle blanch. 'Clients are required to stump up five thousand at the outset – we don't want any unseemly quibbling over bills.'

'I understand.' Carlyle wondered if he should've checked with Helen before asking one of London's most expensive lawyers to take him on as a client. Gritting his teeth, he fished out his wallet. 'Do you take credit cards?'

'Only joking.' Slater let out a throaty laugh.

'Sorry.'

'I'll be happy to take you on, pro bono.' She paused to let the colour return to his cheeks. 'I'm sure when we've finished with them your employers will be begging to pay my costs.'

'They will?' It sounded too good to be true.

'In the end,' Slater promised, 'they'll be throwing money at both of us.'

'And if they're not?'

Slater was briefly thrown by the question. 'If they don't,' she said finally, 'then I won't deserve payment. Based on what you've told me, the claims against you seem very flimsy, to the point of being non-existent. We'll wipe the floor with them.'

I bet you say that to all your clients. Carlyle immediately upbraided himself for being churlish.

'I'll speak to your union rep, Mr Morrow, directly, to get all the documentation from him. Once I've gone through it, I'll contact your employer and request a meeting. I'll make it clear that if they don't drop all this nonsense immediately – and issue you with a full and grovelling apology, as well as paying your costs – we'll sue them for libel, discrimination, harassment and anything else I can think of.' Slater snapped her fingers. 'They'll back down in the blink of an eye. You mark my words.'

'Sounds good.'

'I'll be in touch. You made the right decision in coming to me.'

Having sorted out number one, Carlyle asked, 'How's Hermione getting on?'

'She's doing all right, under the circumstances.' Slater's face clouded. 'O'Sullivan still hasn't found the other guy, though.'

'What other guy?'

'The other guy with Hughes when he threatened her in the flat, Dwayne somebody, an assistant at Perendi Films. They'd go out on the pull together. Rick Ford thinks he's gone back to the US.'

In the wind, Carlyle thought.

'You might want to try to track him down, seeing as it's a *murder* inquiry.'

'I'll speak to the inspector, see what's going on.'

'I'm pretty relaxed about it,' Slater proclaimed. 'Hermione is innocent all day long. The longer you keep her locked up, the bigger her payout's going to be at the end of all this. Plus, there's no such thing as bad publicity when you're a working actor.' Slater shooed him from her office. 'Now let me get on. There's lots to do.'

Sequestered in Totò's, O'Sullivan brought him up to speed. 'Dawson's lawyer's making a meal of bringing him in for a chat.'

204

It took Carlyle a moment to join the dots from Nick Dawson to Reuben Barnwell. 'We could always arrest him . . . again.'

The inspector wasn't keen. 'Dawson seems pretty well protected.'

Carlyle didn't give a stuff. On the other hand, though, he didn't want to create unnecessary problems for his colleague. 'Who's his lawyer?'

'Melanie Wiggins. The Federation uses her quite a bit.'

Carlyle wondered if Alex Morrow would know her.

'I've asked around,' O'Sullivan continued. 'She doesn't seem to have much of a reputation, one way or another.'

'And Dawson, he's no longer embedded with the Rainbow people?'

'They pulled him out,' O'Sullivan confirmed, 'but his cover remains intact.'

'As far as we know.'

'I've spoken to Francesca, making it clear she shouldn't disclose his true identity.'

'I like Angelini,' Carlyle admitted. 'She's going to be a star.'

'Just don't get her into trouble,' O'Sullivan counselled.

'Me?' Carlyle mimed shock and disappointment. 'Why ever would I do that?'

'Do your own dirty work,' was O'Sullivan's final word on the matter, before moving on to Kenny Schenk. 'I've been chasing Dwayne Doud, a runner at the film company.' The guy Slater had mentioned. Trying to keep things simple, Carlyle didn't feel the need to recount the conversation with his lawyer.

'American citizen, trust-fund kid, shit magnet,' was O'Sullivan's summary. 'He was the guy who let Hermione Lacemaker into Kenny Schenk's hotel room. According to Hermione, he was also present when she was remodelling Graham Hughes's skull.'

'And he's done a runner?'

O'Sullivan nodded. 'Got on a plane to New York while we

were questioning Lacemaker at Notting Hill. We didn't manage to get him stopped at the other end. The US authorities are looking for him, but he's gone to ground.'

'So where does that leave us?'

'A report'll go to the CPS in the next few days. In the meantime, Hermione Lacemaker stays on remand.'

Carlyle recalled Slater's compensation quest. 'That could end up proving expensive.'

'Not my problem.' O'Sullivan finished her tea. 'I present the facts as they emerge, although, if it hadn't been for Sweetman, Hermione probably wouldn't have been charged in the first place.' She paused. 'You know, there's a whisper going round the station the assistant commissioner's made a complaint against you.'

Carlyle couldn't be bothered to deny it. 'People have been complaining about me since before you were born. I have nothing to worry about.'

'That's what they all say.'

'Yeah, well, in my case it's true.'

'I believe you.' The inspector's expression grew serious. 'You don't come across as that type of bloke.'

Was that what passed for a compliment, these days? 'You don't know me,' Carlyle pointed out. 'Why should you have a view?'

'Taking a view on people is what being a cop's all about.'

'Maybe. Back in the day. Not now.'

'See?' O'Sullivan teased. 'You're too old, cynical and worn down to be a sex pest.'

'I'm too knackered to be a threat to anyone.' Carlyle was distracted by a familiar face suddenly filling the TV screen on the wall. Underneath the picture a *BREAKING NEWS* banner bore the legend: *Brexit backer murdered.*

'Fucking hell.' Fumbling for his phone, he pulled up the BBC website and started reading a story that had been posted just a minute earlier. 'Christ on a bike.'

'What?'

'Someone's gone and offed Gareth Mills.'

'Who?'

'He's a loudmouth businessman, one of those annoying Brexit guys. His company was bidding to buy those old police stations we're selling off.' Carlyle wondered if Mills's death would somehow invalidate BDS's bid.

'Uh-huh.'

'Says here he was stabbed in the XY Club in Berkeley Square.'

'An establishment well-known to the authorities.' O'Sullivan sounded a bit more interested. 'Did they get the guy who did it?'

Carlyle read down the rest of the article. 'Doesn't look like it.'

'A guy like that's bound to have lots of enemies.'

'You'd have thought so,' Carlyle agreed, his mind turning to one in particular.

NINETEEN

Carlyle marched straight into the commissioner's office to find three bemused civilians. Virginia Thompson did not look surprised to see him.

'Commander Carlyle,' she said wryly, 'I was wondering when you would turn up.'

Carlyle placed the latest edition of the *Standard* on her desk. The front page was dominated by a cheering Gareth Mills waving a little plastic Union Jack. Next to the image, the headline screamed SEX CLUB SLAYING OF BREXIT BOSS.

A look of distaste settled on Thompson's face. After folding the paper, she slowly got to her feet and addressed her guests: 'If you would excuse me for a moment, I need to speak to the commander and then I'll be right back.' She led Carlyle out of the office and into an anteroom. 'Feel free to storm into my office, any time.'

'Thank you.'

'Don't take the piss, Commander.' Closing the door, she folded her arms. 'If you do that again, I'll have you directing traffic in Stratford for the rest of your career.'

When was the last time any cop had been on traffic duty? Carlyle tried to look vaguely contrite.

'You're a right drama queen.'

'Hardly. Nothing was thrown. There wasn't even any

swearing. Even you probably couldn't manage to make another complaint out of it.'

'*That's* what this is about. You must be pretty worried.'

'I'm pretty worried about you making an arse of yourself,' Carlyle dialled up the nonchalance, 'and bringing the Met into disrepute. Not necessarily in that order.'

'A drama queen who loves sticking his nose into other people's business.'

As a wind-up merchant, the commissioner was strictly amateur league. Carlyle wasn't going to let Thompson annoy him. 'The funny thing is, I've never been a very curious kind of a guy – you don't need much curiosity to do this job. Most of the time, all you need to do is keep your eyes open and watch as the shit flows towards you.' Thompson started to speak, but he talked over her. 'I hadn't the slightest interest in the Building and Infrastructure sub-committee or the sale of disused police stations until I, erm, accidentally came across Terry Brunel.'

Thompson rolled her eyes. 'That's one way of putting it.'

'You have one conversation, then another, then another – or, rather, you *listen* to people. And all this crap slowly emerges in front of your eyes.'

'What – you think you're a shrink in a uniform?'

'In a way.' Carlyle scratched his chin. 'If curiosity is overrated in this job, listening is seriously *under*rated. It's amazing what people'll tell you if you let them.'

'Is there a point to all of this?' Thompson made a show of checking her watch. 'I need to get back to my meeting.'

'The point is that Building Design Services is probably gonna cost you your job.'

'Now hold on.' Thompson bridled.

'BDS has spun a web of corruption that could – maybe should – cost you your job and put your husband in jail, where he'll probably be sharing a cell with Bruce Allen.' Thompson made to

209

leave the room but Carlyle blocked her exit. 'What has Allen got on you, by the way?'

'This is outrageous! You—'

'Whoever killed Gareth Mills has done you a big favour.'

Thompson took a step away from him. 'How so?'

'Because now Mills is dead, you can throw everything back into the pot and start again, run the sale process for the police stations properly this time.'

'That'll be a matter for the sub-committee,' Thompson opined.

'Are you saying they're in on the scam?'

'There is no scam,' Thompson snapped. 'I mean, what do you know about running a big property deal, anyway? This bluster is a smokescreen to hide your inappropriate relationship with Victoria Dalby-Cummins.'

Carlyle remained calm. 'If you try to hang me out to dry, it'll backfire badly.'

'Is that a threat?' Thompson made another run for the door and again he blocked her.

'One hundred per cent,' he spat, exasperated. 'But you're missing the point here. I'm no Serpico.'

'Who?'

God, give me strength. Carlyle had to confront the possibility that the woman was even more stupid than she appeared. 'I'm not running a crusade. I'm not on a mission to bring you down. I'm trying to make this mess go away, like the good team player I am.'

'Ha. Bruce gave me a copy of your personnel report. It says a lot of things but the phrase "team player" is conspicuous by its absence.'

Carlyle didn't quibble. 'Bottom line, I'm giving you the chance to keep your job. *And* I'm giving your husband the chance to discreetly withdraw from this deal and avoid a likely jail sentence for pocketing millions of pounds rightly belonging to the Met.'

'I've got no worries on that score,' Thompson parroted. Her face, however, told another story.

'Your decision.' Carlyle turned the knife. 'There's more than enough for an arrest warrant and there are several judges who'll be happy to indulge me. Once the news gets out, you're finished.'

The threat of arrest knocked any remaining fight out of the commissioner. 'Fine.' She held up a hand. 'I'll drop my complaint against you.'

'And get Sweetman's complaint dropped as well.'

'I'll see what I can do. Just leave my husband alone.'

'As long as he cuts his ties to BDS, he'll have nothing to worry about. They're not going to win the auction now anyway, so it's not like he's giving up much.'

Thompson grunted her assent. 'One final condition – find me Gareth Mills's killer. Regardless of the property sell-off, this needs to be sorted out, like, yesterday. The man had plenty of friends in Westminster – I've got half the bloody government on my back screaming for an arrest.'

Carlyle held out a hand. 'Done.'

Thompson shook it limply. 'Good. I'll speak to the chair of the Building and Infrastructure sub-committee about restarting the bid process.'

Carlyle had an idea. 'Maybe you could give me his job.'

'It's a *she*.' Thompson looked genuinely offended by the proposal. 'Don't push your luck, Commander. You've only been to *one* meeting. How could I possibly give you a promotion?'

'Actually, I haven't been to any yet,' Carlyle confessed. 'The last one was postponed.'

'Here's a tip.' Thompson finally managed to get past him to open the door. 'If you don't go to the meetings, you'll never get the top job.'

'Is that how you got the top job?'

'It's a necessary if not sufficient condition.' She ushered him back out of the room. 'You might not be curious, but you need to be *present*.'

'I'm a cop, not a bureaucrat.'

'In that case, get out there and catch me a killer,' Thompson demanded. 'And make it quick.'

Inspector Henry Jones had assumed command at the XY Club. A Welshman, with the accent to prove it, he had arrived in the big city three years ago and had been pining for a return to the valleys ever since. 'London's not what I imagined it would be,' he complained. 'It's so bloody big, you know.'

'Uh-huh.' Carlyle looked around the empty bar. The tables were covered with half-finished drinks and he spied a discarded bra on the small stage. As soon as news of the murder had spread, most people had fled before the police had arrived.

Jones continued prattling on about his personal travails. 'My girlfriend packed it in and went home after a month. She says we can't get married till I get a job back home.' He looked at the commander expectantly. 'You couldn't help me get a move, could you?'

'I'll see what I can do,' Carlyle offered, without enthusiasm. 'Send me your CV.'

'That would be great. I mean, I don't like to have to pull strings but—'

'Everyone does it. No need to be sheepish.' Carlyle wandered towards a door by the side of the stage. 'The stabbing – it happened upstairs?'

Jones froze. 'What did you say?'

'The victim,' Carlyle pointed at the door, 'through there and up the stairs?'

'Before. Did you say something about sheep? I can*not* believe it.' Jones sounded like he was having a panic attack. 'Oh, my God.'

'Are you all right?' Carlyle wondered if the man might be having a stroke.

'You think that's funny, do you, jokes about Welsh people and sheep? It's, like, racist.'

For fuck's sake, I said *sheepish*, you deaf sod. 'Where's the owner?'

'We do *not* shag sheep in Wales,' Jones fumed.

'The owner,' Carlyle repeated.

'Upstairs.' Jones was still clearly stewing at the perceived insult. 'He has a flat on the top floor, a penthouse apartment.'

'Where are the rest of the staff? Is anyone still here?'

'Just the girl who was with Mills when he was killed.'

'Didn't you send her to the hospital?'

'She's fine. The killer didn't lay a finger on her. She was checked out by the paramedics. A bit shaken, as you would be, but no injuries. We're waiting for the interpreter to arrive so we can take her statement.'

'That's me.'

Carlyle looked round to see a small guy, his face partially hidden by round glasses.

'Celso Vallejo. I'm the Spanish interpreter.'

'Spanish?' Jones looked like he was going to cry. 'I asked for *Portuguese*. Telma, the witness, is Portuguese, not Spanish.'

'It's okay.' The interpreter offered up a big smile. 'I can do a bit of Portuguese, as well.'

'A bit?' Jones wasn't having it. 'The poor woman's a victim of crime. This has to be done properly.'

Seeing his job disappearing in front of him, Vallejo became slightly agitated. 'If you don't use me,' he pointed out, 'I don't get paid.'

The inspector was unmoved. 'Not my problem.'

'It'll be fine.' Carlyle led the interpreter towards the door by the stage. 'We'll manage.'

213

Jones's face reddened. 'But it's *my* interview.'

'I'll do it,' said Carlyle, pulling rank. 'You go back to the station and write up your report. And get hold of Inspector Karen O'Sullivan for me. Tell her I want to see her as soon as possible.'

'Is that blood?' Vallejo looked at the mess beyond the police tape, crossing himself and mumbling a prayer at the same time.

Carlyle confirmed it was.

'They're gonna need a new carpet,' the interpreter observed, 'that's for sure.'

Next door, the witness sat on a grubby single bed. Making the introductions, Carlyle felt himself slip into officialdom-mode, a mix of by-the-book-empathy and close observation. 'I'm very sorry for what happened here. No one should have to experience anything like that.'

'Are you the boss?' Telma played with an unlit cigarette. 'I've been waiting for ages.' It was an observation, rather than a complaint.

'I'm the boss,' Carlyle confirmed. He signalled for the interpreter to take the only chair in the room. 'How're you feeling?' For someone who had seen a man bleed out in front of her, the woman seemed remarkably composed. The word that appeared, unbidden, in Carlyle's brain was 'nondescript'. Dressed in jeans and a fleece, she wore no make-up. Her short dark hair was wet, as if she'd just had a shower. Carlyle hoped the forensics guys had taken what they needed.

'I'm fine.' Vallejo started to say something, but Telma talked over him. 'Don' need an interpreter. My English is good.'

Vallejo gave the commander a look.

'The inspector said you needed one,' Carlyle responded.

Telma frowned. 'The guy in the bar with the funny accent?'

'He's Welsh,' Carlyle told her.

She looked at him, surprised. 'You let foreigners join the police?'

'I suppose so, sometimes.'

'He doesn't seem very good. No energy.' Telma paused, giving Carlyle the chance to challenge her assertion. When he did not, she continued, 'He think I need an interpreter, but I never say that. I wanted to speak to someone important, so I told him I would rather wait.'

Vallejo returned to his funk. 'I won't get paid, if you don't use me. And I've already spent two hours getting here.'

'It's all right,' Carlyle reassured him. 'You stay, in case we need you. I'll sign it off. A bit of overtime, too.'

'You don't get overtime,' Vallejo wailed, 'on zero-hours contracts.'

'Put in for whatever you can put in for,' Carlyle snapped, 'and I'll make sure it gets signed off.'

The interpreter accepted the deal and fell silent. Carlyle signalled for the woman to shift along, so he could sit down on the bed beside her. 'You must've had a hell of a shock.'

Telma made a face. 'I'm fine. It was horrible but, you know, like watching a movie. Once it's over, you forget about it.' So far, Carlyle was liking the super-calm Telma fine. 'The guy was very nice.'

'Gareth Mills?'

'No. The other guy – the guy with the knife.'

Trying not to look surprised, Carlyle waited for her to go on.

'I mean,' Telma blushed, 'I see the blood everywhere and I pee myself.' She ran a hand across the thigh of her jeans. 'I had to change after.'

'Yes.'

'Your people, they took my other stuff away. Will I get it back?'

'Yes.' Carlyle crossed his fingers. 'Although it might take a while.'

'It was expensive. Agent Provocateur.'

Carlyle pretended he didn't know the brand.

'I'm more a Pump man myself,' Vallejo chortled. Reaching into his jeans he pulled up the band of his underwear to prove the point.

'Nice,' said Telma.

Carlyle guillotined the pants conversation. 'Tell me about what happened after Gareth Mills was attacked.'

'Sure,' Telma said briskly. 'The guy is on the floor, mess everywhere. He's making a kind of, I dunno, a hissing noise. He kinda looks at me, and then I see he is dead. I look at the man with the knife. He is looking at my feet. I look down and see I have my accident. It is the shock, nothing to be ashamed about, no?'

'No,' the interpreter agreed. 'I'm sure it happens to lots of people.'

'Is one of those things.' Telma sounded philosophical. 'I have a pretty full bladder when it happened. Mr Mills, he liked a golden shower sometimes and I need to be ready.'

Vallejo started to cough.

'Was Mr Mills a regular customer?' Carlyle asked.

'For me? No. I see him maybe four or five times over the last couple of years. But I always try to remember what the customer likes – makes things go quicker. Quicker is always good.'

'Did you know Mills was coming tonight?' Vallejo asked.

'No. Colin told me he was in the bar. I was waiting for him in the room, but if I hadn't been working, someone else would've taken him.'

The interpreter was getting into the Q and A thing now. 'He was a regular of the club?'

Carlyle gave him a frown, inviting him to button it, then addressed Telma, 'Getting back to the events of the evening, the killer sees you've had your, erm, accident, and then what happened?'

Telma let the cigarette fall into her lap. 'He sees what is happening and he puts his knife away. He is very calm, tells me

216

not to worry. He is going to leave and then I should count to a hundred before I leave the room. "You'll never see me again," he said, "so you can tell them anything."'

'"Them" being the police?'

'Yeah. He didn't want me to be afraid. He even told me not to step in the mess.'

'What did you do?' Vallejo asked breathlessly. Carlyle's irritation was offset by the translator making a far better fist of police work than Inspector Henry Jones.

'I counted to a hundred and then ran out. One of the security guys was at the bottom of the stairs, crying with a broken nose. The man hit him on his way out.' Telma let out a little giggle. 'He took his blow, too. I went to find Colin – the boss – and he called the cops.'

After getting his VIPs out of the back door, Carlyle reflected.

Vallejo had another question. 'What did he look like, the killer?'

Telma made a face. 'All men look pretty much the same.' She thought about it for a moment. 'Dark. Foreign.'

'Narrows it down,' Carlyle said acidly.

'Not a black guy.'

'Like an Arab?' Vallejo asked.

'Maybe.'

The conversation began to meander. Carlyle was losing interest when Karen O'Sullivan appeared in the doorway and signalled for him to join her in the corridor.

'In what universe does this become my case?' the inspector asked, clearly narked.

'In the universe where muppets like Henry Jones are allowed to join the Met.' Carlyle gave her a pat on the shoulder, immediately fretting over whether such physical contact was still allowable. 'On the plus side, this is the sexiest case going right now. We break it apart, we'll be heroes.' Realising how lame that sounded, he immediately corrected himself. 'Well, not heroes, but flavour of the month, maybe.'

'Flavour of the week,' O'Sullivan suggested. '*If* we solve it.'

'The Met's clean-up rate for murder is as close to a hundred per cent as you're going to get anywhere, ever,' Carlyle observed cheerily. 'The numbers are on our side.' Sticking his head back into the room, he gave Telma a big bureaucratic smile. 'Inspector O'Sullivan will look after you for the next part of the process.' The interpreter started to talk, but he cut him off. 'Celso will go with you, too, in case you, erm, need him.'

Seemingly happy with the plan, Vallejo leaned forward and patted Telma's knee. 'Don't worry, I'll make sure they treat you properly. They can't kick you out.'

Says *you*. Carlyle bit his lower lip. God knew what might happen to Telma when the system got hold of her.

Telma was unconcerned. 'If they wanna deport me,' she declared, 'it's fine. Saves me the airfare. I'm going home anyway. This place is shit, you know?'

Carlyle stood in the middle of a large living space with massive windows giving an impressive view towards Green Park. 'I've been talking to Telma,' he said. 'She seems to be taking things in her stride.'

'She's a pretty impressive woman.' Dressed in jeans and a pale blue V-neck sweater over a white T-shirt, Colin Holyoak was a tall man, easily over six feet, lean, his head shaven as a response to a pretty severe case of male-pattern baldness. 'I'll be sorry to see her go.'

'She told me she's planning on leaving London, going home.'

Holyoak sipped from a tumbler of whisky. 'This'll be the last straw,' he predicted. 'Which is a shame. Good people are hard to find. The churn I've got to deal with is ridiculous.'

'Maybe you could encourage her to stay.' Carlyle's gaze fell on a large, well-stocked drinks cabinet. 'Offer her some kind of management job – she seems very capable.'

'Maybe. We'll need to get this mess sorted out first.' Following his gaze, Holyoak offered his guest a drink. Carlyle graciously accepted and they settled into facing sofas in front of a vast TV showing a selection of still CCTV pictures from the club.

Carlyle contemplated the frozen images on the screen. 'What are you watching?'

'These are the security-camera pictures from downstairs. I can keep an eye on things from up here if I want to. I don't spend a lot of time spying on people, it's more for deterrence purposes, keeping the staff on the straight and narrow . . . and the adjudication of any disputes. Independent evidence is very handy when it comes to dealing with any he-said-she-said type of arguments.'

'There are cameras in the bedrooms?'

'That would be a bit much. We don't want to put the customers off their stride, so to speak. Most of the rest of the place is pretty well covered, though.' He pointed to the photograph in the top left-hand corner of the screen. 'That's me and Gareth Mills having a drink at the bar ten minutes before he was killed.' He dropped his finger to a smaller image underneath. 'And that's the guy who killed him, going up the back stairs.'

Carlyle felt a little spurt of adrenalin pump through his chest. 'Know him?' he asked.

'Never seen him before in my life. He bowled up and bought a twenty-four-hour membership, in cash.' Holyoak took a gulp of Scotch. 'We're a members-only club but you can become a member for a day. Hopefully, the mug shot can help you catch the bastard.'

'Can you email it to me?' Resisting the temptation to jump to his feet and be off, Carlyle slowly sipped his drink. 'Very nice,' he purred. 'Why don't you tell me about your relationship with Gareth Mills? Take it from the beginning.'

TWENTY

Leaving the club, Carlyle hailed a black cab from the rank on the square.

'Where to?' The driver was a no-nonsense woman wearing a headscarf.

'A club called the Chapel.' Carlyle gave her the address.

The driver jerked her chin in the direction of the door from which he'd just emerged. 'That place not got what you need, eh?'

'It's closed tonight.' Carlyle started playing with his phone, the universal signal for *Let's keep the talking to a minimum, if you don't mind.* 'Nothing doing.'

The driver didn't take the hint. 'People came fleeing out of there like it was on fire after that guy was killed.'

'I can imagine.' Carlyle caught her eye in the rear-view mirror. 'Catch any interesting gossip?'

The cabbie's eyes narrowed. 'You wouldn't be a cop, would you?'

'I am.' Carlyle saw no reason to dissemble.

'Was it a mess, then?' The driver rolled up to a set of traffic lights as they turned red. 'Must've been terrible.'

'It's never good.' Wondering how much cash he had in his wallet, Carlyle eyed the meter uncomfortably until he noticed the card machine bolted to the partition. God bless the cashless society.

'I had him in the back of my cab once, right where you're sitting now.'

What? Carlyle shifted in his seat. 'Who?'

'Gareth Mills.' The driver tapped the mercifully silent radio. 'The dead guy on the news.'

'Right.'

'He came out of the XY Club one night with one of his mates. They were steaming, totally gone. Mills was no trouble – he passed out on the back seat. But the other guy, what a dog he was. You know what he said to me? He said, "Do you want to see a great man's cock?" I said, "What?" And he got it out and started waving it around.'

Carlyle watched the lights change. 'What did you do?'

'I've seen far worse, I can assure you.' The driver moved off. 'I started laughing. It was tiny. And he couldn't get it up. The guy got a bit huffy when I didn't take him seriously, but he zipped himself up and sat back down like a good boy. When we got to his place, he gave me a fifty-quid tip and asked me in. I said, "No fear, mate," and raced out of there like I had a firework up me bum.' She smiled at the memory. 'Bloody hell, what a night that was.'

'What was the guy's name?'

'Sorry, no idea.' Her eyes grew wide. 'You don't think he killed his mate, do you?'

'No. It definitely wasn't him.'

'You know who did it?'

Cursing himself for saying too much, Carlyle parried the question with one of his own. 'What's *your* name?'

'Mehak.' The driver tapped the licence stuck to the dashboard. 'Mehak Sillitoe.'

'Nice to meet you, Mehak.'

'You too, Mr Policeman.'

'I'm Commander John Carlyle. I work at Charing Cross.'

'Nice to make your acquaintance.'

'If I can ever be of help, let me know.'

'Thank you, Commander,' Mehak tutted, as a bus pulled out in front of her, 'but presumably your kind offer comes with strings attached.'

Carlyle didn't deny it. 'The address you took Mills and his pal to, do you think you can remember where it was?'

There had been an accident in Kilburn, and they found themselves caught in gridlock. After making their escape, Mehak drove on past Hampstead Heath, not far from Kenwood House, where Carlyle had first met with Emily Quartz. The meter was making Carlyle fret about his credit-card limit by the time the taxi pulled into The Bishops Avenue.

'Here we are. Billionaire's Row.' Mehak considered the high walls on either side of the street and the dark, hulking mansions behind them. 'One of the wealthiest streets in the entire world and most of the houses are empty.'

As far as Carlyle could see, only one house in the entire street had any lights on. The taxi came to a halt at the kerb outside. 'Here we are.'

'Are you sure this is the place?'

'One hundred per cent,' the driver insisted. 'It was the only place with any lights on then, too. Plus, I remember the security sign.' She pointed to a notice on the ten-foot-high brick wall, which hid the property from prying eyes. Under the legend 'Perryman Protection Services', there was a twenty-four-hour contact number and a King's Cross address. Carlyle slid across the back seat and opened the door. 'Shall I wait for you?'

'Might be a good idea.' Closing the door, he put the meter to the back of his mind. Four feet from the sign was a metal door, with an entry-phone and the ubiquitous CCTV. Carlyle pressed the buzzer, looked up into the camera and waited. After what seemed like eternity, but was probably less than half a minute, a voice came over the intercom: 'Yes?'

'Police.' Carlyle held up his ID to the camera.

'Yes?' Second time around, the question was smothered in an extra dollop of boredom.

Don't mess me around, you fucking minimum-wage monkey. Carlyle held the ID closer to the lens. 'Open the door now,' he hissed, 'or Perryman Protection Services will no longer exist by this time tomorrow.'

It was an empty threat, but it worked. After a short pause there was a click and the lock disengaged. Carlyle pushed the door open and stepped inside.

A young guy in an ill-fitting security guard's uniform slouched down the drive to meet him. The kid looked barely into his early twenties and, up close, appeared ill under the sodium light pollution coming from the street.

'Can I help you?'

Carlyle flashed his ID once more, for luck. 'I want to speak to the owner.'

The kid didn't miss a beat. 'He's not in.' It was the most unconvincing lie the commander had heard in a long time.

'Yes, he is.' Carlyle pointed at the light-fringed curtains coming from what he presumed was a ground-floor living room. 'I'm here on police business and I want to see him. Now.'

'He doesn't want to be disturbed.' A lecherous grin spread across the kid's face. 'It's girlfriend night.'

'I don't care if it's a-dozen-hookers-and-twenty-grams-of-coke night, I still want to see him.'

'That was last night.' The boy let out a nerdy laugh.

Carlyle made it clear he was the only one allowed to crack gags. 'Are you taking the piss?'

'Erm, no, erm, sir.' Fearing he might get a slap for his trouble, the kid took a step backwards, then another.

'Commander.'

'I'm not being funny, Commander,' the boy stammered, 'it *is* girlfriend night. Absolutely no disturbances allowed. The guy who was here before me, he got the sack because—'

'Tomorrow can be girlfriend night.'

'His wife wouldn't like that,' the kid deadpanned. 'Nothing's allowed to disturb girlfriend night, especially not since he started dating Sasha Claremont. You know, the supermodel?' A dreamy look descended on his face. 'She did that Pump advert.'

Pump underwear, as promoted by Celso Vallejo, the talkative translator. 'I thought Pump was for men.' It was out of Carlyle's mouth before his brain could engage.

'Check out the video on YouTube,' was the security guard's advice.

Carlyle realised they were getting off the point. Matter in hand, he admonished himself. Mahek's meter would probably be past three figures by now. There wasn't time for small-talk. 'What's your name?'

The kid thought carefully before answering. 'Steve.'

'Okay, Steve,' the commander placed a hand on the kid's shoulder and gave it a gentle squeeze, not hostile, but containing the vague possibility of violence further down the road if he was in any way messed about. 'I'm gonna go inside now. You can go back to your, erm, command post and—'

Steve pointed at a detached three-car garage. 'It's an office, in there. A kind of prefab thing. Bloody freezing when it gets cold.'

Carlyle stood corrected. 'You can go back to your *office*, nothing to worry about, and get back to your underwear videos or whatever it is you do in there while I'll go and speak to the home-owner.' The kid started up about the supermodel again, but Carlyle hushed him. 'Unless that doesn't work for you, in which case there's a Plan B.'

'Plan B?' The kid looked confused. Was the policeman giving him a choice here?

'You should always have a Plan B, right?'

'Erm, right.'

'Under Plan B, I'm gonna arrest you for obstructing a police officer going about his duties and throw you in the cells for the night.' He pointed at the door in the wall. 'There's a car outside. I can put you behind bars in less than an hour. Maybe lose the paperwork – you can go on a tour of British jails for a week or two before anyone realises you shouldn't be there – whaddya think? You could end up in Manchester, Aberdeen, maybe even Belfast.' He rubbed his chin. 'That would be a bugger, wouldn't it? They kick you out in Belfast and you have to make your own way home without any money in your pocket.'

A constipated look descended on the kid's face. 'But I haven't done anything.'

'You'll make your own way home,' Carlyle repeated, 'without a job to come back to.' His shame at bullying the kid was tempered by the knowledge he wouldn't actually follow through on his threats.

Steve finally relented. Turning on his heel, he headed back towards the garage. 'This way,' he advised. 'I can let you in through the back.'

Carlyle wandered through the empty rooms until he came to a living room the size of a basketball court. The space was decked out like something in one of those porny lifestyle magazines Helen liked to gawp at. In the middle of the room, a man, presumably the home-owner, was chasing a woman, presumably the girlfriend, round a massive coffee-table. On the table a bottle of champagne stood beside a packet of cigarettes and a large mound of white powder. Both participants seemed to have lost various items of clothing in the course of the chase.

A Benny Hill soundtrack started playing in Carlyle's head. He stood in the doorway, warrant card in hand, waiting to be noticed.

It was the man who first registered his presence. 'Who the hell are you?' he asked, giving up the chase. Seriously over-weight, the minimal exercise had left him red in the face.

'John Carlyle, Metropolitan Police.' Stepping forward, the commander let the man inspect his ID before slipping it back into his pocket. 'Steve let me in.'

The man looked at him blankly. 'Who?'

'Your security guard.'

'Not much of a fucking security guard, then, is he?' The woman took the chance of a break in the fun and games to light a smoke.

'Who are you?' Carlyle asked.

'You sneak into my home,' the man roared, 'and you don't even know who I am? What the fuck is this?'

'It's a quiet chat,' Carlyle let his gaze slide across the table, 'unless you want it to turn into something rather more official.'

The man thought about it for a moment, before offering his guest a seat on one of three sofas surrounding the coffee-table. 'I'm surprised you don't recognise us.'

Preparing to be enlightened, Carlyle lowered himself onto the edge of the nearest sofa.

Trying to establish a modicum of control over the situation, Fatso stayed on his feet. 'I'm Sir Christopher Sollerdiche, businessman, thought leader, visionary, patron of the arts and various other good causes.' He introduced his playmate, who was greedily sucking on her fag. 'This is my, erm, friend, Ms Sasha Claremont, the famous model.'

Claremont blew a stream of smoke towards the ceiling. '*Super*model, Chris, please.'

Suitably chagrined, Sollerdiche bowed his head.

Seemingly oblivious to the fact she was half naked, Claremont eyeballed Carlyle. 'I'm assuming you're not here to see me, Officer.'

'Commander,' Carlyle corrected her.

'Whatever. As long as you're not after me.'

'I was after a word or two with Mr Sollerdiche,' Carlyle confirmed.

'Sir Christopher.' The man snapped back into pissed-off mode.

'If you don't need me, I think I'll call it a night.' Claremont floated from the room. Sollerdiche collapsed onto the sofa opposite Carlyle. The commander tried not to stare at the massive tanned belly bursting out from underneath an unbuttoned shirt. His host wore nothing more but a pair of socks and briefs, which looked several sizes too small. The waistband, where not obscured by the man's gut, proclaimed the brand – Pump.

Presumably the girlfriend gets a friends-and-family discount, Carlyle mused. 'Apologies for interrupting the party.'

Sollerdiche drank some champagne. The alcohol seemed to dilute his anger at Carlyle's home invasion. He refilled his glass. 'Help yourself, if you want some.'

'I'm good, thanks. I'll only take a few minutes of your time.'

'Take as long as you like.' Sollerdiche eyed the cocaine but perhaps decided it was best left, for the moment. 'Once Sasha calls it a night, that's it.' He made a chopping gesture with his hand. 'People think being a model is all glamour and flouncing about, but Sasha keeps up a hell of a schedule, let me tell you. The girl has an incredible work ethic. It's one of the reasons we get on so well together. We're kindred spirits.'

'Was Gareth Mills a kindred spirit?'

'That's why you're here, is it?' Sollerdiche raised his glass in a toast. 'One of Britain's finest. Rest in peace, my friend.' Finishing his drink, he reached for the bottle, muttering to himself when he realised it was empty. 'Let me get another.' With some effort, he pushed himself off the sofa and padded across the room, reappearing a few minutes later with a new bottle and two flutes. Handling the glasses to Carlyle, he stripped the foil from the neck and eased off the cork. 'This is a Dom Pérignon 2006. Not the kind of stuff you'd be used to on a policeman's salary.'

Sollerdiche's rapid change of mood, from outraged to jovial, was vaguely unsettling. Carlyle watched as his host filled the glasses. After taking the smallest of tastes, he pronounced it 'very nice' and carefully placed his glass on the coffee-table, well away from the mound of coke.

Sollerdiche put the bottle on the table and sat down rather heavily. 'What were we talking about?'

'Gareth Mills.'

'Ah, yes.' Sollerdiche twirled the champagne in his glass. 'Shocking business. Bloody foreigners.'

'How do you know Mr Mills was killed by a foreigner?'

'Who else would it be?' Sollerdiche slurped his drink. 'Gareth was a true patriot. He stood up for British people, which makes you a lot of enemies these days.'

'It's an assumption on your part, then?'

'If I had proof,' Sollerdiche grunted, 'I'd have been right on the blower to Virginia.'

On the blower? Carlyle tried to remember the last time he'd heard that one.

'In fact, I should probably give her a call anyway.' Sollerdiche took another drink. 'Presumably you know the commissioner. A very fine woman. I take it she's put you on this case because you get results.'

'We have a suspect,' Carlyle confirmed.

'Who?'

'I can't discuss that.'

Sollerdiche did not protest. 'Vicky'll tell me.' He refilled his glass to the brim. 'In custody?'

'Not yet,' Carlyle conceded.

'Well, what the hell are you doing here, man? For God's sake, get out there and do some policing.'

People telling you how to do your job was an occupational hazard. Carlyle didn't feel any need to defend or explain his actions. Instead, he asked, 'Why would anyone want to kill Mr Mills?'

'Why don't you ask the dirty pig who did it?' Sollerdiche shouted. 'People hate success. People hate the truth. People hate this great country of ours. They hate the idea we're finally taking back control. Gareth Mills represented all of these things. Take your pick.'

'I was wondering if the killing might be related to more prosaic matters.'

'Whaddya mean?'

'Could it be related to BDS and the bid for the police-station portfolio?'

Placing his glass on the table, Sollerdiche slumped back on the sofa and closed his eyes. 'Carlyle. Carlyle, Carlyle, Carlyle . . . I know who you are . . . the guy Bruce Allen mentioned, the bent cop on Vicky Dalby-Cummins's payroll.'

'I'm not on anyone's payroll,' Carlyle declared coolly, 'unlike Bruce – or Peter Thompson, for that matter.'

Sollerdiche opened his eyes, rubbed them, and looked at his guest as if he was seeing him for the first time. 'Virginia didn't send you at all, did she? You're here to interrupt my evening and do a bit of fishing.'

'The commissioner has asked me to find Mr Mills's killer as a matter of some urgency. I wanted to see if you might be able to help me with my enquiries.'

Sollerdiche pointed to the door. 'Get out of here before I call security.'

Not much of a threat. Carlyle thought of poor Steve, shivering in the garage. 'I go where the facts take me.'

'Well, the facts in this case take you nowhere near BDS.' For the first time in their conversation, Sollerdiche sounded perfectly sober. 'Leave the deal alone, or I'll squash you like a bug.'

'The sale process needs to be reopened, in the light of Mr Mills's death.'

'We'll see about that.'

'I guess we will.' Carlyle rose to his feet. Pulling a business card from his pocket, he dropped it on the table. 'If you think of anything that might be helpful, do give me a call.'

Sollerdiche grunted.

Carlyle eyed the coke. 'And maybe go easy on the illegal substances.'

'That's Sasha's.'

'It's your house. Don't make me come back with a search warrant.'

'I'd like to see you try to get one.'

'I know plenty of judges.'

'And I know more. I know plenty of politicians, too. Very senior politicians.' Sollerdiche dismissed him with a wave of his hand. 'So good evening, Commander. Thank you for dropping round. I'm sure you can find your own way out.'

Mahek was reading a self-help book by a businessman who wrapped himself in the Union Jack while living in a Caribbean tax haven. An act of kindness meant the taxi's meter had been switched off.

'Get what you want?' the taxi driver asked, as he clambered into the back seat.

Carlyle gave a noncommittal grunt.

Closing her book, she pointed at the fare. 'Want to pay this now, then I'll take you back for free?'

Carlyle fished out his credit card, holding his breath as he shoved it into the reader and entered his PIN. To his relief, after a moment's delay, the payment went through successfully.

'Thanks.' Mahek handed him a receipt and switched on the engine. 'Where to now?'

'The Chapel,' Carlyle commanded, reminding her of the address.

'You got it.' Mahek did a U-turn and they started heading back towards the centre of the city. 'I'll avoid Kilburn this time.'

'Good idea.' Carlyle checked the time on his phone. It was late, not too late to be outrageous but late enough for him to be confident he could call the commissioner without her picking up. Pushing information up the chain of command was never a priority in his book but you sometimes had to give the appearance of making an effort.

To his surprise and dismay, Thompson answered on the third ring. 'I was hoping to hear from you.'

'I've made some progress on the Mills case.' Carlyle paused, trying to give his brain time to get ahead of his mouth. 'I'm pretty sure I know what happened.' Thompson eagerly demanded more details, but he declined to be drawn. 'The important thing now is to see whether I can make a quick arrest.'

'Hm. Quite. We can fill in the blanks later.'

'If I'm right, however, this comes back – again – to Building Design Services and the property deal.'

Thompson groaned.

'It's another reason why we need to go back to square one and restart the auction from scratch.'

'Yes,' the commissioner said wearily.

'And your old man needs to give the whole thing a wide berth.'

There was an extended period of silence and then Thompson asked: 'Is Dalby-Cummins involved in Mills's death?'

Carlyle ducked the question. 'My priority now is to make the speedy arrest you need.'

'Of the right person.'

'Regardless of how things play out, our agreement is more important than ever.'

'Don't you worry about me, Commander. I'm a woman of my word.'

'Glad to hear it,' Carlyle replied breezily. 'I'll be in touch.'

'Don't you ever knock?' Vicky Dalby-Cummins shoved some papers into a drawer as Carlyle strolled into her office.

'Where's Sandro?'

'In prison,' she slammed the drawer shut with a flourish, 'waiting to be deported.'

'Don't lie to me, Vicky.' Carlyle lowered himself into the chair. 'I know Sandro killed Gareth Mills. He's all over the CCTV at the XY Club.'

'Ah.'

'For the moment, no one apart from me knows who he is, but it won't take long for him to get IDed. I need you to hand him over.'

'That supposes I know where he is.'

'I'm assuming you do. Like I'm assuming you're going to give him up to avoid being arrested right here and now, for conspiracy to murder Gareth Mills.'

'I had nothing to do with that.'

'Why else would Sandro kill the man?' Carlyle wondered. 'How would he even know who Gareth Mills was?'

'Do I need my lawyer?'

'Up to you.' Carlyle yawned. 'But make your mind up. I'm knackered. I want to go to bed.'

'I could give you one of our rooms. And one of our girls.'

'Behave.'

'Or two, if you like.'

'You don't get it, do you? The only way I'm any use to you

is if I'm *not* in your pocket. The minute you manage to corrupt me, I'm done.'

'If you get found out.'

'One thing I've learned over the years, the most important thing I've learned over the years, is you always get found out.'

A gleeful question came straight back at him: 'What about Dominic Silver?'

Bloody Teflon man, the exception that proves the rule. Carlyle wasn't going there. 'We're not here to talk about Dom,' he snapped, 'we're here to talk about Sandro.'

Dalby-Cummins said nothing.

'We can do this down the station if you want. I can call a car to take you to the cells for the night.' Talk of the cells put him in mind of Terry Brunel, still locked up in Kentish Town. With so much going on, the contractor had slipped Carlyle's mind. He made a mental note to see about getting him released.

'I need some time to get my head round what's happened.'

'You made it happen,' Carlyle grumbled. 'It's late. I want to go to bed – my own bed. Don't make me regret giving you a choice here, any more than I am already. You've got one minute to make up your mind how you want to play it.'

'What happens next?' she enquired. 'Is poor Sandro going to be shot resisting arrest?' It sounded more like an invitation than a question.

You are a heartless bitch, Carlyle thought. 'We'll pick him up. Make it look like we got lucky. You get him a lawyer. The lawyer gets him to plead guilty, in exchange for a reduced sentence. Come up with some story about a personal grudge, whatever. You promise to bankroll him when he gets out, he keeps his mouth shut. We all move on.'

'He'll be deported when he gets out,' Dalby-Cummins pointed out.

'You'll have to help him deal with that.'

After some further consideration, Dalby-Cummins signalled her consent. 'All very neat and tidy.'

'As long as you don't pull any more stupid stunts.'

'Mills deserved what he got.'

'There was no need to go after him.'

'Getting the smug little shit out of the picture can't have done any harm.'

It's a point of view, Carlyle thought.

'I still want to get my hands on those police stations. Where are we with the auction?'

'The BDS bid will lapse,' Carlyle confirmed. 'We'll start all over again.'

'So, I can make my own bid? New entrants will be allowed into the process?'

'We'll start from scratch. Find yourself a credible partner. And don't kill anyone else.'

'You'll keep me out of the Mills thing?'

'As long as Sandro pleads guilty and doesn't drop you in it, I'll take the quick win and the case will be considered closed.'

'Fine.' Dalby-Cummins scrawled on a Post-it note. Leaning across the table, she handed it to Carlyle. 'Give it twenty-four hours and you'll find him here.'

Carlyle looked at the address. 'Ireland?'

'I have a farm there.'

'I thought it was in Wales, or somewhere.'

'I have more than one. The Irish one's where Sandro'll be holed up.'

'Extradition'll be a bitch.'

Dalby-Cummins was unmoved by matters of international law. 'He could always be shot resisting arrest,' she repeated. 'These things happen.'

Mahek was reading her book, meter off, when he came out of the

234

club. Overriding his half-hearted protests, the taxi driver insisted on taking him home. From the back seat, Carlyle stared vacantly at the empty streets, trying to unpick the different problems he'd accumulated. His mind, however, had closed down for the night.

Unable to think straight, he checked his phone. There were three missed calls from Emily Quartz; the most recent had been less than an hour ago, around the time he was heading into the Chapel. Carlyle had long since given up trying to work out how he managed to miss so many calls. He called the journalist.

'You're working late.'

'I need to get an updated story out. What can you give me? Who killed Gareth Mills? Where does his death leave the police-station deal?'

With the benefit of hindsight, Carlyle regretted going to the press to try to solve a problem that now seemed insignificant. But you either played the media game or you didn't. He had to keep his side of the bargain. 'I know who killed Mills,' he whispered, not wanting Mahek to overhear, 'but I can't give you a name until he's in custody. There'll probably be an arrest in the next couple of days, fingers crossed. You know what these things are like – things can always go wrong at the last minute – but it's fair to say I'm pretty hopeful.'

'Cautiously optimistic.'

After the truth came the lie: 'At this stage, I don't think it has anything to do with Terry Brunel and BDS but that remains to be seen. Obviously, none of this is public-domain information, so treat it carefully.'

Quartz grunted as she made some notes. 'And what happens to the sale of the police stations?'

'I imagine Sir Christopher Sollerdiche will still push for the deal to go through.'

'The guy is so rich you wouldn't have thought he'd be bothered about making a few more million.'

'A few more *hundred* million.'

'Even a few more hundred million. How much does anyone need?'

'People like that,' Carlyle reflected, 'never want to stop. Money's only a way of keeping score and they don't like losing.'

'Sollerdiche is not a guy you want as an enemy.'

'Probably not,' Carlyle agreed. 'But the sale process needs to be stopped. We'll be going back to square one and running it properly this time.'

'Can I quote you?'

'You can quote the commissioner.'

There was a pause.

'Really?'

'Sure. I spoke to her about it in the wake of Mills's death. She is going to instruct the Building and Infrastructure sub-committee to restart the bid process.'

'So BDS is no longer the preferred bidder?'

'BDS can re-bid, but so can anyone else. We want as many credible bidders in there as possible so we get the best price, which, by the way, we have a legal responsibility to do.'

'Sounds good. Can I quote you as a source familiar with the situation?'

'If you must.' Carlyle sighed. Clicking off, he was delighted to see Mahek was pulling into Drury Lane. He told her to drop him at the corner of Macklin Street, they exchanged numbers and he reiterated his promise to repay the favour, in due course.

Mahek stuck the card behind the meter. 'Let's hope I don't need to call you.'

'You never know,' Carlyle advised. As she pulled away, he headed into Winter Garden House. His flat would be empty, but he was too tired to care.

TWENTY-ONE

Sitting in a windowless interview room, Detective Constable Nick Dawson looked exactly the same as Reuben Barnwell, save for the ID on a lanyard round his neck. Beside him, Melanie Wiggins came across as tired and irritable. According to Alex Morrow, the lawyer was sinking under an impossible caseload.

. Carlyle had no compunction about adding to her woes. 'Your client is facing a gross misconduct hearing.'

'You're the ones who should be facing charges,' Wiggins glared at Carlyle and O'Sullivan from behind a pile of papers, 'for sabotaging a long-term, undercover operation.'

Carlyle was having none of it. 'He put his girlfriend in hospital.'

'My client was deployed as an undercover officer against extremists who promoted violence for political ends. He accepted the risks so he could protect law-abiding members of society.'

'There isn't even a complaint,' Dawson piped up. 'Laura wouldn't dob me.'

'I bet she would,' said O'Sullivan, 'if she knew who you really were.'

The default smirk vanished. 'You wouldn't dare.' Dawson looked like he wanted to rip the inspector's face off. 'You clowns sit in your offices, you don't have the first clue about what it's like to be a real cop.'

'Nick, please.' Wiggins placed a restraining hand on his arm. 'Let me do the talking.'

Carlyle addressed Dawson: 'Tell me about James Gillespie.'

'Who?'

'The guy whose head you blew off.'

'The guy in the cell? Nothing to do with me.'

'We found your fingerprints at the scene.'

'I went down and had a look after Laura found him. Nasty.'

'What did you do with the other grenade?'

'What're you talking about? You've lost it, man.'

The lawyer tried to wrestle back control of the conversation. 'The Metropolitan Police Service has taken no action against my client. However, he will cooperate fully with any under-cover policing inquiry established by the commissioner.' There had been talk of such an inquiry for some time, prompted by a scandal in which another undercover cop had fathered children with two unsuspecting eco-warriors. 'Such a forum would be the only proper place for the wider issues surrounding Mr Dawson's duties to be aired. In the meantime, any further harassment from you will not be tolerated.' Packing up her things, Wiggins led her client from the room.

The door clicked shut. 'What did you make of that?' O'Sullivan asked.

'Pretty much as expected.' Carlyle's thoughts turned to Emily Quartz. 'I could make one call to a journalist and all hell will break loose.'

O'Sullivan looked aghast. 'You wouldn't.'

'Probably not,' the commander smiled, 'but they don't know that.'

'I told Angelini not to go there.'

'And she shouldn't. Neither will I, probably . . .'

'Your funeral.'

'I know what I'm doing.'

'Let's hope so. Meantime, the NYPD have tracked down Dwayne Doud, the film company guy who ran off to America.'

'I remember,' Carlyle lied. 'What does he have to say about the death of Hermione Lacemaker's agent?'

'Nothing,' O'Sullivan replied. 'He's dead, too. Run over by a lawnmower.'

'Novel,' was Carlyle's only response.

'A Big Boy diesel lawn tractor, weighing more than a quarter of a ton. Doud was mowing his mother's lawn and drove it off a thirty-foot bluff into a river at the bottom of the garden. He was crushed when it fell on top of him.'

'Never come across death by lawnmower before.'

'It's not as rare as you might think.' O'Sullivan tapped her phone. 'I googled it. On average, sixty-nine Americans a year die in lawnmower accidents.'

'A surprisingly high number,' Carlyle agreed.

'It is when you think the average number killed by Islamic terrorists in the US is only two.'

Carlyle tried to focus. 'What does the absence of Doud as a witness mean for Hermione Lacemaker?'

'The CPS'll decide.' O'Sullivan pointed at her computer screen. 'I'm sending them an update.'

'Fair enough.' Carlyle wondered how Abigail Slater might take this latest development. Badly, presumably, if it deprived her client of a witness who could support her defence.

'Oh, and Graham Hughes's mother's turned up. She's downstairs.'

'A bit late.'

'She lives in Newcastle,' O'Sullivan explained. 'Been on holiday in Florida. Took us ages to track her down. Wanna come and see her with me?'

Carlyle had time to kill. 'Might as well hear what she has to say.' He followed the inspector to an interview room and was introduced to a tanned, heavily made-up Emma Hughes. 'We're very sorry for your loss.'

The woman gave each officer an irritated look. 'It's a bit late for condolences.' Her accent seemed rather affected, what Carlyle's mum would have called a 'telephone voice'. 'What's going on?'

O'Sullivan took a deep breath. 'Well, we're continuing with our investigation.'

'That's not what I meant,' the woman complained. 'When can I get hold of Graham's stuff? He had a nice iPhone. Cost a grand. Not on a contract, see? He won't be needing it now, will he?'

'It's with the digital forensics guys downstairs,' O'Sullivan admitted. 'They're still trying to get it open.'

Sitting back in her seat, Hughes folded her arms. 'I know the password.'

O'Sullivan and Carlyle exchanged glances.

'I know the password,' Hughes repeated. 'It's—' She stopped herself. 'I'll let you know what it is if you give it me back.'

Carlyle shrugged. 'Deal.'

The woman gave a grunt of satisfaction.

'What is it, then?'

'What?'

'The password.'

The woman's eyes narrowed. 'How do I know you'll keep your word?'

'I give you my word as a Metropolitan Police officer of more than thirty years' standing,' Carlyle said solemnly, avoiding O'Sullivan's eye.

'One, two, three, four, five, six in figures.'

'Eh?'

'One, two, three, four, five, six,' Hughes repeated. 'It's Graham's password for everything. He had to keep it simple – his memory was shite. And it was a double bluff. Passwords are supposed to be complicated, right? No one thinks you would use one that simple.'

'Ingenious,' was Carlyle's somewhat sarcastic verdict. 'I like it.'

'Give me a minute.' O'Sullivan rose from her chair. 'I'll go and get it for you.'

As the inspector left the room, Carlyle offered to fetch some refreshments. 'Would you like anything?'

'A coffee would be grand.' Hughes's face lit up like a kid at Christmas. 'And a bacon roll if there is one.'

'Sure.'

'And a Mars Bar, one of the big ones.'

'Here you go.' Carlyle placed a small paper bag on the table. 'A large coffee, *two* bacon rolls and a king-sized Mars Bar.'

Emma Hughes attacked the bag as if she hadn't eaten for months. 'Get any sugar?'

Carlyle had not. He placed his own coffee on the table. 'I'll go back for some.'

'Grand.' Hughes started on the first roll with gusto.

O'Sullivan intercepted him on the way back to the meeting room. She wiggled the shiny iPhone in her hand. 'You've got to see this.' She started a video and placed the phone in his hand.

'What am I watching?'

'One minute twelve seconds of Graham Hughes threatening Hermione Lacemaker. He hits her, then she starts fighting back. I'm guessing Dwayne Doud must've shot it on Hughes's phone. Then he tossed the phone on the sofa and legged it.'

Carlyle let the clip roll through to the end before shoving the phone into his pocket. 'Is this enough to prove self-defence?'

'I'd have thought so. Up to the CPS, though.'

'Get them a copy of this right away,' Carlyle instructed. 'Tell them we need a quick decision. Best to arrange a meeting for us to see the chief Crown prosecutor.'

'Like that's going to happen.' O'Sullivan snorted.

'I know Charlotte Pritchard.' Carlyle wasn't much of a name-dropper, but it seemed appropriate, under the circumstances. 'She did the decent thing in relation to Joey Dunlop.' Dunlop was a classic hard-luck story: single parent with terminal cancer, arrested for use of medicinal cannabis, his daughter put, briefly, into care, creating the predictable media shitstorm. Pritchard had read the file and dropped the charges immediately.

'Didn't have much choice,' O'Sullivan suggested.

Carlyle wasn't having it. 'How often does common sense prevail in our organisation?' he asked. 'Pritchard's one of the good ones.'

'If you say so.'

'I say so. The woman *listens*. Tell her PA we want to see her today. We'll only need ten minutes. If there's a problem, I'll call her myself.'

'What about the mother?'

'I'll handle her,' Carlyle promised.

'Are you going to give her the phone?'

Carlyle scoffed at the question. 'Of course not.'

'But you said—'

'The woman'll learn a valuable lesson.' Carlyle chuckled. 'Never trust a copper.'

He let O'Sullivan disappear before heading back into the interview room. Hughes had finished her 'snack' and the rubbish was strewn around the table to prove it. Carlyle dropped a handful of sugar sachets on the table, watching in dismay as the woman immediately dumped the contents of two in her coffee. 'I'm afraid we've got a problem.' Hughes slurped her coffee and scowled at him at the same time. 'Graham's phone was sent last night to the digital forensics centre in Milton Keynes for further investigation. The people here couldn't do anything with it. I've asked them to send it right back, but it might take a day or two.'

'But I'm on the train back to Newcastle tonight.' Hughes emptied her coffee cup with a succession of gulps.

'I'll courier it up to you as soon as we have it. And we'll get all the rest of Graham's stuff back to you as quickly as we can.'

Clearly not happy, Hughes struggled out of her seat.

'It'll only be a couple of days.'

'Fair enough,' Hughes sighed, 'if it's the best you can do.'

Always the gentleman, Carlyle held open the door. 'You know the way out? Left down the corridor and right at the end.' After the woman had left, he set about clearing up the mess she'd left behind.

Charlotte Pritchard was out of town, attending an anti-terrorism conference in Basel. The chief Crown prosecutor did, however, take his call. After a minimum of small-talk, Carlyle got to the point.

'Hermione Lacemaker.'

'I'm aware of the Lacemaker case,' Pritchard told him, 'as you might imagine.'

'This video puts her in the clear.'

'I've had a look at it, and it's pretty compelling. However, things must run their course. The case officer's on holiday this week. I'll ask her to look at it as soon as she's back.'

It was not the answer Carlyle wanted to hear. 'Meanwhile, Hermione's stuck in Bronzefield.'

'There are worse places to be on remand.'

It was a fair point – HMP Bronzefield was a relatively new prison, with better facilities than most – but not one that would placate Abigail Slater. 'Her lawyer'll go berserk.'

'She's your lawyer as well, I hear.'

Carlyle couldn't hide his surprise. 'Where did you get that from?'

'I heard it on the grapevine.' Pritchard wasn't revealing her sources. 'Isn't it a bit of a conflict of interest?'

'I'm not a client of Slater's.' Carlyle hadn't signed any contract. Indeed, after his conversation with the commissioner, he was hoping that the lawyer's services would no longer be required. 'Your source is mistaken.'

Pritchard didn't probe any further. 'There's still gossip,' was the limit of her observation. 'We must play this by the book.'

'What would happen,' Carlyle asked innocently, 'if the video from Hughes's phone were to turn up on the internet?'

'Don't threaten me, Commander.' Pritchard's tone turned several degrees colder.

'This is still a big story. You saw what happened with those Kenny Schenk pictures. If it came out the CPS was sitting on evidence exonerating Hermione Lacemaker, we'd get a right kicking from the media.'

'We're not sitting on anything,' Pritchard snapped. 'We *are* doing things properly.'

'I know you are,' Carlyle said sympathetically. 'But these things can be spun in different ways.'

'You manipulative bastard.'

'You sound like my wife,' Carlyle joked.

'Poor woman deserves a medal.'

Helen would doubtless agree, Carlyle thought. 'Your case officer, she must have a deputy, right? How long does it take to get a view on a one-minute video?'

'All right,' Pritchard sighed, 'give us an hour.'

'Thank you.'

'In the meantime, you can work on the assumption the case against Hermione Lacemaker will be dropped. I'd have thought Bronzefield should be able to release her tomorrow.'

'I'll get the paperwork ready.'

Pritchard bowed to the inevitable. 'But, Commander, if you

ever try to threaten me again it will be the end of your career.'

'I wasn't—' Carlyle started to protest, but the line was dead.

If his conversation with the chief Crown prosecutor was tetchy, speaking to the commissioner was worse. On speakerphone, from her countryside retreat, Virginia Thompson sounded grumpier than ever. 'Who is this guy Sandro Gassid?'

Carlyle was hearing the guy's surname for the first time. 'He killed Gareth Mills.' Sitting in his office, he contemplated the green walls. Was it too late to change the colour? He whizzed off an email to Joaquin, asking him to find out. 'Some kind of personal dispute.'

'Why am I reading about this online?'

'The Irish police,' Carlyle improvised as he scanned Emily Quartz's story. 'They leak like a sieve.'

'They found him dead on a farm.'

Dead? Carlyle's dismay was fleeting. A dead Sandro didn't need to be extradited; a dead Sandro wouldn't go off message. It looked like another problem had solved itself.

'Shot in the head.'

'Hm.'

'It claims Victoria Dalby-Cummins owns the farm.'

Bloody Emily Quartz. Maybe there were some loose ends after all. That was the problem with journalists: once you'd wound them up, they could go off in any direction. 'I don't know,' he said casually, trying to make it sound like an incidental detail, 'but I've delivered you Gareth Mills's killer in double-quick time, as requested.'

'Doesn't look like you had much to do with it,' Thompson observed.

'Better to be lucky than smart,' Carlyle philosophised.

'Gassid's definitely our man?'

'One hundred per cent. I'll send you a report.'

'I want to be sure he was acting alone and that this has nothing to do with you-know-what.'

You-know-what being BDS and the sale of the surplus police stations.

'It was nothing to do with that,' Carlyle reassured her. 'It was a personal thing. They were fighting over a woman at the XY Club.'

There was a pause, then Thompson said, 'Peter's a member.'

'Sorry?'

'My husband is a VIP member of the XY Club.' The disdain in Thompson's voice was clear. 'Gareth Mills got it for him. They would all go – Mills, Peter, Bruce and Chris Sollerdiche – a regular little boys' night out.'

'He told you this?' Carlyle was amazed at the man's stupidity.

'It was Peter's attempt at damage limitation. Peter claims he only went there maybe half a dozen times, when Bruce Allen dragged him along for a few drinks. He says he never partook of the "additional services" on offer.'

That would explain the woman's foul mood, Carlyle thought. No one likes to hear about their old man hanging out in a knocking shop. 'I could check with the owner.'

'No need. The credit-card statements speak for themselves.'

Cash is king, Carlyle thought. 'We need to keep Peter – and you – as far away from this property deal as possible,' he advised. 'If one thing comes out, everything'll unravel, and it'll all come out.' He paused for effect. 'There's more than enough here to bury you both.'

'I told him I want a divorce,' Thompson declared. 'His business dealings are one thing, but this other stuff is not on.'

Carlyle didn't know what to make of that bombshell. 'I wouldn't be too hasty,' he blurted.

'What are you?' Thompson growled. 'A marriage guidance counsellor?'

'Not at all. Do what you have to do, obviously, but, for appearances' sake, it might be better to wait a bit. Put a bit of clear blue water between actually filing for divorce and ending Peter's involvement in BDS. Make it harder for people to join the dots.'

There was another pause, then Thompson asked, 'Do you think anyone could make the connection?'

'Maybe.' Emily Quartz could, Carlyle thought, if I spell it out for her. 'Why take the risk?'

'Let me think about it. In the meantime, I got a message from Chris Sollerdiche. He says you turned up unannounced at his house and were rude to his girlfriend.'

'Who was off her face on drugs,' Carlyle pointed out.

'It wouldn't surprise me in the slightest.' Talking about the peccadilloes of others seemed to cheer Thompson up a little. 'I've met her a couple of times and she was clearly intoxicated on both occasions. Why she goes out with that whale Sollerdiche is beyond me.'

'Because he's rich?'

'Surely she doesn't need the money. She must've made millions from modelling.'

'There's millions and then there's more money than you know what to do with,' Carlyle reflected.

'I don't get it.'

'What does any model see in a fat, middle-aged billionaire?'

'He's a nasty piece of work, as well as being a pig.'

Carlyle wondered what Sollerdiche had done to offend the commissioner. 'More than ever, he's gonna be the driving force behind BDS now Mills has gone.'

Thompson was mute.

'Have you spoken to the chair of the B and I sub-committee about re-opening the sale process?'

'Not yet. It's on my to-do list, along with a million other things.'

Carlyle had no sympathy. It might be tough at the top, but it was a hell of a lot tougher at the bottom. 'And what about Bruce Allen?'

'Don't you worry about Bruce,' Thompson replied, her grumpiness levels rising again. 'I'll deal with him, like I'll deal with my husband. I'll sort out my loose ends, you sort out yours.'

'Yes.' Loose end number one being Vicky Dalby-Cummins. What the hell was he going to do with her? Before he could come up with any ideas, Joaquin appeared in the doorway.

'Bruce Allen's here to see you.'

'Tell him I'm not in,' Carlyle said reflexively.

'Not a very convincing lie, Commander.' Allen slipped past the PA and dropped into the chair in front of Carlyle's desk.

Muttering to himself, Joaquin stalked off.

'What do you want?' Carlyle demanded.

Allen eyed the phone sitting on the desk. 'Were you speaking to the commissioner?'

'None of your business.'

'Don't think you can get away with this, Carlyle. Virginia's change of heart doesn't alter the big picture. The sale of those police stations is a done deal. If the Met tries to back out now, it'll be tied up in litigation for years.'

'Let me see,' Carlyle rubbed his chin, 'we've got one guy dead, one guy, you, taking backhanders, and another guy, the commissioner's other half, trying to make a fortune out of a deal that will defraud the Met out of hundreds of millions of pounds. Plus, Terry Brunel's in jail.' And you still haven't got him out, he reminded himself. 'All in all, it's gonna make a very interesting court case.'

'The lawyers say we'd have an excellent chance.'

'That's what lawyers always say,' Carlyle scoffed. Getting to his feet, he pointed to the door. 'Now, if you don't mind, I'm busy.'

Allen made no effort to move. 'I understand you went to see Chris Sollerdiche at his house.'

'Hardly surprising, given I was investigating the murder of one of Mr Sollerdiche's close business associates.'

'*Sir Christopher* has made it very clear he expects the BDS deal to close without further ado. He is a very important man, far more important than the commissioner, so I strongly recommend you do as you're told.'

'Thank you for clarifying.' Carlyle again pointed to the door. 'Now piss off.'

Joaquin reappeared after Allen had stormed out. 'He's a very angry man. He should get help.'

'That's not a bad idea.' Carlyle had a minor epiphany. 'Who's his assistant?'

'I don't think he has one. He uses people from the pool.'

'Who do you know over there?'

Joaquin offered a couple of names.

'Why don't you get one of them to book Mr Allen in on an anger-management course?' Carlyle recalled an excruciating course he had been forced to attend, not long after his promotion. 'Maybe throw in a bit of diversity training as well.'

'Mindfulness classes.' Joaquin chortled.

'Perfect.' Carlyle had no idea what mindfulness was, but it sounded suitably crap.

'Unconscious-bias training?'

'Whatever you think'll annoy him most. Make it some kind of residential thing, as far away from London as you can find. A week would be good – get him out of the building for a while.'

'I like the idea,' Joaquin said, 'but he wouldn't go.'

'I'll speak to the commissioner, get her to insist on his attendance as a condition of his continued working in her office.'

'You can do that?'

'Me and the commissioner,' Carlyle held up two intertwined fingers, 'we're like that.'

'Wouldn't it be easier to sack him?'

'Let's make him do the course first, and *then* get him sacked.'

'If you think it'll work.' Joaquin moved on to more pressing matters, for him, at least, 'Aditi's due back from her gastric-band surgery next week.' He pointed at the floor with his pen. 'Personnel says she has to get her old job back or she'll sue us. They want to send me back downstairs.'

'Let me talk to the HR people. I'll get it sorted out.'

'You said that last time.'

'I'll handle it,' Carlyle promised. 'In the meantime, do me a favour, find out what's happened to Terry Brunel, the BDS guy. Last heard of, he was being held in the cells at Kentish Town.'

'They moved him to Bure, locked him up with a bunch of sex offenders.' Joaquin gave Carlyle a thin smile. 'He rang up and complained you hadn't got him out.'

'If he rings back, tell him I'm on the case.'

Joaquin rolled his eyes. 'I hope I never need you to get me out of prison.'

'These things take time.' Carlyle took a moment to contemplate the profound truth he had imparted. 'Where is Bure anyway?'

Joaquin had no idea.

Picking up his phone, Carlyle consulted the definitive database, Wikipedia. 'It's a Category C prison in Norfolk. What's he complaining about? It's basically a holiday camp.'

'I'll remind him next time he starts moaning about having to take a shower with a bunch of paedos.'

Did they put kiddie-fiddlers in Category C? Carlyle doubted it. 'I'll sort him out,' he promised. 'And Aditi. Have faith.'

'Aditi is the priority.' Joaquin jabbed his pen in Carlyle's direction. 'Otherwise, I quit.'

'Rest assured, Aditi is my number-one priority.'

Joaquin gave him a hard stare.

'Well, she's definitely in the top three.' Carlyle made a bolt for the door. 'Tell HR to call me.'

'Yes, sir.' Joaquin clicked his heels together and offered a mock salute as the commander skipped past.

'Good man.' Carlyle saluted back. 'As you were.'

TWENTY-TWO

Walking through Hyde Park, Carlyle took a call from Danny Hunter.

'The last hand grenade's still missing,' the former military cop reported.

'Not good.'

'I got a hit on one James Montgomery Gillespie,' Hunter continued, 'and that's not good either.'

Carlyle contemplated a group of swimmers in the Serpentine. 'Go on.'

'Gillespie grew up in Belfast. He was quite senior in the IRA back in the day.' Largely now forgotten outside Ireland, the Irish Republican Army was the Al Qaeda of its day, Public Enemy Number One. 'He was also an informer for British Intelligence. Special Branch blackmailed him over his taste for sex with men in public toilets.'

'He did well to survive,' Carlyle observed. The IRA was not very liberal when it came to sexual matters. Or snitches, for that matter.

'He'd been living quietly in London for years until he went missing a couple of weeks ago.'

'Sounds like our man,' Carlyle admitted. 'How did you find all this out?'

'Better not to ask,' Hunter advised. 'I'll keep digging but

go carefully on this one, John. If Gillespie's old comrades – on either side – are involved in this, we're talking about some seriously dangerous people. Do not get in their way.'

Carlyle tried to laugh off the warning. 'I can look after myself.'

Hunter was not fooled. 'Tread carefully, my friend.'

Half a dozen riders were taking Rotten Row at a gentle pace. One looked in Carlyle's direction and started to wave.

'I've been expecting you.'

Carlyle came to a halt at the iron railings running alongside the bridle path.

Victoria Dalby-Cummins looked down on him from her grey mount. 'We need to talk.'

Carlyle agreed.

'You know the Cromwell Club?' She jerked a thumb over her shoulder. 'Down the road.' Carlyle had never heard of it. 'You'll see it – it's got three flags hanging outside – on the far side of the Albert Hall. Tell them you're my guest. Order a drink, and a snack, if you like. I'll see you there in about half an hour, after I get back from the stables.'

In the event, Carlyle was kept waiting for more than an hour. Deep into his third Jameson's, enjoying people-watching in the opulent surroundings of the Cromwell Club's Hambleton Bar, he minded not a jot. Finally making an appearance, Dalby-Cummins meandered across the room, acknowledging a number of fellow members before arriving at his table.

'This is some place.'

'You're making yourself at home, I see.' She had showered and changed into a pair of jeans, torn at the knees, with a white T-shirt under a Chanel jacket.

'Just enjoying watching how the other half live.' It sounded chippy but he couldn't be bothered to hide it.

'It's how the other one per cent live, these days, Commander.' Dalby-Cummins dropped into the chair next to his. 'I fear you might be a bit out of date.'

'Showing my age,' Carlyle conceded. 'But this is a very nice place. I'd never heard of it before.'

'It opened a few years ago. Harry paid some astronomical sum for a lifelong founding membership, which turned out to be not so very long in the end.' She lowered her voice. 'The owners were a bit embarrassed about it, so they transferred his membership to me. You can't tell anyone, though. They're worried about the precedent.'

Carlyle promised he would keep schtum.

'I don't think Harry was ever here more than a handful of times but I'm managing to get his money's worth. The place has become a bit of a home-from-home for me. Like riding in the park, it's one of the things that make living in London a bit more bearable.'

'It's definitely a step up from the Chapel, no offence.'

'None taken.' Dalby-Cummins pointed to a bunch of promotional brochures spread on the low table in front of them. 'Last time I looked, it was ten grand to join and then six grand a year, if you're interested.'

Carlyle let out a low whistle. 'I think I might pass.'

'I could speak to the owners. They'd probably consider waiving the joining fee.'

'Still a bit rich for my blood, even on a commander's salary.'

'A hundred and ten thousand's not bad.' Dalby-Cummins displayed a surprising knowledge of the Met's pay scales.

'Don't forget the two grand London weighting.' Carlyle laughed mirthlessly.

'Two thousand, three hundred and seventy-three pounds.'

He professed surprise at her grasp of such a detail.

'I did some research before we first met.'

'When you wanted to put me on your payroll?' Carlyle sipped his whiskey.

'The offer's still there.'

'No, thanks.'

'Stubborn.'

Carlyle lifted his glass in salute. 'One of my better qualities.'

'Seriously, you shouldn't look a gift horse in the mouth.'

'You should *always* look a gift horse in the mouth,' Carlyle asserted. 'And then send it on its way. At least, you should if you're a cop.'

'I don't think the commissioner takes that approach.'

'I disagree. I think Thompson is straight. The problem is her husband.'

'Husbands can be difficult,' Dalby-Cummins agreed. 'I hear she's filing for divorce.'

Carlyle played dumb.

'The word is she's gay. The marriage has been a sham for some time.'

'Blimey. I suppose you never know what's going on in someone else's relationship.'

'What about you?' Dalby-Cummins enquired. 'Any dark secrets?'

'None.'

'Maybe we could create some.'

'Such as?'

'I could make a donation to your wife's charity, like you suggested.'

Carlyle vaguely recalled the ill-considered proposal. 'That idea's a non-starter. I floated it before things got . . . out of hand.'

'Out of hand?' Dalby-Cummins arched her eyebrows. 'This business with the police stations is nothing compared to some of the things I could tell you about.'

'I don't want to know.' Carlyle meant it.

'Perhaps, but I would still much prefer it if we had a stable and sustainable basis for our working relationship.'

Carlyle was irked by the business-speak. 'Which means what?' he asked.

'Which brings us back to my original proposition.'

'Which brings us back to my original no.'

'So puritanical.' She looked around the bar. 'A bit more pragmatism and you'd be able to join this place, no problem.'

Carlyle took a tiny sip of his drink. Three was his limit and he was trying to make it last. 'It's nice to visit, but I can live without it.'

'Why deny yourself? That's the Scots Presbyterian in you.' He shot her a look and she shot him one right back. 'Your salary wasn't the only thing I researched, obviously.'

'Let's not keep going back over old ground. What about you? You seem to be settling into London life very nicely.'

'Business is business. I need to be here most of the time. There's only so much you can do on the other end of a phone. I haven't been back to the farm in months. To be honest, I don't miss it nearly as much as I thought I would.'

'The place in Ireland?'

'Wales. I also have a place in Spain, one in Sicily and two in Argentina. My father collected them. It was a hobby that ended up getting a bit out of hand. Collectively, they make a small profit so I'm happy to keep hold of them.' A waiter appeared and she ordered some sparkling water and a chicken sandwich. 'Do you want anything else?'

Carlyle held up his glass, which still had a coating of whiskey in the bottom. 'I'm good.' He had a nice buzz going on which had taken the edge off any irritation he might otherwise have felt at such a lengthy preamble to the matter in hand. Once the waiter was out of earshot, he asked, 'Why did you have Sandro killed?'

'Why do you think? It's safer that way. Not to mention cheaper.'

Her total lack of bullshit was genuinely disconcerting. 'I thought you wanted to give him a chance.'

'Not everyone can succeed in this life.'

'Not when someone puts a bullet between your eyes.'

'Look,' she pouted, 'it's not like the boy had a lot to look forward to: prison, then deportation back to Syria, where they'd have killed him anyway. After torturing him for a while. His family is all dead.'

'A shit hand,' Carlyle agreed.

'When you get a shit hand, you fold. We've done the poor sod a favour, saved him a lot of pain.'

We?

'Plus, this outcome saves you a lot of work. And it's a great result for the taxpayer.' The waiter arrived with her order and Dalby-Cummins nibbled at her sandwich. 'What's done is done. We move on.'

'The Irish have launched their own murder inquiry.'

'Good luck to them. If and when they wish to speak to me, I'll be happy to oblige, even though I know nothing. In the meantime, what matters is that the Mills case is now closed. I gave you a great result there.' She offered Carlyle a moment to challenge, then asked, 'What's the latest on our property deal?'

'It's not "our" deal.' Carlyle sucked the last of the whiskey from his glass.

'You know what I mean. I've already had some meetings with prospective partners. People want official confirmation the process is being reopened.'

'It's coming.'

She waved her sandwich in the air. 'As soon as you like, Commander.'

***

A reception for the Royal Ballet wasn't his thing. Bruce Allen stood sullenly at the bar, sipping a glass of warm champagne.

'Cheer up. It might never happen.' Sir Christopher Sollerdiche, sponsor of the evening's event, placed an empty glass on the bar.

'Ready to leave?' Allen asked hopefully.

'I'm hosting this thing – it cost more than seventy grand for the champagne alone. I need to stick around.'

'They could have at least chilled it properly,' Allen griped.

A barman handed Sollerdiche a fresh glass, allowing him to ignore the barb. 'These dancers can drink like you wouldn't believe.' He paused to slurp. 'You'd have thought they'd be more abstemious, looking after their bodies type of thing.'

'Free booze is free booze.'

A tiny waitress appeared, offering a tray of mini hamburgers. Sollerdiche shovelled one into his mouth. 'Thanks. I'm starving.'

'Dinner would be good.' Allen still had hopes of a nice Malbec and a bloody steak at the nearby Rules restaurant.

'I told you, I can't leave early, I'm the host.' Sollerdiche snaffled another couple of mini burgers, tossing them into his maw like peanuts. 'Plus, I've got to wait for Sasha.'

Allen cursed. He would never complete a sensible conversation with his boss if he had to play gooseberry. 'I didn't know she was coming.'

'Why wouldn't she?' Sollerdiche reached for more food but the waitress had already turned her platter towards another group of guests. Muttering to himself, he consulted the massive watch on his wrist. 'Although she's more than an hour late.' His irritation stepped up a notch. 'Sash was never very good at timekeeping but, I swear, she's getting worse. Sometimes, I think she's even worse than my bloody missus.' He finished his drink and helped himself to another. 'I think she's gonna dump me, you know.'

The wife or the girlfriend? Allen kept the question to himself.

'Every so often, Sasha goes off and has a quick fling. Last

258

time it was with some Dutch war photographer barely older than her son. She's been very eclectic in her tastes. Doesn't go exclusively for older men.'

'Hm.' Allen felt himself blushing. Alcohol was clearly loosening his patron's tongue. He had never heard his boss discuss such matters before and it was making him feel deeply uncomfortable.

'I've come to accept it. There's no point in being possessive. If I want another woman, I take her. It's the same with Sasha. We're very alike in that regard. It's an on-off relationship. I can see another off-period looming.'

'Uh-huh.' What Allen knew about personal relationships you could write on the back of a fag packet. Technically speaking, he had lived with his mother until well into his thirties. His limited physical needs were met through a combination of online dating and Punternet. Mostly Punternet. Intellectual stimulation came from the crosswords in *The Times* and the *Spectator.* Emotion was for keeping under lock and key. He'd never had a 'partner' in his entire life. 'I didn't realise it was such a long-term thing with Sasha,' he stammered.

'A true meeting of minds is hard to find,' Sollerdiche declared. 'It would be hypocritical of me to stop Sasha having her fun. At the same time, I'd be very sad if she went off one day and never came back.'

If the girl had an ounce of sense, Allen thought, she'd run for the hills. Then again, there was no evidence to suggest she did. 'I'm sure Sasha'll be here soon. Meantime, we should catch up on business matters.' Resigned to not being properly fed, he resolved to keep their conversation as short as possible. 'Shall we go somewhere a bit quieter?'

'Here's fine.'

Allen looked around in dismay. 'It's not very private.'

'Trust me, no one in this room has the slightest interest in the sale of a few police stations. What's the latest?'

Allen leaned closer, trying to keep his voice as low as possible while still being audible over the buzz of conversation. 'The commissioner has agreed the auction will be reopened. There's no reason why BDS can't take part, but we'll need to submit a new, higher, bid.'

'But we've already won,' Sollerdiche growled. 'They're moving the goalposts.'

'It happens,' Allen said philosophically.

'Not to me, it doesn't.' Sollerdiche jabbed a fat finger into Allen's chest, causing him to wince. 'I've already got buyers lined up for half the sites. When we flip those, we'll already be in the money. There's no going back now. If those fucking coppers try to stiff us, we'll sue their arses off.',

'They've checked the contracts. Legally, they're entitled to stop the process and start again.'

'Doesn't matter.' Sollerdiche gave a dismissive wave of his hand. 'My lawyers can tie them up in court for years, decades even. They won't be able to sell a thing. Not raise a single penny piece for their coffers.'

'That wouldn't look good in the press. Plus, it wouldn't get us what we want any time soon.'

'I want those fucking police stations.' Sollerdiche smacked his palm on the bar. 'Speak to the commissioner, get her to change her mind – again. Otherwise, as well as unleashing the lawyers, I might buttonhole the home secretary. He's a guy who has enough common sense to do what I fucking tell him.'

Allen looked doubtful. 'Is he gonna be around much longer? There's talk of a reshuffle.'

'There's always talk of a reshuffle,' Sollerdiche observed, 'not that it matters. I can talk to this home secretary or I can talk to the next one. If I decide Virginia Thompson is past her sell-by date, she'll be out of Scotland Yard in less time than it takes to say, "You have the right to remain silent."' He laughed at his own joke. 'How long has she been in the job now?'

'Two years, as of last month.'

'Well, if she wants to make it three, she'd better stop messing about and show some bloody leadership. Show some *backbone*. The deal should've closed in days. Instead, it's taken months . . . years, held up by public-sector pen-pushers at every turn. It's not good enough.'

'It's rarely as simple as that.'

'Stop telling me how hard everything is, Bruce. It's always the same with you: problems, problems, problems. I need solutions.'

Allen's face reddened. 'The solution, it seems to me, is to deal with the meddlesome Commander Carlyle.'

'The little shit who turned up in my house the other night.'

'Carlyle's putting the squeeze on Virginia Thompson, threatening Peter with corruption charges if BDS were to win the auction with a lowball bid.'

'It wasn't a lowball bid,' Sollerdiche insisted. 'It was fair value. Well within the range given by the independent expert valuers.' That roughly translated as *It was more than a hundred million below the number randomly generated by the agents you paid to come up with the lowest price that was remotely credible.*

Spare me, Allen thought. He had heard the fat man's self-serving political analysis far too many times already. 'What about Peter?' he asked. 'He's the weak link in all this. Virginia's trying to play it cool, but I can see Carlyle's got her spooked.'

'We'll drop her husband as an adviser,' Sollerdiche said. 'Problem solved.'

Allen was unconvinced. 'Carlyle'll still come after both of them.'

Sollerdiche rubbed his chin. 'Well, maybe we hire Carlyle as an adviser. Make him an insider.'

'That's what Dalby-Cummins tried to do. He wouldn't take the money.'

'Maybe she didn't offer him enough.'

261

'Carlyle's not as stupid as he looks.'

'He looked pretty fucking stupid to me,' Sollerdiche grunted.

'All through his career, he's somehow just about kept on the right side of the line.'

'Everyone's got a price.'

'No one's found his yet. He's definitely in cahoots with Dalby-Cummins but she's not paying him.'

'Is he fucking her, you think?'

'Happily married.'

'Strange bloke,' Sollerdiche mused. 'If money and sex don't work, what are we going to do about him?'

About bloody time, you bastard.

'I'll take that as grateful thanks.' Sitting in a café near Golden Square, Carlyle deleted the text from the newly released Terry Brunel, crossing the builder off his mental to-do list.

Next was a message from Virginia Thompson. The commissioner confirmed she had spoken to the chair of the Building and Infrastructure sub-committee. The sale process regarding the surplus police stations would be restarted. Everything would go back to square one.

Carlyle finally turned his attention to the one problem that remained insoluble. Personnel had confirmed Aditi was entitled to return to the precise job she had held prior to her sick leave. Carlyle's protestations that the woman should never have been put in his office in the first place were met with stony silence.

Parking that problem, he rang Slater.

'Commander, I was about to call you.' The lawyer lied with such a complete disregard for any attempt at sincerity that it was impossible to take offence. 'Hermione was released from prison a couple of hours ago. I wanted to convey her thanks to you, as well as my own.'

'Sorry it took so long.'

'Ye-es. It's a shame you didn't find the video on Mr Hughes's phone rather earlier, but I suppose these things happen.'

'It took us for ever to break the password.' Carlyle didn't go into the details other than to complain, 'Bloody Apple were no use whatsoever.'

'Better late than never,' Slater offered graciously. 'I know you did your best, as did Inspector O'Sullivan. I'll make sure you're both left out of the civil claim – as far as is humanly possible.'

'The civil claim?'

'Wrongful arrest, illegal incarceration, loss of earnings – it's quite a list. I would estimate the shameless rush to put Hermione Lacemaker behind bars is going to cost the Met somewhere north of seven figures.'

'You've got to be kidding.' Carlyle groaned.

'You know me, John,' Slater purred, 'I don't joke. If the Met has any sense, they'll settle out of court. Luckily, most of the blame can be conveniently laid at the door of Gina Sweetman.'

Fine by me, Carlyle thought.

'Speaking of the assistant commissioner,' Slater continued, 'I think it's probably best if I don't represent you after all.'

'You're dumping me?' Carlyle tried to sound suitably miffed. In reality, he was delighted Slater was terminating their embryonic relationship before he'd got down to doing so. He adopted a weary tone. 'I suppose it would make things too complicated.'

'I can recommend a couple of other lawyers . . .' Slater paused '. . . although they might not be able to provide a pro bono service.'

'Send me their details and I'll think about what I want to do.'

'Sounds like a plan,' Slater agreed happily.

As she ended the call, a calendar alert popped up on Carlyle's screen. 'Shit, what day is it?' Pulling up his diary, he did a double-take. How the hell could I forget? Muttering to himself, he hustled out of the café, heading for the tube.

He arrived at Terminal Five with almost ten minutes to spare, only to find Helen's flight was delayed. By the time he finally spotted his wife emerging through Arrivals in her Avalon-branded T-shirt, he was in a foul mood.

Looking tanned and healthy, Helen embraced him warmly. 'I wasn't expecting you to come.'

'I was able to bunk off.' Feeling his spirits rising, Carlyle gave her an extra squeeze before releasing his grip.

'Good for you.' Helen fished a jumper out of her backpack and pulled it over her head. Next came a fleece, then a coat.

Carlyle rolled his eyes. 'Got enough layers to put on?'

'It was thirty-six degrees when I left.' Helen handed him the backpack and a smaller holdall. 'This is a shock to the system.'

Taking the bags, he led her towards the lifts for the Underground platforms. 'How was the trip?'

'Oh, you know, the usual mix of inspiration and despair. The charity is doing some great work, truly wonderful stuff, but it's not even a drop in the ocean. Bottom line is there's not enough cash to cover even a fraction of the things we need to do.'

Carlyle wondered how much Vicky Dalby-Cummins might have donated to Avalon. Probably not enough to make a difference, and certainly not enough to make the risk worthwhile. 'I was thinking we could go out to dinner.'

Helen gave him a weary smile. 'Not tonight. I just want a hot bath and then go to sleep in my own bed.'

'How's Alice?' Helen asked, as they waited for a train.

'All good,' was Carlyle's response, crossing his fingers.

She looked up at him, the irritation in her face obvious. 'Bloody hell, John, you haven't spoken to her in all the time I've been away, have you?'

'Well,' Carlyle looked guiltily at his feet, 'she's doing her own thing. I don't want to dog her every step. If she had a problem, she'd let us know.'

'You're hopeless,' Helen complained.

'It's a question of getting the balance right.'

'It's a question of showing an interest in your only child. What's so important you can't even give your daughter a call?'

'The usual.'

'It's always the same with you,' Helen complained.

Carlyle gritted his teeth. It was going to be a long, slow journey into London on the Piccadilly line.

At least they were each able to get a seat. Fiddling with his phone, he discovered a text from Emily Quartz: *I need a quote about Victoria Dalby-Cummins.*

Carlyle frowned. *Why?* He sent the reply, then realised, underneath the airport, without any coverage, it would be going nowhere.

'I don't suppose you've done any shopping while I was away, either.' Back at the flat, Helen gave him a list of items to get from Sainsbury's before taking herself off for a soak. Typing it onto his phone, he remembered Quartz and re-sent the earlier text.

The reply arrived as he was going down the stairs: *Because she's dead.*

TWENTY-THREE

Emily Quartz read from her notes. 'She was halfway across when an old guy in a Skoda took her out.' The journalist pointed at the zebra crossing outside the Chapel. 'An eighty-six-year-old man was questioned at the scene but released without charge. He claimed he never saw her. He must've been going at quite a lick, though. He sent her across the road and right under the wheels of a bus. It was a mess, by all accounts.'

RIP Vicky Dalby-Cummins. Live by the sword, die by the pensioner.

'She was going for a smoothie.' Quartz pointed to the juice bar on the far side of the road. 'Her PA offered to get it for her, but she wanted to go out for some air.'

'Unfortunate decision,' Carlyle observed.

'I know, random, huh?'

'Yeah.' Was this genuinely an accident? Looked at another way, it was as close to the perfect murder as you could get. People were run over all the time and no one gave it a second thought. Even if a case went to court, juries rarely convicted, and if they did, the perpetrator was probably looking at a suspended sentence, as long as they weren't on their phone, or drunk.

Easy.

He turned to Quartz. 'And this is a story for you?'

'Crime queen dead at thirty-eight – it'll make a great part of my series on London's semi-criminal underworld.'

The term 'semi-criminal' made Carlyle scowl. In his book, you were either criminal or you weren't. 'You're doing a series?'

'I am now. I was gonna start with Terry Brunel, but Victoria Dalby-Cummins just became a bit more topical.'

'Your call.' Carlyle wasn't going to tell the woman how to do her job. 'Whatever you write, remember to keep me out of it.'

'I always look after my sources.'

'Glad to hear it.'

'I still need a quote. An unnamed source talking about what the woman was really like.'

'Make it up,' he suggested.

'I can't. It would be in complete breach of our editorial standards.' She looked at him expectantly.

'Okay.' Clearing his throat, Carlyle took a moment to compose his thoughts. 'What about "Vicky was a bit of a surprise package. A self-proclaimed country girl, she came to London to take over her husband Harry's business interests – *business interests* in quotation marks – and went into partnership with Vernon Holder"?'

'Is that it?' The reporter was unimpressed. 'Feel free to add a bit more colour.'

'Like what?' Carlyle asked, exasperated.

'What about Holder?'

'Vernon Holder,' Carlyle said dully, 'was an old-school gangster and the man who was suspected of having Harry killed.'

'And where is he now?' Quartz asked, trying to tease more out of her reluctant source.

'That,' Carlyle admitted, 'is a bit of a mystery. No one has seen or heard from Vernon in ages. The suspicion is Vicky lulled him into a false sense of security with their partnership, then took her revenge.'

Quartz pointed towards the Chapel. 'One of the girls told me there was a rumour Vicky fed Vernon to her pigs.'

'Sounds a bit far-fetched to me.'

'Maybe.' The journalist was clearly torn between wanting it to be true and knowing it was almost certainly bollocks. After reading back his quote, she asked, 'How would you sum her up?'

'A smart businesswoman with some dodgy associates.'

'Good.' More scribbling. 'And her legacy?'

'Legacy?' Carlyle made a face. 'Buggered if I know.'

Inside the club, he found Chief Inspector Trevor May, the officer in charge of the investigation into Dalby-Cummins's death, propping up one of the bars. Carlyle flashed his ID and the women melted away.

'What d'you want?' May demanded grumpily. 'I'm off the clock.' He was a small man of late middle age, with the air of a burned-out cop waiting for retirement. 'My shift finished more than an hour ago.'

'What happened?'

'The woman got run over. End of.'

'An accident?'

May slurped lager from a pint pot. 'What's it to you?'

'I'm your superior officer. Humour me.'

'I've already filed my report.'

'Gimme the highlights.'

'The highlights.' May let out a sigh of such profound weariness you might have imagined he'd been asked to climb Everest solo, without oxygen. 'The deceased was *accidentally* struck while crossing the road by a Mr Alfred Sunderland, driving a Skoda Octavia.' He paused to take further liquid refreshment. 'The car knocked Ms Dalby-Cummins into the path of a 158 bus, heading towards Blackhorse Road. The bus driver was a Hazel Norris. The front right wheel of the bus went straight over the victim's head and . . . splat.'

'Game over.'

'It was a hell of a mess, I can tell you. Ms Norris had just finished her lunch. Most of it ended up back on her lap. The smell was fucking terrible.' May wrinkled his nose. 'She was covered in puke and hysterical – you can probably see it on YouTube already. The fucking passengers were laughing and joking and filming it on their phones. One of them was such a cunt he wouldn't stop filming until I waved a pair of cuffs in his face and told him he was about to get nicked. Meanwhile, the bloody driver's doing her nut. The paramedics had to give her an injection to calm her down. They took her off to hospital – she might never drive a bus again, they reckon.'

'Some people take things like that very badly.'

'Some people are twats,' was May's verdict. 'Anyway, those were the highlights. Now, if you don't mind, sir, I need to be off.' Finishing his drink, he made to leave, but Carlyle blocked his way.

'Tell me about the Skoda driver.'

May clearly wanted to tell him to fuck off. Instead, he swallowed his annoyance and said, 'Alfred Sunderland, been driving for more than sixty-odd years. This was the first accident he'd ever had. Never even had a parking ticket. Says he didn't see her. Wasn't speeding, wasn't on his phone, wasn't intoxicated, of sound mind and body, as far as you can be at that stage of the game. He was very calm and composed about it all. Not like the bloody bus driver.'

'Where was he going?'

'He has a cousin in Epping. They get together every month or so. He's driven along this road hundreds of times.' May spread his arms in acknowledgement of the random nature of the universe. 'The victim was very unlucky. Shit happens.'

'No charges against Mr Sunderland, then?'

'No charges,' May confirmed. 'I've basically had to waste

my entire shift on a sodding traffic accident.' He eyed Carlyle suspiciously, asking again, 'What's it to you?'

Carlyle ignored the question. 'Don't you need to be somewhere?'

As May slouched out, Carlyle tapped the Twitter app on his phone and typed in 'London traffic death'. After a little searching, he found a link to a video showing the aftermath of the accident. The forty-second clip had been shot by a gawker on the pavement rather than a bus passenger. May made a fleeting appearance, as did the unfortunate bus driver, but there was no sign of Dalby-Cummins or the Skoda driver. A bit more digging yielded three other videos. One was of particular interest. After a couple of attempts, he managed to pause the video at the point where it showed a tall elderly gent in a flat cap and black fleece, standing next to May.

Alfred Sunderland, I presume. Given the quality of the video, it was impossible to make any judgement about the man's demeanour. Blowing up the image, Carlyle peered at the red capitals over the left breast of the fleece. 'ACP'.

'Can I get you a drink?'

Carlyle looked up from his phone to see Dalby-Cummins's office manager standing in front of him. To his relief, he remembered her name: Karolina. It looked like she'd shed a tear or two for her boss.

'How're you doing?'

'Oh, you know.' Slipping behind the bar, Karolina helped herself to a large vodka. 'It's a hell of a shock.'

Carlyle wasn't going to let her drink alone. He pointed at a bottle of Jameson's on a shelf behind the bar. 'Did you see it?'

'I was upstairs.' Karolina reached for the bottle and dumped two inches of whiskey into a tumbler. 'Ice? Water?'

'Always neat.'

'Good man.' She handed him his drink.

'Thanks.' Carlyle took an appreciative sip. 'You were in the office?'

'Yes.' Karolina raised her glass. 'To Vicky.'

'To Vicky.'

'I heard the screaming.' She took a mouthful of vodka and swallowed. 'By the time I got to the window it was kind of all over.'

'What did you see?'

'The aftermath of an accident. Some people were in the road, trying to help but the police were there very quickly. The ambulance too.' Karolina let her gaze drift off into the middle distance. 'I knew it was Vicky – I could see her lying there – but I didn't want to go down. I kept thinking it should've been me. I mean, I offered to go and get her a juice, but she wanted some air. How random is that?'

'Pretty random,' Carlyle agreed. He looked around the empty bar. 'Not opening tonight?'

'I guess we should, but a lot of the girls are too stressed, you know?' She gunned the rest of the vodka and poured herself another.

'I'd go easy on the booze.'

Her look said, *Mind your own business*.

'What'll happen to the club, now?'

'That's the question we've all been asking. I've no idea. I suppose we'll keep it going until it gets sold, or whatever.'

'Ah, well, good luck.' Finishing his drink, Carlyle dropped a business card onto the bar. 'If I can be of any assistance, let me know.'

'Sure.' She stuck the card into the pocket of her jeans. 'I will.'

'The Metropolitan Police Service,' Carlyle offered, as he headed for the exit, 'is always here to help.'

'Have you been drinking?' Helen wasn't cutting him any slack. 'Where's the shopping?'

Carlyle had to confess he'd been side-tracked by a matter of life and death. 'I've still got the list, though.' He waved his phone, Exhibit A for the defence.

'Well, go and get it, then,' she demanded. 'And bring me a latte on the way back in.'

'Certainly, my sweet.' He planted a gentle kiss on her forehead before turning on his heel and heading back out of the door. 'My pleasure.'

TWENTY-FOUR

The Building and Infrastructure sub-committee held a minute's silence for Superintendent Susan Moran. By Carlyle's estimation, it lasted forty-four seconds. With the chair waylaid by an unspecified family crisis, the deputy chair brought them to the meat of the agenda: the proposed sale of the decommissioned police stations.

'Before we go any further,' he announced, in a voice so low Carlyle struggled to hear, 'there's a motion to postpone the meeting.'

Carlyle immediately smelt a rat. 'A motion from whom?' he demanded.

All heads swivelled in the direction of the new boy.

'The chair proposed it,' the deputy chair managed to raise his voice a tad, 'and I seconded it.'

'But the chair's not here.' Carlyle's complaint generated a mixture of amusement and dismay around the table. 'We need to crack on. This is a very important issue.'

'That's why the chair wants to postpone our discussion.' The deputy chairman was clearly narked by Carlyle's unwillingness to back down. 'He wants to be present when any decisions are made.' When Carlyle started to protest further, he was ruthlessly cut off. 'Let's take a vote on it.'

***

This is why I don't go to bloody meetings. Carlyle's frustration was laced with satisfaction at the vindication of his view of committees as a complete waste of time. Voting to call a halt to proceedings by ten to one, his colleagues had fled quicker than a bunch of fifth-formers at the school bell. 'You're a berk for even trying,' he admonished himself. Taking out his phone, he re-watched the Alfred Sunderland video. Having given the matter some thought, he'd decided the 'ACP' on the elderly driver's fleece had to be a clothing brand or perhaps the name of a company or some other organisation.

Time to do some primary research. He tried searching for brands called ACP, with no joy. When it came to companies, Google helpfully came up with more than thirteen million listings, including the Association of Clinical Pathologists, the American Christian Party and a California-based outfit called Alternative Cannabis Providers Inc.

'O-kay.' Lifting his feet onto the table, he sat back in his chair, stroking his chin, a parody of a man in thought. After a while, he typed in 'ACP' and 'Sollerdiche' and was rewarded with a far more manageable 114 results, the top one being for Antigen Capital Partners.

'Of course.' Why hadn't he made the connection immediately? Clicking on the link, Carlyle wandered around the ACP website until he came across a short biography for a strategic alternatives consultant called Olly Sunderland. Could Olly be the son of the Skoda-driving Alfred? More likely the grandson, Carlyle decided, unless the guy's photograph had been airbrushed to the max.

Carlyle imagined how an elderly relative of one of Gareth Mills's employees could have been used to run down Victoria Dalby-Cummins. It was, he had to admit, quite a clever ploy. Proving such a thesis would be impossible, however, and he had to remain focused on the matter in hand. His priority was still to ensure that the low-ball bid for the police stations was torn up and the auction process restarted.

Back in the office, he found Joaquin tapping away at his computer. The PA peered at him over the top of his monitor. 'Have you sorted out the Aditi situation yet?'

'I've told HR they've got to sort it out.' Joaquin looked sceptical but Carlyle had more pressing concerns. 'Can you get hold of the commissioner for me? I need a word.'

Grumbling, Joaquin picked up the phone. After a bit of chat back and forth with Virginia Thompson's PA, he informed Carlyle that the commissioner had left the building. 'She's gone to a private meeting – not to be disturbed under any circumstances. Her diary's crazy and she's off on holiday next week, but I can try to get you a slot with her when she gets back.'

'Great.'

'If you can't wait that long, you could try gatecrashing her private meeting.'

'I could,' Carlyle agreed, 'if I knew where it was.'

Joaquin gave him a big smile. 'It's at Pakenham's.'

The club had a timeless, airless quality, which suggested its many clocks had stopped sometime around the early 1950s. Sitting in the lobby, Carlyle was reminded of nothing so much as the setting of an Ealing comedy. All colour had bled out of the place, to the point where the commander almost imagined he was seeing the world in black-and-white.

Getting this far had been a minor triumph. His warrant card had cut no ice with Pakenham's doorman, and only after an amount of petulant foot-stamping, 'Do you know who I am?'-ing and threats of one sort or another was he allowed to pass beneath the *A Deo rex* logo – From God the King – inscribed over the entrance.

Inside, further progress was blocked by an officious man in

full penguin suit who asserted the lack of a tie round Carlyle's neck prevented access to the inner sanctum. An extended discussion and another show of petulance from Carlyle led to a tie being produced from the club's 'emergency supply'. The stained green and blue item depicted a bunch of grapes on the vine.

Carlyle contemplated it with considerable dismay. 'Haven't you got anything else?'

The man's expression indicated he'd like to use the tie to strangle his unwelcome guest. 'It is only a temporary loan,' he pronounced solemnly, 'you will need to return it on your way out.'

Carlyle reluctantly put it on.

Satisfied the dress code had been respected, the manager led Carlyle to a lobby area. 'Please wait here.' He directed the commander to take a seat on an ancient sofa. 'Someone will attend to you shortly.'

Next up was an elderly retainer, who moved at a glacial pace and spoke in a whisper. 'Are you looking for someone, sir?'

Summoning the patience of Job, Carlyle confirmed he was, indeed, looking for Commissioner Thompson.

'Is he a member?'

'She,' Carlyle corrected him. 'Commissioner Virginia Thompson. Of the Metropolitan Police.'

The old fella's confusion grew. 'We don't have women members at Pakenham's.'

'Presumably she's a guest.'

The possibility seemed to intrigue the old-timer. 'Excuse me while I check.' Chuntering to himself, he shuffled off. Several minutes later, he reappeared, inviting Carlyle to get to his feet. 'It would seem you are correct, sir. The commissioner is on the premises. Please follow me.'

'What a horrible tie. Where the hell did you get it from?' Sollerdiche mocked.

'It's from the emergency stash,' Bruce Allen pointed out with a smirk.

Carlyle wasn't in the mood for any banter. 'Where's the commissioner?'

'Virginia's powdering her nose.' Allen indicated over his shoulder. 'She'll be back in a minute.'

'And what brings you here?' Sollerdiche enquired.

'I know about Alfred Sunderland. You had Vicky Dalby-Cummins killed.'

'Not so much a drive-by,' Allen chortled, 'more of a drive-over.'

Carlyle raised his eyebrows. 'You admit it?'

'No more than you admit you were in the woman's pocket,' Allen spat, 'or her bed, or both.'

Carlyle jumped forward, ready to give him a smack, but Allen danced out of reach.

'Now, now, gentlemen,' Sollerdiche intoned. 'No brawling on the premises. The last duel in here was almost two hundred years ago. The Duke of Southwold and the Earl of Somewhere or Other went at it with rapiers.'

'It was the Earl of Huntingdon,' Allen chipped in. 'They had a disagreement over a gambling debt. For the record, Huntingdon lost the duel. He died of his wounds three days later.'

'All very interesting,' Carlyle growled, 'but I'm more concerned with the here and now.'

'What are you doing here, Commander?' Thompson appeared at his shoulder. 'I gave my office very clear instructions I wasn't to be disturbed under any circumstances.'

'He's claiming Dalby-Cummins was deliberate,' Allen informed her.

'It was a normal traffic accident.' Thompson's voice was tight with tension. 'The case is closed. I don't want to hear about that bloody woman ever again.' She jabbed an angry finger at Carlyle. 'You've pushed your luck too far on this thing.'

'Be a good boy and call it a day.' Allen's eyes sparkled with alcohol-fuelled mischief. 'And, by the way, thank you for signing me up for that awareness course. A week in the Algarve,' he mimed swinging a golf club, 'an excellent chance to work on my handicap.'

The Algarve? I'm gonna need some anger-management therapy myself, Carlyle thought unhappily. 'You can't just brush me off.'

'We just did,' Sollerdiche proclaimed.

'You're lucky you're keeping your job,' Allen added.

'If you had any sense,' said Thompson, 'you'd take your pension and call it a day. But sense is not your strong point, is it, Commander?'

Carlyle flexed his jaw. 'What about the sale of the police stations?'

'That's going ahead,' Thompson confirmed. Before Carlyle could express his outrage, she added, 'The legal advice was that any backtracking could leave us open to being sued. The Met could be left with a very large bill for damages and the sale process would be delayed for years. The unequivocal advice is we should proceed with BDS as the preferred bidder.'

'And don't bother to threaten her husband,' Sollerdiche added. 'Peter's been seconded to another project of mine, in Doha. He'll be nowhere near this when it goes through.'

'If that's all, Commander, I'm sure you can find your own way out.' Allen pointed towards the door. 'Don't forget to hand back the tie at the door.'

Leaving Pakenham's, he got a call from Emily Quartz.

'Did you see my story on Dalby-Cummins?'

'Yes,' Carlyle lied reflexively. 'A good read, I thought.'

Quartz took it as her due and moved briskly on. 'I need another quote. Same basis as before. A few words on Peter Thompson and the conflict of interest at the heart of the police-station sales.'

'That's kinda gone away a bit.' Carlyle gave her a quick update, trying to make it sound as boring as possible.

'Sounds like it's more of a story than ever,' the journalist proclaimed. 'Francesca's expecting eighteen hundred words ASAP. She wants to put the story up tomorrow. They might run a version of it in the *Guardian* and Channel 4 News is interested.' The reporter seemed excited at the prospect of appearing on TV.

'My fingerprints'll be all over it.' With the benefit of hindsight, introducing Quartz to Terry Brunel hadn't been a clever move. 'I'd be too exposed.'

'You're doing the right thing.'

'Doing the right thing gets you killed.'

'You're scared for your life?' The idea seemed to excite her almost as much as the possibility of going on Channel 4. 'Seriously?'

Carlyle had been speaking metaphorically. Still, he found himself saying, 'You saw what they did to Vicky Dalby-Cummins.'

There was the sound of a keyboard being bashed. 'I thought it was an accident.'

'Maybe it was, maybe it wasn't.'

Quartz typed some more. 'This whole thing is getting right out of hand,' she declared. 'We need to nail these guys.'

TWENTY-FIVE

'Rick Ford has sold Perendi Films to a company called Antigen Capital Partners.'

Carlyle feigned ignorance.

'Why would anyone buy it?' O'Sullivan wondered. 'Last time I looked, there were seventeen civil cases pending against the company and the estate of Kenny Schenk.'

I'm sure they have their reasons. 'How're things?'

The inspector gave a heavy sigh. 'It's all a bit boring.'

'Boring is good.'

Neither of them believed that.

'I can't believe I'm being sued myself over this Hermione Lacemaker thing,' O'Sullivan blurted.

Carlyle offered a bit of reassurance. 'You're not being sued. The Met is. You were only doing your job.'

'Yeah, but it's a hell of a lot of money. If we lose, I'll get the blame. My career will be screwed.'

'That won't happen.' Carlyle crossed his fingers. 'If there was the slightest hint you'd crossed the line, you'd have been up in front of a disciplinary hearing like a shot. And I should know. I've had more than my fair share of them.'

The inspector seemed to appreciate the reassurance. 'Thanks, Commander.'

'Any problems, come straight to me.'

'Thank you. I hope we get the chance to work together soon.'

'Me too.' Seeing Joaquin standing in the doorway, he rang off.

'Sorry, I was going to call HR and I got distracted.' He waved his phone in the air. 'I'm gonna do it now.'

'Don't worry. The problem's resolved itself.' Joaquin did a little jig of triumph. 'Aditi's not coming back. She choked on a hamburger and ended up back in hospital.'

'I suppose the gastric-band thing didn't work.'

'She's going on long-term sick leave.'

'For choking on a hamburger?'

'She reckons she's got a complex mixture of long-term dependency and psychological issues that cannot be solved in the toxic environment of the workplace.'

'I could've told you that months ago,' Carlyle said ungallantly.

'It looks like I'm staying here,' Joaquin declared happily.

'Result.' Carlyle's enthusiasm was genuine.

'You've got a meeting in twenty minutes.'

Carlyle's reply was interrupted by a call from his lawyer, Alex Morrow.

'Inspector Henry Jones,' was the lawyer's opening gambit. 'He's made a formal complaint. Says you racially abused him at the XY Club. Something about having sex with sheep.'

'Welsh guy,' Carlyle recalled, 'wants me to help him get a new job. I told him not to be sheepish.'

'What?'

'I didn't—' Carlyle stopped mid-sentence, lacking the will to try to explain. 'Don't worry about it. It's not worth fighting.'

'Really?' Morrow's surprise was obvious.

'Sure. Let the powers that be have a free hit. I mean, what's the worst they can do?'

He took a call from the commissioner while standing in his

kitchen. If Thompson had read Quartz's story about her husband, she didn't mention it. Instead, she said, 'I've agreed a deal with the assistant commissioner. The Moran complaint will be dropped and Hermione Lacemaker's claim settled quietly, while Gina retires with her pension. The Met will also pay for a residential stay in a rehab clinic. In return, she drops her complaint against you.'

'All very neat.'

'I'd have thought you'd sound a bit more grateful,' the commissioner said testily.

'I am grateful,' Carlyle insisted. 'And I appreciate you letting me know.'

'Yes, well, it's been a difficult period for all of us. Hopefully now we can move on.'

'I'm sure we can.'

There was a pause. Then Thompson said, 'Have there been any developments on the Nick Dawson thing?'

Carlyle smiled. The undercover policing inquiry had yet to be announced and the commissioner was clearly trying to kick it as far down the road as possible. 'No,' he said soothingly, 'that's all gone away.'

'Good. Let's hope it stays that way.'

Carlyle made himself a cup of tea and wandered into the living room, determined to make a start on the Jo Nesbo novel he'd picked up in the charity shop at Elephant and Castle. By page two, however, came the grim realisation he'd read this one before. He tried to console himself with the thought that his three quid had gone to a good cause. The book itself could easily be recycled in the Oxfam shop on Drury Lane. What should he read next? There were a couple of Peter Temple paperbacks in the bedroom. Jack Irish was a more than acceptable substitute for Harry Hole. Before he could get up, his phone started to vibrate across the coffee-table.

'What's up?'

'Laura Taylor's missing,' Angelini blurted. 'I'm downstairs, waiting for you.'

Minutes later, Carlyle clambered into an unmarked SUV from the station carpool. 'Where are we going?'

'Dawson lives in Essex . . . with his wife and two kids.'

That's all gone away. Carlyle shook his head as they drove out of the city. 'Me and my big mouth,' he muttered, under his breath.

'Talking to yourself, Commander?'

'Going senile,' Carlyle joked. 'Tell me what happened.'

'Laura Taylor was supposed to attend her younger brother's birthday party. When she didn't turn up, the parents contacted one of her mates in the Rainbow Front. They hadn't seen her for a while, so they called the station and asked for me.'

Carlyle frowned. 'By name?'

'They said they wanted to speak to the kick-ass cop who took down Reuben Barnwell.'

Carlyle laughed.

'Switchboard put them straight through to my mobile.'

'You're already a legend,' the commander declared.

'I don't know about that,' the sergeant blushed slightly, 'but I do want to deal with the bastard properly this time.'

Chez Dawson was a nondescript semi on the edge of a suburban housing estate. The door was opened by an amiable girl called Amy, who announced that her mum and dad were both out. Angelini politely said they would wait. After showing them into the living room, the girl disappeared upstairs to finish her homework.

'Nice kid,' Angelini observed.

'Delightful.' Carlyle inspected a row of photographs on the mantelpiece. Aside from the usual family holiday pics, there were a couple of Dawson holding up large fish of some sort.

Angelini appeared at his shoulder. 'Looks like the guy's a keen angler.'

'Don't see the attraction.' The last photo on the row was the smallest, and the oldest. An armed soldier standing on a street corner. Carlyle picked it up and showed it to Angelini. 'Dawson's dad?'

'Maybe his wife's.'

In the background of the photo was some graffiti on a wall demanding *Brits Out*. 'Could be Belfast . . . in the seventies.' Carlyle's thoughts turned to the complex figure of James Gillespie.

'*Way* before my time.'

'Yeah.' A car pulled up outside. Carlyle carefully put the picture back in its place. The front door opened, then slammed shut. A moment later, a small blonde woman stormed into the room.

'What're you doing in my house?'

'Amy let us in. She said we could wait.'

'You're the bastard who shopped Nick.' The woman jumped across the room and slapped Carlyle in the face.

'Ow.' Before the commander could respond, Angelini had the woman face down on the floor and was snapping on a pair of handcuffs.

'There's no need for that.' Carlyle waited for the sergeant to remove the cuffs before helping the woman to her feet. 'What's your name?'

The woman looked at him like it was a trick question.

'Name,' Angelini barked.

'Lizzie . . . Lizzie Dawson.'

'Okay, Lizzie, this is your lucky day – you've had one free hit, next time the cuffs stay on.'

The woman didn't show any gratitude. 'Whaddya want?'

'I'm sure we've got lots to talk about but, right now, I need to find Nick. Where is he?'

She stared at her feet. 'Dunno.'

The sergeant waved the cuffs in front of Dawson's face. 'I arrest you, put you in the cells and call Child Services to take the kids . . . or you answer the question.'

'He's gone fishing,' the woman said sullenly. 'We have a cabin up at the Eco Lakes.'

After more cuff-waving by Angelini, she coughed up the details.

'That wasn't hard, was it?' Carlyle pointed at the picture on the mantelpiece. 'Who's the guy in uniform?'

'Derek, Nick's dad. He died over there.'

'Belfast?'

She shook her head. 'Londonderry. 1978. Just disappeared. The bastards never told us where the body is.'

'Hm.' Carlyle started for the door. 'We'll speak later. Don't tell Nick we're coming, or my sergeant *will* come back, arrest you and put the kids into care.'

'*My* sergeant?' Angelini smirked as they drove away.

'Just an expression,' Carlyle replied. 'Don't read anything into it.' He called Hunter and asked him to see if he could find out anything about Derek Dawson. 'MIA in Londonderry in 'seventy-eight.'

'The IRA disappeared him?'

'If James Gillespie was an informant, he might've had something to do with it.'

'And this is the son taking revenge? If Gillespie was working for the army, why would he be responsible?'

'It's just an idea. We have to compile the pieces of the puzzle before we can try to put them together.'

'Okay,' Hunter replied. 'Leave it with me.'

Eco Lakes was a series of man-made ponds on the site of an old quarry. The place had originally been turned into a holiday camp for working-class Londoners back in the 1930s. The clusters of cabins, built in woodland east of the water, had been rebranded as cheap yet environmentally friendly second homes a decade or so ago. Dawson's cabin was in the Green Quarter, a dozen properties, each built on a quarter-acre plot. As they approached, the place seemed deserted. It crossed Carlyle's mind that they hadn't seen a soul since arriving on site.

'This is it.' Angelini pulled up in front of the address Lizzie Dawson had given them. 'I wonder if she tipped him off.' Her question was immediately answered by a bullet shattering the windscreen. Tumbling out of the SUV, they took cover at the rear of the vehicle.

'Better call Armed Response.' Flapping at his jacket, Carlyle cursed when he realised his phone was still in the car.

'No time.' Angelini popped the tailgate. 'Anyway, I brought some toys of my own.'

In the boot was a selection of body armour and a large metal trunk. The sergeant handed Carlyle a vest. 'Put this on.'

The commander was only too happy to oblige. After slipping into her own, the sergeant unlocked the trunk and flipped open the lid.

'Take your pick.'

'Bloody hell.' Carlyle surveyed the selection of weapons in front of him. 'You came prepared for a small war.'

'Dawson's losing it. He's had firearms training. He's licensed to carry weapons. It seemed only prudent.'

'When were you going to mention the firearms training?'

'Didn't want to freak you out.' Angelini slipped a magazine into a machine pistol and handed it to Carlyle. 'How about you, know how to handle a gun?'

Another couple of shots slammed into the engine block, followed by a third whistling over their heads.

'I know how to point and shoot,' was as far as Carlyle would go.

Angelini frowned. 'Leave the safety on.'

'Good idea.' Carlyle watched Angelini select a carbine. 'Presumably you're, erm, proficient in the use of firearms?'

'Sure am,' Angelini grinned. 'Essex Gun Club champion three years running.'

That was reassuring, at least. 'What's the plan?'

'Nothing fancy,' Angelini kept low as she slid round the side of the car, 'we'll go straight in, through the front.'

'Great.'

'Don't worry, he's only trying to scare us off.'

'How do you know?'

'Because if he wanted to kill us, we'd be dead by now.'

TWENTY-SIX

Angelini smashed through the door of the hut as if it was made of matchwood. Carlyle followed, coming to a halt in a large, sparsely furnished room. Laura Taylor sat at the far end of a long dining-table. For a woman with a gun to her head, the young activist seemed remarkably composed.

Behind her, Nick Dawson hopped from foot to foot. 'You couldn't leave it alone, could you?' He pressed the barrel of his pistol into the nape of Taylor's neck. 'You just had to stick your nose in.'

Angelini kept her weapon trained on the rogue cop. 'Put the gun down, Dawson, and we'll sort this out.' She took a cautious step forward. 'No one else needs to get hurt.'

'People are always getting hurt,' Dawson grunted. 'One more won't make any difference.'

'We'll go first.' Angelini dropped her weapon to her side. Carlyle realised he'd never raised his in the first place.

'Are you all right, Laura?' Angelini asked.

'I'm fine.' The reply was cool, the voice unwavering.

The scales have fallen from her eyes, Carlyle thought. She knows she's been conned, and conned by a lunatic at that. 'You won't get away with this, Dawson.'

'Won't I? Those ponds are pretty deep . . . Maybe I'll just turn you into fishing bait.' He chuckled at the thought.

'Put the gun down and we'll sort this mess out.' Angelini was trying to play the good cop.

'I don't think so.' Dawson waved his pistol at them. 'Put your guns on the floor.'

Carlyle ignored the demand. 'Everyone knows we're here,' he said calmly. 'The cavalry will arrive soon. Better this is sorted out amicably before they get here.'

'Bollocks.' Dawson squeezed off a round. Bisecting the two officers, it flew through the smashed door and lodged in the grille of the hapless SUV.

'The carpool sergeant's not going to like you.' Dawson giggled. He pointed his gun at Carlyle. 'Next one goes in your head, moron. Weapons on the floor, *now*.'

'Okay, no problem.' Slowly moving onto her haunches, Angelini placed the carbine at her feet. Coming back up, she looked at Carlyle.

The commander caught a glimpse of resolve in Taylor's eye. He imagined her telling him not to give up his weapon.

'Last chance.' As Dawson took a bead on the commander's forehead, Taylor sprang out of her chair and smashed an elbow into his face in a fluid, almost balletic movement.

'Ow.' Dropping the gun, Dawson retreated under a hail of blows.

'You lying bastard.' Taylor spat in his face. 'You fucking *shit*.'

Carlyle leaped forward, careful not to be hit by Taylor's falling limbs, and kicked Dawson's gun under the table. With Taylor still in attack mode, the commander stuck out a strategically placed leg and sent the backpedalling Dawson sprawling on the floor. Before he could get up, Carlyle placed a boot firmly on his chest. 'Nick Dawson, you are under arrest. You do not have to say anything but it may harm your defence if you do not mention when questioned something which you later rely on in court. Anything you do say may be given in evidence.'

The blood pouring from his nose prevented Dawson from offering an intelligible response.

Over his shoulder, Carlyle called to Angelini. 'Cuff him.'

The sergeant said nothing. Instead, a deep Cockney voice said, 'Put it down, son.'

The two large men standing in the doorway must have been well into their sixties but they were still intimidating bastards, not least because of the Glock 17s in their meaty hands.

'Looks like the *Gunfight at the OK Corral.*' One of the men laughed. Covered by his comrade, he stepped into the room. After retrieving Dawson's weapon, he helped the battered cop to his feet and led him out of the door.

'He's under arrest.' Carlyle's announcement provoked considerable mirth among the new arrivals.

'We're leaving now,' said the remaining guy. 'A word to the wise, forget this ever happened.'

Carlyle glanced at Angelini but the sergeant was giving nothing away. He took a step forward and a round slammed into the floor, six inches from his foot.

'The next one takes you down. Count to five hundred, then you can leave. Any earlier and the first one out gets a bullet in the head.'

'I'm a police officer,' Carlyle wailed.

'We know you are.' The man smiled as he followed the others out of the door. 'Fuck off, copper.'

Carlyle was in no hurry to step outside.

. . . 497 . . . 498 . . . 499 . . . 500 . . .

. . . 501 . . . 502 . . .

Angelini looked at him expectantly. 'Shall we call it in?'

'And say what?' How the hell was he going to explain this? Best to start sweeping things as far under the carpet as possible.

With their SUV out of action, he called Hunter to come and pick them up.

Waiting for their ride, Taylor explained how she'd been on the way to her brother's birthday party when she'd spotted Dawson heading into a bar. Inside, she'd found him chatting up some 'blonde bimbo' and flown into a rage. He'd bundled her into a car and brought her to the cabin.

'Did he threaten you?' Angelini asked.

'He told me he was a cop, then to keep my mouth shut or he'd get rid of me,' she clicked her fingers, 'just like that.' It wasn't clear whether Taylor was more annoyed by Dawson being an undercover cop or a love cheat. That he'd threatened to kill her had yet to sink in.

'You did well,' Carlyle said.

'I should've shot him. We'd been, like, you know, an item for more than three years and I didn't even know his real name.'

Angelini sympathised. 'Men can be such total bastards.' She shot Carlyle a look. 'Cops especially.'

Leave me out of it. 'You helped us get out of a tricky situation,' he told Taylor. 'Thank you.'

Taylor shrugged. 'What exactly happened? I mean, who were the old guys?'

'I don't know,' Carlyle admitted.

'Will you do what the guy said,' Taylor asked, 'and forget about it?'

Carlyle looked at Angelini. 'For the moment,' he replied, 'I think it's best if we just keep this to ourselves.'

They drove back to London in silence, dropping Taylor at her parents' house before returning the weapons. Hunter looked on admiringly, as Angelini lifted the trunk onto her shoulder and marched into the armoury.

'She seems like quite a woman.'

'Interested?'

'Maybe . . . if I was twenty years younger.'

Carlyle laughed. 'Let's go and get a drink.' Reaching the West End, they stopped at a bar off Golden Square, where Carlyle gave Hunter a blow-by-blow account of what had happened.

'The old guys would be ex-special forces,' Hunter concluded. 'There are plenty of people for whom the war in Northern Ireland's never really ended.'

'Dawson's been undercover for years.' Carlyle swallowed his whiskey and ordered another, 'but it seems like he's been looking for the guys who killed his father for even longer.'

'I got some more on that.' Hunter signalled to the bartender that he was happy with his existing bottle of lager. 'The *theory* – all you ever get with this kind of stuff are theories – is that James Gillespie gave up Derek Dawson to protect his own cover. Nick wasn't even born at the time.'

'You can see how that would screw with his head.'

'Gillespie dropped out of sight for decades. Then he started talking to a few journalists and even appeared on a TV documentary about Bloody Sunday.'

Carlyle knew about the civil-rights march that had turned into a massacre.

'Some of Derek's old comrades – maybe the guys you just met – saw the clip, tracked Gillespie down, and got in touch with Nick. They probably grabbed Gillespie and took him to the police station.'

'So all Dawson had to do was pull the pin on a grenade and blow his head off.'

'Killing him in Paddington Green was a nice touch. Gillespie was held there for a week, back in 1979.'

'The squat provided nice cover, as well.' Carlyle stared at the fresh drink, which had been placed in front of him. 'A nasty postscript to a nasty war.'

Hunter savoured a mouthful of Peroni. 'What happens now?'

Carlyle lifted his glass to his mouth, 'Fucked if I know.'

Laura Taylor managed to keep her mouth shut for a couple of weeks. Suitably outraged by her revelations, the Anti-Capitalist Rainbow Front held a press conference to protest the use of 'spy cops' such as Nick Dawson. No one was particularly interested. Emily Quartz and her colleagues had seemingly lost their appetite for yet another bad-cop story.

The world moved on. Dawson himself had vanished. Lizzie Dawson took the kids to stay with her mother in Cyprus. O'Sullivan and Angelini turned their attention to other crimes. Even Abigail Slater was no longer on Carlyle's case.

In short, things had become rather boring.

Sitting in his office, the commander reluctantly turned his attention to the pile of mail that had been left to grow in his in-tray. The only item that piqued his interest was a fat padded envelope marked *Private and Confidential*. Casually tearing it open, he shook out the contents.

'Oh, shit.'

The grenade bounced on the desk, before lazily rolling onto the floor. Outside, the hum of traffic continued, unconcerned.